AN IDIOT IN MARRIAGE

Also by David Jester

An Idiot in Love
This is How You Die

AN IDIOT IN MARRIAGE

A NOVEL

DAVID JESTER

Skyhorse Publishing

Skyhorse Publishing books may be purchased in bulk at special discounts for sales promotion, corporate gifts, fund-raising, or educational purposes. Special editions can also be created to specifications. For details, contact the Special Sales Department, Skyhorse Publishing, 307 West 36th Street, 11th Floor, New York, NY 10018 or info@skyhorsepublishing.com.

Skyhorse® and Skyhorse Publishing® are registered trademarks of Skyhorse Publishing, Inc.®, a Delaware corporation.

Visit our website at www.skyhorsepublishing.com.

10 9 8 7 6 5 4 3 2 1

Library of Congress Cataloging-in-Publication Data

Names: Jester, David, author.
Title: An idiot in marriage : a novel / David Jester.
Description: New York : Skyhorse Publishing, 2017.
Identifiers: LCCN 2016052465 (print) | LCCN 2016056197 (ebook) | ISBN 9781510704343 (softcover ; acid-free paper) | ISBN 9781510704411
Subjects: LCSH: Husbands--Fiction. | Parenthood--Fiction. | Marriage--Fiction. | Domestic fiction. | BISAC: FICTION / Family Life. | FICTION / Humorous. | GSAFD: Humorous fiction.
Classification: LCC PR6110.E79 I35 2017 (print) | LCC PR6110.E79 (ebook) | DDC 823/.92--dc23
LC record available at https://lccn.loc.gov/2016052465

Cover design by Lilith_C (lilithcgraphics)

Printed in the United States of America

To Yiota—For providing encouragement, love, and support. And for putting up with my shit for eleven years.

You're a saint.

Contents

Prologue

I was pouting, a glum expression I had been wearing all morning. My arms were folded over my stomach and I was slumped in my chair, looking like a petulant teenager as I waited to be called to the principal's office.

Ahead of me was a small child, no more than ten or eleven, fidgeting like his pockets were full of firecrackers. His mother sat next to him, looking worse for wear and watching all of his movements out of the corner of her eye as she read an upside-down copy of a *Wonder Woman* comic. The kid was well dressed, his clothes neatly ironed, his collar turned down, but she appeared to have dressed herself in bed. Her clothes were tattered, ripped, and so stained it looked like she'd been caught in the middle of a food fight, while her hair resembled a neglected Chia Pet.

She stared at her child, a look of contempt, misery, and murderous intent in her eyes. It was the look of a woman who regretted not raising her child the right way. The look of a woman who wanted to spend some quality time with that child, just her and him, but couldn't think of any activity besides a murder-suicide. The kid was moving so fast he was almost vibrating. She looked like she was ready to pass out from the stress of everything. Although she might have been suffering from motion sickness.

"Kieran, straighten up. Look smart!" a voice beside me ordered, swatting at me as if I were a fly.

I turned to face my mother, twisting my petulance into a look of disdain. She had clearly been studying the partially comatose mother and her entirely irritating child. I knew how her mind worked, and I knew she had spent the last few minutes comparing herself to that mother and comparing me to that child. The obvious age gap wouldn't have concerned her.

She had always insisted she didn't care what people said or thought, but she would go out of her way to give people reason to say and think good things. It didn't matter who they were or whether they were paying attention. She wouldn't answer the door in her robe, and while she wasn't quite snobbish enough to refuse to eat at McDonald's, she did insist on getting dressed up for the occasion.

She also refused to fart, burp, or admit to any other bodily emissions in public. That's not to say that she didn't do those things, because she most certainly did; she just didn't take responsibility for them. My father had become so accustomed to taking the blame for public flatulence he had admitted to everything from dog farts and squeaky chairs to a bad smell wafting from a nearby Turkish restaurant. Whenever he heard it, whenever he smelled it, he gave my mother one cursory glance, assumed she was guilty—she has one of those faces—and then held up his hand to claim ownship.

My mother wasn't a bad person, nor was she vain or self-centered in any way. She just had a habit of comparing herself and her family to everything she saw on TV and in film, focusing on the impossibly kind, loving things that she saw in dramas, action, and romance flicks, and conveniently ignoring the trashy behavior shown on reality TV, talk shows, and other trash television—also known as real life.

That was the reason my father tried to avoid watching soppy films with her, because whenever she saw a man do something romantic for a woman, she became angry that *he* had never done anything like that for her. At the end of *Titanic*, following a lengthy argument, and as several dozen moviegoers looked on, he had to promise her that if their cruise ship ever capsized and the ice-cold waters didn't kill them immediately, then he would do as the protagonist had done and sacrifice his life for her. Although, by that point he was annoyed, embarrassed, and ready to go home, so what he actually said was, "Yes I'll let your fat ass have all the life raft to yourself, even if there is enough room for the both of us."

"Straighter," she instructed as I tried and failed to match her standards of sitting.

I corrected my posture and straightened up. My mother then turned briefly to the woman opposite, smiling a content half-smile before turning back to me and nodding proudly. *We showed her,* that look said.

I rolled my eyes. Life had taken a strange turn for many of us over the last few years. My dad had retired and turned his life into an endless cycle of playing golf and complaining about the home owner's association. My friends had become involved with married life, having children, and trying to get as much free time as they could—which they used to get as far away from their marriage and their children as possible. And my mother had turned into Mrs. Grundy.

"Why am I here?" I asked her.

"You know why," she said cryptically.

"If I knew, why would I ask?"

"Because you like to ask questions and be annoying." She paused to scan an assortment of outdated magazines on an adjacent coffee table. "You always have," she added before casually picking up a tattered magazine on interior decorating.

I'd always been told that an inquisitive child was an intelligent child. But it was my father who told me that, and he usually followed it up with, "But you ask a lot of questions, and look how you turned out."

I grumbled a note of discontent and then turned to face the front again, just as a handsome young woman walked out of a nearby room and strode toward me. She was wearing a formal suit with a skirt and black tights. Her legs seemed to stop at her neck, which was hidden by a tall, open collar. He hair was pinned into a ponytail and although she was smiling, she didn't look very friendly. She wouldn't have looked out of place in a fetish catalogue, posing in a leather costume as she gripped a man's testicles and waved a terrifying contraption at him.

"Mr. McCall?"

I nearly jumped out of my seat when she said my name. I had hoped she would walk straight past me, that she was part of my imagination and my guilt, or that she had stumbled into the wrong building on her way to an orgy. The expectant look on her face told me otherwise.

With my hands unconsciously safeguarding my crotch, I stood and greeted her with a meek smile. She gave me a sharp nod and then turned around without uttering a word. I looked at my mother expectantly, as though waiting for her permission, but she shrugged in reply. I looked at the door, seeing the bright morning light streaming through the glass-paneled entrance. It beckoned me into the parking lot, into the open air, into freedom, but just as my excitement increased, the image of freedom was replaced by my mother's face, popping into view.

"Don't you dare," she warned, her eyebrows raising so high I thought they would disappear into her hairline. She then whispered, "You're embarrassing me," while glancing at the stressed mother opposite. The poor woman had paid no attention to anything this prudish woman said. She hadn't heard a single word and probably didn't care either. She clearly had other things on her mind and was probably contemplating suicide that very moment, even as she stared at a poster that advised against it.

I sighed, lowered my head, and then followed the psychologist into her office. This wasn't the first time I had seen a psychologist. I had even spent time in a psychiatric hospital, an episode that led me to my beloved wife, Lizzie, but things had changed a lot since then. After marriage, and after spending time doing all of the things that married couples do—arguing, shouting, bickering, making up, arguing—things had taken an ugly turn. That was why I was now staring at the straightlaced features of an expectant psychologist, preparing to tell all about the breakup and the happy times that had preceded it.

I was in my mid-twenties, and although life had been a roller coaster ride in my early years, the last few had been plain sailing. I had no career to speak of and moved from odd job to odd job. I always ended up with positions I didn't want, bosses I hated and, as a result, contracts that barely lasted to the first paycheck. Aside from that, and from a few minor blips elsewhere, life had been kind. Great, even. But then, just a few weeks ago, the nightmare that was my adolescence had returned.

"From what your mother has told me," the psychologist began, "you have quite the story to tell." She spoke with a smile curling the corners of her lips. She found it amusing and that annoyed me, but in truth I couldn't blame her. Many people had found my version of events amusing, but my wife, her family, and I didn't find it very funny at all.

"You could say that," I said meekly, before settling back and preparing to tell her a story that I dreaded reciting.

1

Prenatal Hogwash

"Having a baby is a big deal in anybody's life. It's a time of great change, of great reward, and of great healing."

She had an infectious smile. She probably thought it made her look saintly, but it actually made her look simple. That's the problem with nirvana, with a state of ultimate divinity and wisdom—it's always a few wrinkles away from the smile of a stoner who just found a melted Kit-Kat in his pocket. The only reason it's so infectious is because it's hard *not* to smile at someone when they look at you like that, even if you're secretly wondering whether their happiness comes from a life of bliss or from a bottle of blue tablets the doctor said would keep the voices at bay.

"It is a time when many people become one, when many bodies combine and many hearts merge, creating two big and lovely halls of fun."

I smirked and looked around to see if anyone else had heard that, but they were either asleep or pretending to be. I turned back to the front, letting out a gentle sigh. Beside me I could hear Lizzie's soft breathing. She hadn't spoken a word for nearly twenty minutes. She hadn't cried, hadn't screamed, and hadn't threatened to leave me because I cheated on her in her dreams. That's the thing with pregnancy; yes, a baby can be a great thing—or so I've heard—and yes, it can make a family complete, but the process of acquiring one makes me doubt that it's worth it.

I adore watching the World Cup, I adore bacon cheeseburgers, cold beers, and lazy sunny afternoons, but if someone told me they could give me all of those things if I just tortured myself for nine months and made everyone around me miserable, I'd tell them to get lost. It got so bad that I'd spent the last few weeks waking up at 6:00 a.m., quietly sneaking out of the house and spending the day at Starbucks. When Lizzie thought I was at work, I was drinking an unhealthy amount of caffeine and harassing hipsters. I told myself that I did it because I was ashamed to let her know I'd lost my job. Again. She still thought I worked at the local newsstand, which had fired me for what they described as "gross incompetence." I had lost a lot of jobs in the last few years. Even in the last few months. I had been perpetually late. I had fallen asleep on the job. I had insulted customers (albeit accidentally; I wasn't to know she wasn't pregnant). This time, I thought I was actually doing the right thing. I hadn't been paying attention when he was showing me how to work the till, so I took the initiative, worked everything out in my head, and kept the money under the counter. In the end, we narrowly avoided being robbed, only to discover I was terrible at math and that we'd been robbing ourselves all morning.

The bank of Mom and Dad kept me going from failed job to failed job. They kept Lizzie out of my hair and ensured we would still have enough to look after our baby when it finally arrived. But life had been a struggle and, as much as I liked to believe otherwise, it wasn't going to get any easier.

I didn't want to put too much pressure on my son-to-be, but he had a lot to live up to.

"It is also a time—"

I grumbled under my breath, an instinctive sound borne of frustration. Everyone was too high on their own spirituality to notice me. Even the teacher at the head of the class didn't look up. I lowered my head until my chin touched my chest and prayed this nightmare would be over soon.

Her name was Mrs. Divine, or so she said. Before the class began, I had asked her what her first name was, and the vacant expression she gave me suggested that she had either forgotten it or she was trying to make one up on the spot. Her entire lesson seemed to have been made up on the spot, loosely based around "helping" a few expectant parents cope with their imminent bundles of snot, puke, and curiosity, but more focused on separating them from their hard-earned money.

A sickly sweet incense burned nearby, prickling the back of my throat and making every swallow taste like Christmas. Smoke hung in the air and I got the impression that every fetid breath of burned wood had already passed through the lungs of everyone else in the room. The curtains were shut, the lights off, but what seemed like a million candles burned away, adding to the toxicity of the air and throwing odd and ineffective lights around the room. It seemed like a waste. Candles don't come cheap, and beeswax candles are even more expensive. For a woman who prided herself on being in touch with nature, she was doing a very good job of burning half of it. And she could have gotten the same effect by turning on a light and plugging in an air freshener.

The candles had bugged me since we arrived. They were the main reason I hadn't been able to absorb myself in the class like the others had. One of my many, many previous careers involved selling handmade candles out of a pop-up store. I hated myself for it. The store popped-up, stunk up the mall, and then disappeared, leaving one guilty employee, dozens of broke customers, and a smell that lingered for years.

The candles weren't the only reason I couldn't absorb myself in the class. It didn't help that the teacher had the demeanor of someone who couldn't make it through a sentence without having a stroke.

"But it is also a time for personal reflection, for looking within your-self and for finding your beating soul, and your pulsing whole."

I rolled my eyes and checked my watch.

The lesson was supposed to last an hour, and in that time you were supposed to "take a step toward enlightenment." But it was nearly halfway through and I was still none the wiser. It was supposed to be a class to help first-time parents embrace their children and their rapidly changing lives, or at least that was the spiel written on the leaflet. So far we'd just sat on our asses, listening to a hippie who made as much sense as a Glaswegian astrologer. I hadn't sat with my legs crossed since elementary school, when they inexplicably made us sit on a hard and dusty floor while some extraordinarily boring teacher read announcements that had no bearing on any of the three hundred children and their rapidly developing hemorrhoids.

My ass had been killing me for weeks, around the same time I realized the only peace I got was when I was on the toilet. I'd let Lizzie believe I was constipated just so I could spend a good hour sitting on the toilet reading comic books, but then karma decided to fuck with me by giving me hemorrhoids and guiding me toward the only hippie in the world who didn't own a fucking beanbag. I spent my days on a hardwood chair in a coffeehouse and my nights trying to sneak into the toilet to feign constipation.

They would have been fine in most situations, but stuck on a solid floor for an hour was not one of those situations, and I knew that if the lesson dragged on any longer, I could be joining Lizzie in the hospital—as they removed a bundle of joy from her, they'd be trying to force a bundle of much less joy back into me.

She was due in a week, but it still amazed me how they could know such a thing. I didn't trust my local hospital one bit; too many horror stories, too many problems. And if they could confuse a cold with cancer and struggle to perform surgery without leaving half of the surgical table in the patient, how could they be so precise about pregnancy?

"It's fine, stop worrying so much," Lizzie had told me.

That's also what the nurses had told me when I expressed my concern about the birth itself, and about me being there. They told me everything was going to be okay, that many weaker men than me had made it through. Which I struggled to believe on several counts. In their infinite wisdom, they then decided to tell me all the things that could go wrong, things I had never even contemplated and would have been happy to remain ignorant to.

"Do you know you'll shit yourself?" I had said, releasing my shock on Lizzie as soon as we arrived home from what had been a check-up for her and an eye-opener for me.

"I won't really shit myself," she had said. "But I will go to the bathroom, if that's what you mean."

"On the bed, as you give birth."

"Yes."

"You have a very strange definition of what a bathroom is."

They also asked me if I wanted to keep the placenta. Several months prior to that, I might have said yes, always reluctant to turn down a freebie, but then I found out what it was. If keeping the placenta had been mandatory then I would have canceled the birth there and then.

"Some people eat it," they had told me. "Some people preserve it and keep it for when their kid gets older."

Of course, and some people also sleep with their siblings and shoot their parents. The fact that some people like to eat their own placenta does not tell me it's normal; it only confirms my suspicions that people are fucking insane. It is a waste product that leaves the human body, something that serves its purpose and then departs. There is no difference between that and the crap you leave in the toilet bowl every morning, and in my opinion, if you don't eat that, then you shouldn't eat placenta, and if you *do* eat that, then why not, go for it, because eating placenta would clearly be the least disgusting thing you've done all day.

The pregnancy had been a crazy experience overall, and one that had us both on our last legs, but it was nearly over. Just a week left and then the baby would come and the ordeal would be over, with another, greater ordeal taking its place. But at least there would be more satisfaction, at least there would be an end result, because after a long day, we would see a cute and dimpled little smile, or hear a sweet little laugh. Whereas after a long day during pregnancy the best I could hope for was a nuclear fart that threatened to strip the wallpaper and end life as we know it.

This class was another part of the crazy experience. There had been prenatal classes, parenting classes, and pre-pre-pre-school classes, the purposes of which still baffled me. It was like being back in school. Mrs. Divine's class was one of the most tedious of them all, an endless torrent of bullshit and cinnamon-scented smoke.

Lizzie was happy, though, and I liked to think that I was happy because *she* was happy, but if I mirrored her moods then our house would look like a scene from a poorly written Hallmark drama, one where tears of joy and tears of sadness were the same thing, and where the acceptable response to running out of peanut butter was to break down and declare that life was not worth living anymore. Our life had been like a soap opera—just as surreal, just as needlessly dramatic, and just as irritating. Some men say that pregnant women are beautiful, that they glow, but only because they're worried about the ramifications of telling the truth.

"Now, are we all sufficiently relaxed?"

Mrs. Divine clapped her hands, a signal that woke up the legions of victims around her. They all opened their eyes, fixing placid smiles on their faces as they did so. The smiles were fake, they had to be. If candles, incense, and bullshit was that effective then there would be no need for drugs.

"How was that?" Mrs. Divine asked, surveying the room with a smile that never faded. It was a curious smile—not quite utter contentment, not quite deviousness, but a strange mixture of mischief and delight, like a toddler who'd just farted and was listening to his parents as they blamed the dog. If what they say is true, that if you make faces and the wind changes then they'll stick, then Mrs. Divine had been doing something very unsettling on a very windy day.

"That was fantastic," one person lied.

"It was, it really was," another insisted with a nod.

It was like they wanted her approval, like they were fighting to be the biggest idiot in the room. One of them, a very annoying woman who hadn't shut up since we arrived, was clearly the happiest and the most content, or so she wanted everyone to believe.

"I was so deep in a trance, I was so gone. It was amazing."

She clearly enjoyed being the center of attention and excelling at everything, even if there was nothing to excel at. But the irony was that her husband, a man who looked as downtrodden and as suicidal as they came, actually looked like the one who had enjoyed it the most. The melancholy had all but vanished from his eyes. The last thirty minutes had probably been the only peace he'd had in years.

"And you?"

I was looking at the content man, as happy for him as he was for himself. I didn't really know his wife, but she was one of those people you immediately hated, so I felt great pity for him. Only when he turned to me did I realize that Mrs. Divine was talking to me and that the class was waiting for an answer.

"Excuse me?"

"Did you enjoy yourself?" she asked, the smile still there.

"Did I *enjoy* myself?"

She nodded patiently.

Did I enjoy myself listening to you prattle-on like a hippie with an agenda while I tried not to choke?

"Yes," I lied, jumping into the pen with the other sheep.

"You didn't look very relaxed," she noted.

I shrugged. "It's been a difficult few months. It's hard for me, what with the pregnancy an' all."

I heard Lizzie clear her throat.

"And her," I added. "It's probably been hard for her as well."

Mrs. Divine nodded, Lizzie sighed.

Mrs. Divine gave Lizzie a long and sympathetic look. She clearly didn't have kids, so she probably couldn't relate. I'd learned that the only people who were actually excited about children, and the only people who were optimistic about their arrival, were those who didn't have them or had never met them.

Mrs. Divine piped up again. "It's a hard time. There's a lot of stress, a lot of uncertainty, a lot of pain, suffering, and sleepless nights."

I nodded. "And don't forget the hemorrhoids."

Lizzie was silently shaking her head as Mrs. Divine gave her another sympathetic look. "You have hemorrhoids, Lizzie?" she asked. "I'm sorry to hear that."

"No, I'm the one with the piles," I told her, wondering why the attention had so suddenly and so rudely shifted to my wife. "And you're right, it is a hard time and there is a lot of stress, I mean she thinks—"

I felt Lizzie nudge me. "Kieran, she wasn't talking to you, she was talking to me."

I turned back to the teacher. "Really?"

Mrs. Divine nodded.

And to think I was beginning to like you.

"The birth of a child is a hard time for the father, as well," she said in my defense. "It is a time of great uncertainty, a time of great—"

I groaned again, feeling another lecture coming on. I checked my watch for what felt like the hundredth time, and I tried to drift away, but not successfully. The annoying woman and her down-trodden husband had their say at one point; she tried to convince everyone that not only had her pregnancy been the worst ever, but that her doctor had declared her to be a super specimen who was capable of birthing a million babies. Or at least that was the gist of it. Her husband's role in the relationship was clear: he was there to sit still and be quiet until his wife nudged him and said, "Isn't that right, Frank?" at which point he came into his own with a nod that said *yes* on the outside, but screamed *kill me* on the inside.

Another couple looked like they were carbon copies of Mrs. Divine. They both wore equally creepy expressions and told everyone how their baby would be born with no drugs, no needles. They also made a point of telling everyone that they didn't trust hospitals. I was with them on the last one, but I had a feeling that drugs played a bigger part in their lives than they were letting on.

Another couple sitting next to us looked more like father and daughter than man and wife. He was touching sixty and she looked around the same age as me, which was more than half his age. I have no issue with such discrepancies; I just found it odd. I could see the appeal for the man, and a small part of me, the masculine part—which was often overshadowed by the part that liked sweet scented shampoos and moisturizers—was proud of him, but what did she get out of it? The fact that they were having a baby was also odd. His retirement years would be spent changing diapers and wiping shitty asses. On the plus side, when the kid hit his or her late teens, they could return the favor.

Seeing so many relationships made me happy that mine and Lizzie's was as sane and as normal as it was. Fair enough—we did meet when we were children, ignore each other for many years, have a fling as teenagers, and then bump into each other as adults in a psychiatric hospital—but everyone has their quirky stories. Life was crazy then and it was even crazier before then, but she calmed me down—she centered me, as Mrs. Divine and her slack-brained friends would probably put it. Life had been fairly uneventful since our marriage. We were happy together and—

I heard a noise from Lizzie and felt her grab my arm. I yelped, gaining the attention of everyone in the room. While I was in the process of hiding my embarrassment and thinking of an apology, they all turned to Lizzie, looking alarmed. I followed suit and saw the fear and the pain on her face and the sweat that had quickly formed on her brow. Her entire body had tensed up.

"Kieran, I think we need to go." She looked down, directing my attention to the liquid that had soaked through her dress. She had wet herself before, a few drops from laughing too hard, and a few more when the act of wetting herself made her laugh even more. But this was different. I was prepared for this.

I'd worried about her going into labor early. I'd worried that it would happen when I was out, and that I wouldn't be there to help her or to stop her from having the baby on the kitchen floor. I'd worried that it would happen in the dead of night, when I was too tired to function. I'd never imagined that a premature birth would be anything but inconvenient, but as I saw the gaping stares of many silent parents, and the worried expression of Mrs. Divine—who had finally lost her divinity—I realized that there was no better time, because it meant I wouldn't have to endure another second of this tedium.

I grabbed Lizzie by the arm and helped her to her feet. "I'm sorry," I told them all, even though I really wasn't. "We're going to have to scoot."

"No, no, of course, please—go!" Mrs. Divine panicked.

We rushed out of the room and out of the building, puffing and panting all the way with Lizzie doing her best to waddle at speed. I didn't drive and Lizzie was in no fit state. We had taken a taxi to get to the class and managed to hail one to take us to the hospital, as well. The driver was fairly nonchalant about the whole ordeal, looking like a man who regularly drove heavily pregnant women to the hospital. I got the sense that if we were stuck in traffic, he would roll up his sleeves, say, "Let's have a look," and then deliver our son in the backseat. That made me feel a bit more secure, but it didn't seem to do anything for Lizzie.

We made it to the hospital before the taxi driver was given a chance to play the hero, and before long Lizzie was being prepped. The panic on her face and the haste at which the doctors and the nurses moved made me worry. It was finally going to happen, the moment that I had been waiting and worrying about for so long.

I had worried that something would be wrong with him and that the crushing blow of losing a child so early would end what had been a very happy relationship. I worried that I wouldn't be a good father, that the kid wouldn't like me or that I would do something wrong, something stupid. I was an adult, a grown man, a married man, but I still felt like a child. There had been no induction into adulthood, no point at which I was handed a certificate that said, "You're an official adult." There was no training, no tests, nothing. To say I was unprepared would be an understatement, and if I couldn't handle my own ascension into adulthood, how was I supposed to handle becoming a father?

I'd had these thoughts before, but in the panic of the hospital setting, with so much furor around me—people shouting, people running, people giving orders—it made things worse. I knew I was going to fuck up fatherhood. It was inevitable.

Why did I let myself do this?

Why did I agree to this?

Is it too late to turn back?

I was still a child. I still watched cartoons. I still had no idea what APR meant.

"Are you okay?" I stepped out of my panic to see a nurse staring at me, wide-eyed and worried. "You look a little pale," she noted.

I nodded. "I heard the doctor say not to give my wife any drugs."

"That's right, not yet, but—"

"If she's not using them, can I have them?"

"You need to stay strong. For your wife. For your child."

She left after that. No drugs, no words of sympathy. And of course there wasn't, because this had nothing to do with me. This was about Lizzie, because as scared and as uncertain as I was, I knew that those feelings would be amplified in her. She was suffering more than I was, and she needed me to stay strong, as difficult as that was going to be.

I waited by her bed, giving her a hand to squeeze and some bones to break. I also let her scream at me as the pain took hold. She said some horrible things, but I found most of it amusing, and I had been told to expect such things. "It's like *The Exorcist*," my best friend, Matthew, had told me. He didn't have kids of his own, thank God, but he made it his duty to know everything about women. "She's the psychopathic little demon girl and you're the priest."

Not until I was standing by my wife's bedside did I realize that Matthew had referred to my son as the devil, waiting to be purged from my wife's body, but I tried my best not to think about it. I'd already worried about enough things—would he be sick? would he hate me? would he support Manchester United? —the last thing I needed to worry about was that he would be born with horns and religious contempt.

At some point, the adrenaline kicked in and the worry went away, replaced by a hazy veil and a sense of dissociation. I remained by the bed, and at some point, they put up a screen, which I was happy for. After hearing about the horrors of birth, I had no desire to see them. I wondered if the screen was for my benefit, but reasoned that the screaming woman beside me was probably equally averse to watching half of her insides became outsides.

When Lizzie was given the drugs, she settled down somewhat, but she was still suffering. Her face looked like it was ready to explode. I had vowed I would never see my wife, the woman I love and the woman I am very much sexually attracted to, sit on the toilet suffering from constipation, trying to squeeze one out. That image is enough to ruin any sexual attraction, which is why there is an unspoken bond between most couples that they will never see each other in that position. But as I stood next to her, watching her push out our baby, I realized that that was exactly what I was witnessing. As these thoughts ran through my head, accompanied by other random images that had nothing to do with my impending responsibilities and thus were exactly what I wanted to think about, I heard a different screaming, one that didn't come from Lizzie.

I turned to see the nurse bury her head in my wife's vagina. I popped my head around the screen with a smile of anticipation on my face, but what I saw wiped that smile clean off.

They say that giving birth is a beautiful, wonderful thing. I can only assume that, seen through the eyes of an endorphin and morphine rush, the excess shit, mucus, and slime isn't as disgusting to the mother as it is to everyone else.

Through the mess of gunk that slid unceremoniously out of a place I had once enjoyed—and never would again—was a small blue head. The shoulders and arms came next, squeezed out like an old, limp turtle trying to emerge from its shell. I'd heard people compare birth to a sunset on a tropical island, the same people who named their kids after fruit or days of the week and seemed to think that sandals were perfect for all occasions. I had also heard it compared to a drug-fueled orgy, an intoxicating mix of emotions and inebriation that climaxes when everyone in the room has had their fill. But at that moment, I realized Matthew was the closest of all.

"It's the most disgusting, freakish, God-awful thing you could ever possibly imagine," he had told me. He was doing something with his hands, turning them over and over, but when he realized what he was doing, he stopped, stared at them for a while, and then shrugged. "I can't even explain it, mate," he said with a shake of his head. "Put it this way, you remember how much you loved pussy when you were a kid? Remember all of those nights in your teens when you stayed awake just thinking about how great the female vagina was?"

I had given him a curious frown. "I think we had different childhoods."

"Anyway," he had continued, offering me a sympathetic shrug. "This is almost enough to make you want to bat for the other side."

I didn't believe him, of course, but now I had seen it for myself. The noise, the chaos, the blood. I tried to smile, tried to feel how I knew I should be feeling, but no matter how hard I tried, I couldn't feel anything but repulsed.

Lizzie looked relieved and was softly groaning to herself. Considering what she had just unloaded, I wasn't surprised. Following a diet of pain pills and fast food after I had broken my wrist, my bowels had been blocked for weeks. For the first week or so I was too out of it to care, but by the second week, I began to feel it. And by the third week, it felt like a small child was hiding in my intestines. But when it finally came out, it was the most relieved I had ever felt and the joy that came afterward was like the best drug ever.

I'm not saying that my three-week bout of severe constipation was like giving birth, but there were a lot of similarities. There was also some blood at the end of it, although considerably less than what had just plopped out of my wife.

The nurse had my baby in her arms, wrapped in a blanket, his alien features hidden. She was chatting to him, uttering soft and soothing words. He was still screaming.

"You're so lovely, aren't you?" she said in a saintly whisper, rocking him back and forth. "So, so beautiful."

All babies are ugly. I like kids, don't get me wrong. They can be cute, amusing, but it usually takes a year or two for that cuteness to develop. At birth, pretty much all babies look alike: they're small, blue, slime-coated creatures with squinted eyes and wrinkled skin. They say that the reason humans are so attracted to bunnies, kittens, and puppies is because they see their own babies in them. They look at their big eyes and small heads, think of babies, and then the protective instinct kicks in. I say give me puppies, kittens, and bunnies any day.

The nurse smiled at me and then back at the child whose cries seemed to be subsiding somewhat. "There we go," she told him, stroking a finger across his cheek. "Nothing to worry about. You're out now, welcome to the big wide world."

He started crying again. Those words would have made me cry, too. The poor bastard had been kicking back for nine months in a warm and cozy spot where he was drip-fed everything he could ever need and had nothing to do all day but sleep and dream. Now he had been introduced to a cruel and cold world where, over the course of a few years, he would suffer the indignity of pissing on himself, having his ass wiped, and not being taken seriously as he tried his best to learn the language. Once school started, he would be forced into a regime of mandatory learning, bullying, and peer pressure, topped off by puberty, at which point he would become a raging mass of sexual desire and hand cream, followed by rejections from every girl he liked and erections at inopportune moments.

Or maybe that was just me. Maybe life would be easier for him.

The nurse was back to coddling him, back to stroking his blue, slimy cheek and staring lovingly into his eyes. I wasn't sure if she was trying to calm him down or if she was getting ready to steal him. "You look just like your father."

"I hope you're fucking joking."

"Kieran!"

I turned from my wife, her face red, flustered, sweaty, and annoyed, back to the nurse, who looked slightly bemused as she held my son in her arms.

"Sorry," I said with an impish smile.

The nurse walked around the bed with the demon child in her arms. It was screaming constantly, barely stopping for breath. My mother said that I cried a lot as a baby. She said when the nurse first gave me to my dad, I screamed the hospital down and he asked for a refund. He was joking, but I could see where he was coming from.

I didn't want to hold him. He was small, fragile, breakable, and he seemed pissed off. I didn't want to add to that. But I also didn't want to displease anyone. Lizzie was glaring at me, and the doctor and nurses were looking on expectantly. There were half-smiles on their faces, stuck in transition, prepared to go either way.

I swallowed thickly, held out my arms, and waited for him to drop into them. I was so expecting him to be placed in my outstretched arms that I actually felt some weight on them and I thought he was there, but it turned out my brain was just fucking with me. When I opened my eyes, about to say how light he was and how much easier it was than I thought it would be—as if holding a baby was something to be proud of—I saw that they were still looking at me, their half-smiles now transitioned into bewilderment.

"What?" I said.

"He's *your* baby," Lizzie barked, angered by my unwillingness to hold him.

"I know that," I said with a nod. "We've been through this. That was what all the screaming was about. I put my 'dirty penis' inside you and should have 'stayed the hell away' from you."

Lizzie looked embarrassed. "Sorry about that. I was caught up in the moment."

"It's okay, I was actually turned on a little."

The lack of sleep really was doing something to my brain. "I'm so sorry," I told the waiting nurses, before adding, "but I'm sure you've heard worse. And it's not like I should be embarrassed, is it? I mean, you know babies aren't delivered by storks, you know what went down nine months ago, and you—" I smiled at the doctor "—you were staring at my wife's vagina for an hour."

"Kieran!"

She usually stops me long before then, but she'd also had a long day. She was probably just as tired as I was.

"Are you going to hold him now?"

"Do I have to?"

I could see she wanted to kick me at that point, but the glare she gave me was enough.

"I mean, yes, of course I do."

I took the initiative and retrieved the child from the nurse's arms. I would like to say that at that moment I fell in love, and that all my problems melted away, but the only thing swimming though my head was how he looked like the chest-ripper from *Alien*. I did relax with him in my arms, though, and as I sat down on the edge of the bed and took some weight off, and as the baby stopped his high-pitched wailing, I felt a gentle euphoria wash over me. It was over, Lizzie was okay, and the baby, my son, was also okay.

"So, have you two thought of any names yet?" the nurse asked.

I nodded. "I quite like the name Ezra."

"We're not calling him Ezra," Lizzie said sternly.

"Keanu?"

"Hell no."

I turned to the nurse. "We haven't decided yet."

"But I quite like the name Ben," Lizzie added.

"Oh, what do you know, we've decided after all," I told the nurse. "He's going to be called Ben."

Lizzie had a few names in her head but had always insisted that she was going to go with what suited him when he came. She thought Ben was apt, and I had no idea why. I was just surprised she picked a human name.

I did get some say in the naming process though and was told I could give him the middle name Ezra, only to watch her write Michael on the birth certificate.

"What about Ezra?" I said, a little hurt.

"That's *your* middle name for him," she told me. "That's not his *real* middle name."

"Oh." Because obviously that made sense.

I'm calling the next kid Fred, I thought bitterly. *Regardless of whether it's boy or a girl. That'll show her.*

2

The Baby Tour

By the time we took him home, Ben looked a little more human and a little less terrifying. He had lost all the goo. He was still a little wrinkly around the edges, but I get the same when I stay in the bath too long, and he'd been in the womb for nine months. He would straighten out in time.

Lizzie had taken some time off from work. When I met her, she was a part-time art tutor at a psychiatric hospital—which I had discovered after running naked down the corridors of said psychiatric hospital—but soon afterward she was offered a full-time position at a local college. She still offered her time helping children with special needs and adults with mental illnesses, giving up her Saturdays to teach them art and other creative pursuits, but she would be focusing one hundred percent on Ben's special needs for the next few months. And mine. Because I had also taken some time off work, by which I mean I had told her about accidentally robbing the newsstand and losing my job.

The first few days were difficult and dramatic to say the least, and both of us were on edge constantly. Lizzie stripped me of most parental duties on the insistence that I was neither mature enough nor competent enough. But eventually she relented, letting me change his diaper unsupervised. Although she didn't really have a choice. She needed to look after Ben and do the ironing. And while she didn't trust me with heat or humans, she knew it had to be one or the other.

I regretted her decision as much as she did. That was the first time I discovered the abhorrent marvel that is baby poop.

I had shouted Lizzie in from the other room, and she came bundling in to see me standing over the diaper with a horrified look on my face. I had dropped it in shock and some of the contents had sprayed onto the carpet, but we had bigger things to worry about.

She followed my finger and looked at the brimming diaper. "You realize that's normal, right?"

"Normal?" I spat, incredulous. "It's fucking green. What have you been feeding him?"

I lay Ben back onto the changing mat. He looked up at me and grinned, mocking my stupidity. He looked just like his mother.

The demon child and his fluorescent excrement continued to demand our attention night and day. It's amazing what such a small human can do to a pair of adults, and what the ablutions of said human can do to a home. Prior to Ben, I was of the belief that Febreze could fix everything. I can't believe I was so naive.

We got nearly two weeks of relative peace—if you don't include the screaming and the insomnia —before Lizzie decided that it was time to show him off.

"He's not the Super Bowl," I told her. "I don't think they'll be holding a parade for us."

"I know my parents," she said. "Trust me, a parade is the least we can expect."

Two days of very little sleep had turned me into a depressed zombie. I had no idea how I was going to get through the next few months.

"Do we *have* to show him to your parents?" I asked.

"What do you think?"

"That depends. If I think we should stay home, then can we stay home?"

"No."

"Then of course we should let your parents see him." She was taking advantage of my weakened state, but I was too weak to resist.

It was as good of a time as any to let Ben know that he had two creepy, stuck-up grandparents who would make the next few years of his life an unbearable deluge of condescension. I was convinced that they had never seen a baby before, let alone would know how to deal with one. He didn't work. He wasn't educated. He wasn't on speaking terms with his parents. Throw in an Adidas hoodie and he was everything they hated and everything they spent their days moaning about.

Since our marriage, I had tried to avoid her parents as much as possible. We saw them on special occasions, but only when I wasn't ill, working, or sleeping, which happened a lot. I had tried to be sociable with them in the past, especially with her dad, but it didn't end well. I'd also had what I thought to be a special and private time with her mother, but that had turned into something else entirely.

We had been drinking with her, a supposedly relaxed, laid-back night that I had spent on the edge of my seat, trying my best to suppress my farts and avoid saying anything stupid. Lizzie, content that I was behaving, left me alone with her as she walked to the shop to get more booze. I had spent the better part of forty-five minutes talking to her, doing my best to be polite and to treat her like a normal person, instead of the witch that she was. She seemed responsive and I even began to change my mind about her, only for her to tell Lizzie that I had spent the night trying to hit on her.

"I told you he was a bad husband, I told you that you made a mistake."

Of course, she didn't say any of this in front of me. She was subversive, devious. She was the devil in storebrand clothing.

Luckily, Lizzie didn't inherit any insanity from her parents. In fact, she'd gone out her way to try and be as little like them as possible. But she loved them and they were still alive, so we had to keep up appearances.

"They are cooking dinner for us," Lizzie announced. "I also said we would stay and watch their vacation videos."

Life, it seemed, wasn't going to get any easier. I'd been promised that a child would complete both mine and Lizzie's life, but those same sadistic liars had then told me that I would need to wait a few years before I could settle into the routine of never sleeping, never eating, and never having sex. It wasn't a routine I was keen to follow, but I didn't have much say in the matter. I'd eaten nothing but fish sticks for two days, and it had been six months since we had done anything in bed that didn't involve sleeping, gossiping, and, occasionally, farting and then forcing her head under the covers.

"Where did they go?"

"I told you," Lizzie said, sounding frustrated, failing to realize that nothing anyone had told me over the last few weeks had sunk in. "They went to see where my mother grew up."

"I didn't know they were letting tourists into hell these days."

"Hull," Lizzie said, sounding annoyed.

What's the difference?

"And why do we have to be subjected to their videos? What could they have possibly taken that would be of *any* interest to *anyone* ever?"

The look she gave me didn't go a long way to answering any of my questions, but it did suggest that if I didn't stop asking them then I would regret it.

"Okay, vacation videos it is," I told her reluctantly. "But if I see any homemade porn on there, you're disowning your parents and I'm committing suicide."

"Deal."

Lizzie's mother had a big smile waiting for us, one stitched together with a combination of Valium, Prozac, and plastic surgery. "It's so lovely to see you!"

"Well, if it isn't my favorite mother-in-law in the world!" Lies, lies, all lies. She was my only mother-in-law in the world, but she still wasn't my favorite.

We hugged. We kissed. I died a little inside.

I gave Lizzie's father a strong handshake and a nod. He preferred that. No talking, no theatrics. He hugged and kissed his daughter, of course, but he liked her.

Dinner wasn't as painful as I thought it would be. Ben took most of the attention, so no one noticed when I spilled wine on the floor or used a pristine white tablecloth to wipe gravy stains from my mouth. Such incidents would have caused problems in the past, so being able to get away with them made me feel invincible.

That invincibility faded when the home videos began. They were a little inebriated by that point, and nothing alters the personalities of the upper middle class like copious amounts of alcohol. They spoke to me like I was a family member and not a vagrant who had just murdered their dog. It threw me off guard and for a moment I forgot I was in the devil's domain talking to his underlings.

"So, how's the sex life now then, eh?" her father said jokingly, nudging me as he did so. "I bet you're glad that has started again?"

He made a face at Lizzie, showing her that he was trying his best to embarrass her. She rolled her eyes at him. I thought it was a little inappropriate, but I decided to play along regardless, not realizing that whatever they had going on was supposed to be just between the two of them.

"I'm not touching that thing again," I joked. "If you'd have seen what came out of it, you would know why. We'll find a way, though."

I was laughing, but my comment was met with silence. It did occur to me that I had probably taken it too far, but I was uncomfortable, tipsy, and tired. It could have been worse.

They averted their eyes. Her father cleared his throat and checked his watch. Sensing a need to make myself understood and to clear the air, a need that had never done me any favors in the past, I proceeded to jam my foot further into my mouth.

"No, no, I didn't mean anal." I heard Lizzie groan and saw her bury her head in her arms, but I was determined to explain myself. "I just mean like, you know. Then again, I suppose if she wanted to. . . . I mean, I'm not going to force it up there or anything."

Her father quickly interjected. "I think we've heard enough." He gave me a look of pure hatred, as though I were trying to disgust him and annoy him on purpose.

"Are you sure? Because I wasn't finished."

Okay, that was on purpose.

"I think you should leave."

Excellent!

I shot to my feet and swooped in to take Ben from his grand-mother's lap, narrowly avoiding her horns on my way down. I then nodded to Lizzie and gave her a look that said, *Hurry up; places to go, people to see, babies to show.*

My parents were next. By that time Ben was asleep, so they were getting the sloppy seconds. Luckily, they had already seen him in the hospital, a day after his birth. This was something Lizzie's parents had refused to do, possibly because hospitals are too common for their tastes. Lizzie's parents also lived further away, and she had warned me that if we didn't go to see them then they might not get to see Ben during the first six months of his life.

"They know where we live," I had argued.

"You know what they're like—"

Evil. Psychotic. Manipulative. Bat-shit crazy.

"—they don't like to impose."

"Ha!"

She had glared at me.

"Sorry."

"Anyway," she had continued. "If we hadn't gone to them, then they might not have seen him until the christening."

"And what about church?" I asked. "I mean, is she allowed?"

"What's that supposed to mean?"

"Nothing."

My mother did her best to subtly wake up the baby, after which she blamed his wakening on my father and then spent the next hour doting over him and pretending to try and rock him back to sleep, probably pinching him when no one was looking. She was a sweet woman with a lot of love to give, and she lived with my father, who didn't really have any, so this was her only outlet.

She unleashed an endless torrent of sweetness, with smiles, baby-talk, and cute names. My dad, on the other hand, sat on the other side of the room, only getting up once to hover over him and mumble, "He looks just like you, Kieran."

"Thanks, Dad."

"Poor bastard."

He sniggered to himself and then sat down. He later told us that the baby actually looked like Lizzie, which was a huge compliment, as my dad adored Lizzie. He never had a bad word to say about her, saving all of them for me.

When Ben drifted off again, my mother carefully placed him in his carrier, spending several minutes standing over him and grinning before eventually turning to me and wiping that smile off her face. "I hope you're going home after this," she warned. "The boy needs some rest. He's had a long day."

I nodded. "Of course."

We'd all had a long day, but these days anything longer than several hours felt like a long day. In fact, every morning, as I woke to the sound of screaming, still half in a dream state, my legs barely able to carry me, the day already felt twenty hours long.

We left Ben to sleep, and as soon as we got back we tried to get some sleep as well, but that didn't last. We arranged to take it in turns, which meant we could see to him throughout the night and in the morning, but that rarely panned out. If Ben wasn't the one to wake up the parent who was off duty, then the parent who was on duty was.

The following morning, we opened the house to Lizzie's friends, a bundle of excitable women who, judging by the sounds they were making, had never seen a baby before. I did my best to stay out of the way; a penis in that company was only acceptable if it was attached to a small baby.

My own friends came over to see him later in the day, with Max at the head of the line. Max was my oldest friend, but far from the best. He wasn't very bright and had somehow dulled with age. "He's so much of an idiot that he makes you look intelligent" was how my dad often described him.

Max's family had money. He was given some big opportunities at an early age and, to everyone's surprise, he didn't mess them up. He was now rich beyond belief, his idiocy now irrelevant and completely hidden behind his designer clothes, his designer haircuts, and his designer girlfriends. He had offered me a job on several occasions, but I couldn't bring myself to work with, under, or anywhere near Max. He was a nice guy, but there was nothing but wax and air between his ears.

He showed up with a dazzling brunette on his arm. I didn't even bother to ask her name; I knew I wouldn't need to remember it. Max wasn't a womanizer, certainly not as much as Matthew had been. Many of his girlfriends were with him for his money, and when those relationships inevitably broke down, there were always several more waiting to take their place. I still wasn't convinced that Max knew what went where in the bedroom. Matthew had once put such a question to him and, following his answer, it took us several minutes to realize he was talking about home improvement.

"Who do you think the baby looks like then?" Lizzie had asked Max.

Max studied Ben for a while. His girlfriend was sitting on the sofa trying to look elegant and nonchalant and failing horribly in both cases. I'd already caught her pulling her knickers out of her ass and grimacing when Lizzie mentioned the labors of pregnancy. Obviously, I tried my best not to be drawn in by Max's girlfriends, but I was still amazed that the little idiot who had sat next to me at school, failing at every subject and at life in general, could be such a babe magnet.

"Matt Damon," Max said eventually.

Lizzie rolled her eyes. She usually had a lot of patience for Max, but since the birth, she seemed to be always one syllable away from murdering someone. "Me or Kieran, I meant."

"Oh," he nodded slowly and looked like he understood, but I knew Max better than that.

"No, he definitely looks like Matt Damon."

I always felt strange having Max in my house. This was a man who had more money than he knew what to do with, a man who made more in a day than I made in a year. But despite that, he never acted like he was too good for me and was always just as polite and as friendly as he had always been. That was one of the reasons I still counted him as a close friend.

He didn't talk about money or about work, and he didn't brag. He was an all-round great guy, and one who life and karma had treated very well.

"Has Matthew seen him yet?" he asked.

Matthew was my closest friend, but they didn't get along. Matthew had issues, bags of them, and he took a lot of his anger out on Max. Most of them stemmed from the fact that Max had everything that Matthew had ever wanted and had used only a quarter of the brain power to get there. Max was a better man than Matthew in that respect. He was not as petty, but he wasn't as much fun to be around either.

"He's coming soon."

"I should go."

"You don't have to go just because he's coming."

Max waved a dismissive hand. "Trust me, I'm not. I like watching him squirm. I just have work to do."

He shook my hand and gave me a hug, which felt a little awkward. "You did good, Kieran. The baby is adorable."

"Thanks."

He walked past me and I froze when it was his girlfriend's turn. She held out her hand as if she expected me to kiss it, perhaps mistaking me for someone who gave a shit and mistaking herself for royalty. I turned her hand around and shook it, reveling in the appalled expression on her face.

Matthew arrived after Max had left. He wasn't a big fan of children, something he made a point of mentioning as soon as he walked through the door.

"So, what brings us here? I hope you got a new pool table or an Xbox, because if this has anything to do with the baby, then I'm going home."

His wife, Sharon, shoved him and hissed at him. She was the one who kept him on the straight and narrow, the one who had reeled him in and stopped his playboy ways, but keeping him on a short leash was a full-time job. The only reason they didn't have a kid themselves was because Sharon couldn't see herself looking after two children who only wanted to whine and suck her nipples.

In a move that had shocked everyone, including his parents, Matthew had married before me. To this day, his parents still thought the marriage was some sort of elaborate joke, unable to believe that Matthew would settle down and that Sharon would allow him to settle down with her. They were opposites in every way. She was smart, well-read, and well-educated; he finished school at the bottom of his class and had never read anything that wasn't large print and illustrated. She was polite, generous, forgiving; Matthew once stopped speaking to me for three weeks because I borrowed money to pay for a pack of gum and forgot to pay it back. I'd never imagined that opposites could ever attract, but somehow they did. Max had once speculated that Sharon made up for Matthew's downsides and he made up for hers, like they were two incomplete jigsaws that provided the parts needed to complete each other, and that marriage was the box that brought them both together—of course, this was Max talking, so I'm paraphrasing. But while I could see Sharon's jigsaw completing Matthew's, I couldn't seem him contributing to hers.

It wasn't like I thought my friend had no good points, but rather that I had known him long enough to *know* that he had no good points. In fact, between all the obscenities, the crudeness, the name calling, and the fact that he was constantly trying to make me look like an idiot, I had no idea why I was friends with him. But somehow I knew that all those reasons were *exactly* why I was friends with him.

Their marriage had been facing difficulties, with Sharon depriving Matthew of sex. But with his sexual appetite, I couldn't blame her. She probably needed a rest.

Once the pleasantries were over, we took them to see Ben, who had fallen asleep in his crib. Sharon was ecstatic; Matthew was a little less impressed.

"You've seen one, you've seen them all," he stated.

"And when was the last time you saw a baby?" Sharon asked.

Matthew shrugged. "Does television count?"

I laughed it off, but Sharon didn't seem to find it as funny. She glared at him momentarily and then turned away, the smile only returning to her face when her husband was no longer in view.

"So how is the sex life?" Matthew asked as soon as we all sat down.

"Really?" Sharon was ready to take another shot at her husband. "That's the first thing you ask?"

Lizzie and I both felt the tension, and we both tried to laugh it off, but it didn't work. I also tried to change the subject, but Sharon cut me short, her attention fully on her husband, her tone even more annoyed than before.

"What else am I going to ask?" Matthew wondered. "How fun the diaper changes have been? How many sleepless nights they've had? If anything, sex talk *lightens* the mood."

"It's always sex, sex, bloody sex with you, isn't it?" Sharon said.

"Not in our house it's not."

I heard a sharp intake of breath from Lizzie. "So . . ." She stood quickly, slapping her thighs and making sure everyone was paying attention to her. "Can I get you guys another cup of coffee?"

They both looked down at the cups they had just placed on the coffee table, both brimming with scolding hot coffee.

"No," they said simultaneously, giving her a worried look.

"Tea?" she asked, her voice loud, her tone high.

"No, no," Matthew said, eyeing her, most likely wondering what she had taken and if she would give him any. "We're good, thanks."

"I'll get you some cookies then."

Matthew rolled his eyes. "Sure."

Lizzie waited, still standing. Then, happy with the silence that followed, she ducked into the kitchen. As soon as she was gone, the bickering couple turned back to each other, but before either of them could utter a word, Lizzie popped her face around the door.

"Chocolate Chip or Sugar?"

Lizzie's bizarre behavior did its job. After spending some time wondering what had gotten into her, and dealing with all her requests, they had completely forgotten what they had been arguing about. Once the cookies, the cake, and the sandwiches came, a friendly atmosphere returned.

When they were ready to leave, before they kissed and hugged their goodbyes, and while Sharon was upstairs with Lizzie saying a silent goodnight to Ben, I felt Matthew's hand grip my arm.

"I need your help."

There was a pleading, desperate look in his eyes. "Sorry?"

He released me from his grasp, paused to check on the noises coming from upstairs, and then ran a hand through his hair. He looked like a man in distress, and for a moment, he had me worried, but as was always the case with Matthew, whether he was happy, sad, angry, or ecstatic, there was always one prevailing cause. "I'm horny as hell," he whispered.

I took a step back. "I can't help you there."

"Trust me, mate, even if I was that way inclined, you wouldn't be my first choice."

I was a little hurt by that. "What do you mean?"

"You're not my type."

I understood. "You'd prefer them more feminine."

He looked like he was struggling to suppress a laugh. "Yeah, sure. I like them *more* feminine." He paused to look up the stairs again, content when he heard the two women gossiping, seemingly stuck in an argument about how adorable the sleeping baby was. He grabbed my arm again and dragged me away, into the hallway and out of earshot.

"It's been three weeks now." His voice broke toward the end of the sentence, as if hearing it aloud was painful for him. "I don't know what to do with myself."

"Well . . . there are a few things."

"Ah, believe me, I've been wanking so much that I'm worried it's going to fall off. I have friction burns down there. At least, I hope they're friction burns."

"Let's not get into that, please."

"I need you to help me get laid."

"With Sharon?"

He shrugged. "At this point, I don't care. Anyone will do. Whatever you can get; whatever it takes."

"You realize I have a small baby to look after now, right?"

He looked a little confused. "You have a wife for that."

Sometimes Matthew's blatant sexism surprised me. Most of the time it made me question just why I kept him so close and how Sharon, Lizzie, or any other woman in his life hadn't killed him. But I knew him well enough to know that he said those things *because* they annoyed me, and I kept him around because he amused me. And because I didn't really have any other friends.

"I can't expect Lizzie to do everything."

"How many diapers have you changed? How many times have you woken up in the middle of the night to help? Come on, mate, I know you and I know Lizzie. Everything you do to help is probably supervised by her. You probably get in the way more than you help. She'll be happy to get rid of you."

I thought about calling him a liar and defending myself, but he was right. "Okay, I'll help."

He clapped his hands. I flinched more than I would have liked. "Remember, *anyone* will do."

"Let's stick with Sharon for now, seeing as you did commit to love, honor, and obey an' all that."

"Okay, whatever. Just help me."

3

Desperate Measures

I spent the next few weeks in a haze. I wasn't sure if minutes or days had passed, because I wasn't convinced I was even awake most of the time. I might have been supervised and I might not have done as much as Lizzie, but I heard those screams as much as she did; I helped to clean up the vomit, the poop, and everything else that came out of our little bundle of joy; I was also tasked with running to the shop to get whatever Lizzie wanted or told me that the baby needed (although I have my suspicions that the 11 p.m. Snickers was for her and not him). I avoided the local newsstand, on account of the abuse I got from the owner, and trekked the extra mile to another shop. But in doing so, my tired brain got confused, going back to an old routine. On two separate occasions, I ended up at Starbucks, ordering enough caffeine to power an army and glaring at hipsters.

But even though I had a new baby to look after, an older baby became just as demanding of my time. Matthew had spent that time assuming I was looking for an unfortunate woman to sleep with him, and then getting very angry with me when he realized I was putting the needs of my newborn baby ahead of his.

I had avoided his texts and his Facebook messages, on account of the fact that I couldn't find my phone and couldn't look at Facebook without getting angry at people who were sleeping and living normally. A few weeks after the night he had been introduced to Ben, he managed to get me on the phone. He sounded even more desperate and frustrated than he had been when he begged for my help. Once we got the pleasantries out of the way, which consisted of him swearing at me for not responding to his messages, and reminding me that he had known me for years, while Ben had only known me for five weeks, he got straight into his sex life.

"She just refused me again," he said. "I don't know what to do. I tried everything. I tried brushing up against her, I tried just going for it, but she just blanks me at every turn."

"Brushing up against her?"

"In bed," he clarified. "After all else had failed. I figured I'd just sort of slap her in the ass with my penis."

I had heard many stories about Matthew's bedroom antics. The majority of them sickened me, but the thought of a desperate Matthew slapping his cock against a disinterested wife and looking perplexed when she didn't immediately ravish him amused me. "And that didn't work?"

"No."

"*Amazing.*"

It was equally amazing that Matthew used to be such a hit with the ladies. I didn't know if it was just because he was younger, because *they* were younger—and therefore too naive or too horny to commit to any real flirting—or if Matthew had just lost his touch over the course of his marriage.

"I had to resort to masturbation again," he said, giving me an image that I definitely didn't find amusing. I had once stumbled upon Matthew while he was masturbating. He stopped what he was doing to berate me for catching him, telling me that I shouldn't be disgusted because it was perfectly normal, that what a man does in the comfort of his own house is no one else's business, and that, if anything, it was all my fault for following him when it was blatantly obvious what he intended to do. Which is all fair and well, but we were in McDonald's at the time and I'd only popped into the bathroom to wash Big Mac sauce off my hands.

There was a pause and I suspected that he was contemplating hanging up so he could pleasure himself again. Horny, unsexed men tend to get turned on by the merest mention of sex or naked women. But it didn't even take that much for Matthew. The thought of himself masturbating was enough to get him excited and make him masturbate again. It's a continuous cycle that only stops when he runs out of lubricant or his balls retreat back into his body.

"It's not right," he said eventually, seemingly rejecting the idea of more alone time with his hand. "Marriage is a commitment between two people who signed a verbal contract that neither one of them should ever need to masturbate again."

"I don't think that's quite what marriage is."

"If I need to unload, then she should be ready to receive me."

"Is this what you tell Sharon?" I wondered. "Because I think I may have found your problem."

"Don't be stupid. Even if she did listen to me, I wouldn't tell her that."

I pitied him. He was breathing heavily now, and there was a tone of what appeared to be worry in his voice. It sounded like he was getting ready to cry, or doing his best to avoid crying. I had never known Matthew to be affected by anything that anyone ever did or said. He was like a robot with a penis.

"I need your help," he reiterated.

"I don't know—" I paused; his breathing had changed again and I could hear something else. "Are you okay?" I asked. "You sound a little—what's that noise?"

"I told you, I had no choice but to come downstairs and beat one out."

"You're doing it *now*!?"

"Is that a problem?"

"While you're on the phone with me?"

"I have two hands, don't I?"

"Are you fucking kidding me?"

"I don't see—"

I hung up, pressing the call-end button way more times than was necessary and feeling a desperate need to shower immediately afterward.

To say he had a skewed view of the world would be an understatement. He recently tried to convince me that Jehovah's Witnesses were secret government agents sent to catch you masturbating, insisting it was more than a coincidence that they only showed up when he was in the bathroom trying to knock one out. He didn't seem to acknowledge that ever since his wife stopped showing an interest in sex, he was barely out of the bathroom.

"And why would they want to catch you masturbating?" I had asked him.

"Exactly!"

He had tapped his nose and I'd shook my head. The excessive masturbation was definitely doing something to his brain. For most men, masturbation was a private act. Something they did away from the rest of the world and something they kept to themselves. For Matthew, it was as natural as clipping his nails or making cereal, and I'm fairly confident he had masturbated while doing both of those things in the past.

It could have also been the lack of sex rotting his brain. Matthew had always been a sexually active guy, more so than any man I had ever known. He lived and breathed sex, and he had been that way for as long as I had known him. Take that away from him and he just wasn't the same man. Like Samson without his hair, or Professor Hawking without his wheelchair.

Matthew invited himself around the following morning. He looked tired, like he hadn't been sleeping and had been up all night doing something else, which was exactly why I refused to shake his hand. I had actually slept. Ben hadn't been as troublesome. He had slept through the night, woke for his breakfast, and was asleep again in my arms as I stood in front of Matthew, trying to cover Ben's ears when Matthew spoke, just in case anything got through to his developing brain.

"You look like shit," I told him.

"You don't look so smooth yourself, prick."

Matthew isn't very good at taking criticism.

He brushed past me and I heard him talking to Lizzie in the living room, polluting her mind with his filth before she even ate breakfast. I had only left him alone for a few seconds, but that was more than enough time for him to offend someone. When I entered the living room, Lizzie was on the couch, one of her breasts on show. She had just fed Ben and was now using an alien contraption to suck out some breast milk for later. She looked half-asleep and very annoyed.

"Do you know what your perverted little friend just said to me?" she said when she remembered how to speak.

Matthew was looking quite happy with himself, so although I hadn't heard, I could have made an educated guess.

"He asked me if he could have a suck," she said, gesturing toward her breast, which she now made an attempt to cover. "Then he told me to get in the kitchen and make him some breakfast."

"Toast will do," Matthew chimed in. "But if you want to make some cornflakes and squirt some of that on them, that'd be great."

"You disgust me," Lizzie said bitterly.

"Thank you." As bad as he was with criticism, he considered that a compliment. I was sure that he got a kick out of being insulted by women. If he had his way, small talk would be banished and replaced with dirty talk. He'd get a sexual thrill out of every conversation, and it would also make the world a little more interesting.

Lizzie made an annoyed grunting noise and then slowly climbed to her feet, doing her best to scowl at Matthew on her ascent before leaving the room and slamming the door behind her.

Matthew rubbed his hands together and I had flashbacks of the previous night. I'd actually dreamed about that, and in my dream I hadn't been able to escape as Matthew followed me around, waving his penis about and threatening to slap me with it. No matter what I did, I couldn't get away from him and his insatiable needs. If he wasn't harassing me on the phone like some sexually perverted creep, he was invading my dreams like an exhibitionist Freddy Krueger.

"Right, now that she's out of the way, let's get down to business." He frowned at me as I moved to cover Ben's ears. "Why do you look so scared?"

"Nothing. No reason."

"Okay. So, what's the plan?"

I had no idea. Although Matthew liked to think of himself as the center of the universe and had no doubt been expecting me to stay awake all night contemplating how to get him laid, I hadn't given it a second thought. In fact, I had been so haunted by the phone call that I hadn't been able to think of anything else.

"If I don't have sex soon then I'm going to explode."

"When you phoned me last night, it sounded like you were making an effort to release some pressure."

"Believe me, if there was any *pressure* left in there, it's gone. Like completely. I don't even use tissue anymore. I use a duster."

That was my fault. I engaged him, so I asked for it. I tried to shake these new haunting images out of my mind, worried that they would also invade my dreams.

I sat down next to him, careful not to wake Ben. I didn't want him to wake up and find an irritable Matthew sitting next to him. It was an experience that countless girls had been through and one I wouldn't wish upon anyone, let alone my five-week-old child.

"I think that we should start by talking to your wife, get her side of the story."

"Are you fucking crazy?" He spun around on the seat, his red eyes glaring angrily at me. I had images of him whipping out his penis and chasing me around the room.

"Language!" I hissed, probably looking a little more scared than I would have liked, on account of the penis imagery.

"He's a baby, he won't understand."

I glared at him.

He rolled his eyes, mumbled a "fine," and then continued. "She's been off it lately. Stressed, working late, snappy as hell. I'm not sure if something's not right with her or if I'm so desperate for sex that I'm projecting and making her like that. Either way, I can't just openly talk to her."

"Why not?"

"Because it's fu—it's insane."

"You're right," I said, nodding slowly and not breaking eye contact. "Talking things over with your life partner is insane. It makes much more sense to book a hotel room and hire a prostitute."

The sarcasm couldn't have been laid on thicker, but Matthew bypassed it, thinking with his penis again. I saw his eyes widen as a smile broke out on his face.

"I was joking," I said quickly.

"No, no, it's a great idea."

"It's not. It's really not, I mean, for one thing, it was *my* idea and ideas are not my forte."

"Stop blabbering," he said, swatting at me limply as if I was a fly trying to spoil his picnic, which in some ways I suppose I was. "You get online and find a nice hotel, not too expensive, though; the less I spend on linen and amenities, the more I can spend on tits and pussy, the things that matter."

Oh God, what have I done?

"While you do that, I'll go and get ready. I'll pack an overnight back and get the number of an escort agency from a friend."

I knew I could trust Matthew to have those sort of friends.

"You really want to do this?" I asked as he stood up, looking excited.

He nodded. "I don't want to, I *need* to. If I don't get sex soon then I'll explode. If I don't get sex soon then my marriage might even be in jeopardy. I don't know how much longer I can hold out. I need to do this for myself, for my sanity, and for my balls, but I also need to do this for Sharon and for our marriage."

I covered Ben's ears. "You're a regular fucking hero, aren't you?" I said softly.

"Quit your moralistic bullshit," he said bitterly. "I need this. Find a hotel, I'll be back shortly."

I found a fairly expensive hotel, making sure that it had its own private hot tub and porn on pay-per-view. I secretly hoped that that would be enough to satisfy his needs and stop him from ruining his marriage, but knew that it was a long shot.

"It was the cheapest they had at short notice," I told him when he saw the price and complained, mentally deflating the breasts of the woman in his head. He was probably adding a mustache and a few warts, as well, but it didn't really matter. He was desperate enough to poke his penis in a female Chewbacca.

He hit on the girl at reception, but he seemed different suddenly. Not like the Matthew I had known for many years. He was just as crude and just as forward, but it wasn't as innocent now that he was a grown man. He was less Jack-the-Lad and more Peter-the-Pervert. The woman at the desk flattered him as she was wont to do, but I saw the look she gave him when she thought we weren't looking. It was a shame to see how far he had fallen, but at the same time, he didn't *need* to be any good with women; he had a beautiful wife who loved him and still fell for his bullshit. She was all he should need, all that *anyone* could *ever* need, but he had been blinded by his penis.

In the hotel room, as I prepared to show him the hot tub and the pay-per-view channels, he went straight for the phone and dialed a number he had written on a slip of paper. I stood over him with my arms folded, hoping I could somehow pressure him into actually doing the right thing.

"I would like to order a girl, please," he said, grinning. "To be delivered."

He chuckled lightly and I heard the woman on the other end of the phone do the same, even though it was probably the creepiest joke she had ever heard.

"My name is Kieran," he said, winking at me, a gesture that I didn't return. He gave the address of the hotel, gave his preference as, "face is not important, just give me a nice pair of tits and a firm ass," and then moved onto the extras. "Maybe just some foreplay, some kissing, and maybe a little light spanking, if the mood strikes."

Maybe he *wasn't* going to go all the way after all. Maybe he just wanted female company, maybe—

"And potentially some fisting, and some anal, but we'll probably go for straight-up sex first and then see how it goes."

He hung up with a grin and then turned to me. "What's wrong with you?" he asked. "If *that* disgusts you then I need to show you some of my home movies."

I was back to realizing that my best friend was just as twisted and soulless as he had always been. "So, what did she say?" I asked.

"She's game for it, what do you expect?" he said with a noncha-lant shrug. "It's money, that's all that matters." He paused, lost in thought momentarily. "She actually sounded quite hot. Maybe I should ask her if she'll come around instead."

"She's not the escort?"

He looked at me like I was an idiot, a look I was accustomed to. "It's an agency, she's just the admin. She speaks to the clients, arranges the bookings, finds the right girls—don't you know *anything*?"

"I'm not as experienced as you are when it comes to prostitutes."

"*Escorts*," he said, stressing the word.

"What's the difference?"

"Usually bigger tits," he said, pressing his hands to his chest to mimic breasts, in case I didn't know what they were either. "And more stamina. I think it's all about quality. Prostitutes are skinny, poor, and usually addicted to drugs; escorts are a little higher class so they tend to be better."

I had no idea how that related to breast size, but I wasn't about to question a master on his favorite subject, a man who had probably slept with every working girl in the city. Matthew had had so many sex partners that I was surprised he still found sex entertaining. If I do the same thing too many times, it loses its appeal and becomes dull and boring, regardless of how fun it was to begin with. That was the reason behind my recent indifference toward M&Ms.

"Do you want me there?" I asked him.

"Do I want my best friend beside me while I spend the night with a beautiful girl who wants to have sex with me?" He put a finger to his lips. "Hmm. You know what, I think I'll pass."

"You don't have to be a dick about it, you know. I'm just trying to help. You asked me to help you, remember? And yet I haven't really done anything but stand by while you find, phone, and then potentially fuck a prostitute."

"*Escort.*"

"Whatever."

"You have a kid at home, remember."

"Do I remember? You're the one who seems to keep forgetting, having me run around and do your dirty business when I should be tending to my new child."

"And why aren't you?" he said, a cheeky smile on his face that suggested he somehow knew what the answer would be.

"Because Lizzie said I was useless and needed to give her and Ben a break."

He laughed. I glared.

"So, why *did* you want me here?" I pushed.

He shrugged. "Maybe I just needed you for moral support."

"That's bullshit."

"Maybe I just wanted to give you something to do. I know you must feel useless not having any work to do."

"I feel useless? And I suppose you feel perfectly useful working every day, making all that money, and achieving all that you achieve," I said, knowing that Matthew was just as pathetically unemployed as I was.

"That's low," he said.

"I agree. You deserved it."

He sighed. "Okay, the truth is that I needed you to be the sane one, to let me know that all of this is okay," he admitted honestly. "I am potentially cheating on my wife, and I don't trust my own morality, so . . ." he shrugged. "That's your job. You have a conscience, or so you're always telling me."

"But all of this *isn't* okay. I never said it was. In fact, if you're taking my advice on this then I think you should leave this hotel right now! Go home, talk things out with your wife, and—what are you doing?"

Matthew was sitting on the bed, remote in hand. "I'm ignoring you."

"But—but—you can't do that. You asked for my help and—what is that—*porn*? You're watching porn? Are you fucking serious?"

I should have known he would find it. He has a built-in vagina radar.

"Like I said, I'm horny, I need my fix."

"You're unbelievable," I told him.

"Thank you."

"That wasn't a compliment. And just so you know, I'm not leaving."

That got his attention. He sat up on the bed, muting the moaning on the television. "You can't stay," he said.

"Watch me." I sat on the chair in the corner, spreading my legs and folding my arms across my chest.

"Are you really going to sit there and watch me have sex with an escort?"

"I'm going to sit here," I said. "As for the sex, well, we'll see. I'm hoping that the person I have called my best friend for a number of years now is not some sex-hungry pig who always puts his penis first. I'm hoping that the man who promised to love, honor, and obey Sharon will do just that, and won't look to stick his filthy dick in the first prostitute he sees."

"*Escort.*"

"Whatever!" I spat, throwing my arms around wildly and feeling a little silly for doing so. "You call them what you want. I'll sit here while you do that. So when you're peeling off her panties and preparing to fill her full of STDs, just remember that I'll be sitting here watching every move you make; when you whisper sickly sweet nothings into her ear and promise to rock her world, just remember that I'll be able to hear every single word."

I could see I was getting through to him, and I could see the doubt and the regret coming through, but I could also see that he was going to do his best to hide it. "You're disturbed," he said.

"You sicken me," I told him. "You should phone this girl up right now and tell her that you're married. Tell her that you can't look at her face without thinking about your wife and therefore you can't bring yourself to sleep with her."

He thought about that for a moment and then exhaled slowly. "You're right," he said eventually.

I shot forward in the chair, surprised. "I am?"

He nodded and slowly picked up the phone. "I wouldn't feel right looking at her face, seeing Sharon and feeling the betrayal."

"Right!" I cried happily. "*Finally!*"

He picked up the phone and I watched as the glum expression remained on his face while he waited for it to ring. I stood above him, looking and feeling proud.

"Hello," he said. "I phoned a few minutes ago requesting a girl. My name is Kieran?"

I beamed at him, feeling proud as he prepared to admit defeat, to retreat. I had conquered a beast that seemed untamable. Many had tried and failed before me, but I had finally—

"I want her to wear a mask."

"What?" I hissed under my breath.

The woman on the phone must have asked him the same question because he quickly reiterated. "A mask, any will do, but something that covers her face entirely. It's a thing, I'm sure you understand."

I slumped back into my chair, and the smug smile that had been wiped off my face slowly transferred to Matthew's.

"There," he said, hanging up. "Problem solved. Now, you can stay there all you want, but I'm going to continue watching this to get me in the mood, then I'm going to bang the living daylights out of a hot escort. So if you *do* insist on staying, then at least take some pictures so I have something to look at later."

When she knocked on the door, Matthew didn't even acknowledge me. He simply turned off the television, checked himself in the mirror, and then opened the door. I couldn't see the woman, but I heard Matthew speak and I didn't hear her reply. He spoke again and this time he stepped away to invite her in, revealing her to me. She wore a long coat, clearly to disguise the fact that she wore very little underneath, and she also wore a Venetian mask that obscured her features. Her hair was tied back tightly, giving her the appeal of a secretary or even a dominatrix, both of which I knew would turn Matthew on. Although it didn't take much.

She hesitated and seemed fascinated by Matthew, perhaps unable to believe his confidence and the fact that he was so open about all of this. It certainly made me feel creepy, and I imagined that for anyone who was new to it, expecting their client to be submissive and somewhat anxious, Matthew was a shock.

"Are you going to come in or what?" he asked her.

She looked at him, cleared her throat as if she were about to speak, and then entered. She walked straight up to me and then pointed at me.

I shook my head and nodded to Matthew. "It's him you're here to see," I told her. "But don't worry. I'll get out of your way."

I had intended to sit and pester him as much as possible, but I knew he was going to have sex with her either way and I couldn't bring myself to watch. She was also very timid and as well as hurting Sharon, I didn't want to damage another female.

"Not staying for the show?" Matthew asked as I shuffled past him.

The look I gave him said more than words could. He knew what I felt, he knew what I was thinking; the rest was up to him.

I shut the door behind me, stood outside for a moment, and then slowly rested back against the door, sliding down until I was sitting on the floor. I listened to him flirting with her on the other side of the door, and I felt sicker and sicker the more I heard. But then something caught me off guard, something wasn't right. Because when he should have been rubbing his dirty self all over her, or at least undressing her, he was actually complaining.

"If you don't undress then we can't do anything."

"Why the rush?" I heard her ask.

There was a contemplative silence before he answered. "Maybe you're right."

They mumbled after that, their voices reduced to barely audible tones. I lowered my head into my knees, stared at the floor, and thought about how I would feel if Lizzie had done that to me, or how she would feel if I had done that to her. Sharon had known about Matthew's ways before they married, but she loved him regardless; she forgave him and she trusted him.

I decided that I couldn't bear it any longer. I couldn't wait for the mumbles to turn into groans, and for the groans to turn into something much more sordid. He had a habit of narrating when he was having sex, describing himself in the third person, and although it had been hilarious the times I'd overheard in the past, it would be somewhat less amusing now.

I stood and prepared to leave, but then the tone changed and I was sure I heard Matthew sob.

That can't be right.

The only time I'd ever heard Matthew cry was when England were knocked out of the World Cup, and even then it had been brief. This was so much worse. I pressed an ear to the door and listened.

He is crying.

Holy shit. So this is what it feels like when hell freezes over.

"I just don't know what to do." He was speaking through sobs. "I love her, I really do, but I don't think she wants me anymore. She just isn't interested in me."

The woman didn't seem to be replying, but I imagined her consoling him, probably while secretly wondering if this was a fetish she hadn't encountered before.

"I'm sorry, I can't have sex with you. It would have been great, I know. But I just can't. This was a lie, an act to make her jealous and to get back at her, but I can't. I just can't."

Really?

I took a step back and double-checked the room number.

"It's okay," the woman said. "Believe me, I understand." She sounded familiar, and just as I put it down to the sound of her voice being distorted by the door and the wall, she spoke again.

"Matthew, I think we have to talk."

Matthew? But—

Without thinking, I opened the door and burst in. I saw Matthew sitting on the edge of the bed with his wife, the mask now in her hands. Matthew was gawking at her, and he didn't even acknowledge me as I entered.

"Sharon?" he spat.

She looked to me and then back to Matthew before hanging her head. "I didn't want anyone to know," she said softly.

"You're a prostitute?" I asked, perplexed.

"Escort!" Matthew snapped before turning back to his wife. "You're an *escort*?"

She gripped his hand tightly, her head still lowered. "Dominatrix mostly, and also some fetishes, never sex, although . . ." She looked into his eyes. "Tonight was going to be my first. The jobs have been drying up and they said that to stay on at the agency I needed to do it."

"But your job at the university . . ."

She shrugged. "They fired me."

"When?"

"Weeks ago. I know we were relying on that income to get by, so . . . I didn't think there was any other option."

"There's always an option. I mean, God, if I know that things were that desperate, I would have gotten another job and I would have made it stick. Hell, I would have sold my body before letting you sell yours."

I laughed, a little too loudly. They both stared at me, I pretended to be looking at my phone.

"I'm so sorry," she said to Matthew, their eyes locked once more. "I should have been honest with you."

"Well, I wasn't exactly helpful either," Matthew admitted.

"No, you were amazing, you always are."

It's amazing what bullshit people will tell each other when they're upset.

They were both in tears now, their hands locked together as if they were trying to squeeze each other to a pulp. There was no tension or hatred, both of them were in the wrong, and both of them looked like they were getting the cathartic release they'd been wanting for some time.

"So, the sex?" Matthew asked.

"I couldn't bring myself to do it. I haven't slept with the clients, but what I did still made me feel dirty. I just, well, I guess I didn't want to pass that onto you when I got home."

"This is like Jeremy Kyle," I said, my mouth hanging open, my eyes wide.

They turned to look at me again.

Did I say that out loud?

"I'm sorry, I'll go now."

I turned the corner and pressed myself up against the wall, closing the door with my foot while remaining in the room.

"He hasn't gone, you know," Matthew said." He's hiding around the corner, too dumb to realize there's a mirror there."

I turned to the mirror and cursed, but I stayed where I was, at least giving them the illusion of privacy.

"I'm so sorry," Sharon said, putting a hand on Matthew's cheek.

"No, *I'm* sorry."

He reciprocated and they stared into each other's eyes. In moments, they were kissing, a deep and passionate kiss. It made me smile, made me feel happier than I had felt all day. That smile turned to embarrassment when she stood and removed her coat, exposing nothing but a lace bra and knickers, but it was still a happy moment.

She jumped on top of him and before long he was getting his wish, and he wasn't doing it at the expense of his marriage.

"Dude!" Matthew spat, staring at me through the mirror, pausing just as Sharon was preparing to take the final step. "Can you fuck off, please?"

I held up my hands. "Sorry. Can I first just say that I'm really proud of you, of you both really, and—"

"*Kieran!*" Sharon said, twisting to face me. "Listen to the man, we're busy here!"

"You make such a lovely couple."

"Get out!" they both screamed.

I left the hotel room a happy man. The screams of a very horny and sex-starved couple who were finally getting their release followed me.

So romantic.

4

The Blind Leading the Blind

After their problems, and after the night in the hotel room when I came close to playing the third wheel in some rather heated love-making, Matthew and Sharon settled down, their issues departing on a sticky, slippery course of endless sex and adoration. They were like honeymooners all over again, unable to leave each other alone and constantly trying to rip each other's clothes off.

Matthew told me that they even did it in the elevator of a busy building, and because there were only two floors, he spent a lot of time hitting the button and giving some rather baffled onlookers an apologetic smile. They had sex in the changing rooms of a swim-ming pool, where I assume the smell of chlorine and the constant threat of warts was a turn-on; and they had sex in a phone booth, which are essentially modern toilets that advertise prostitutes, porn, and the Yellow Pages.

They had also done it in a shoe shop, something he never stopped bragging about. Personally, I can't think of a more boring place to have sex, or a more boring place, period, but maybe that was the allure for him. For both of them.

She didn't give up her job as an escort—she just made a slight deviation. With Matthew's help, she set herself up as a professional dominatrix, catering for people who liked to be spanked and spat on, as opposed to sucked-off and ridden, as Matthew so eloquently put it. He wasn't one to talk, of course, as he was as kinky as they came. In fact, I was sure that the main reason he became his wife's pimp was so he could get her to warm up to the idea of turning their spare bedroom into a sex dungeon and being able to write it all off as a tax expense.

Matthew became very happy with his sex life, but he still believed that he was God's gift to women and he wanted to prove that. He found an unwitting man that he could mentor, someone who he could show his creepy, chauvinistic ways and pass on pearls of wisdom to, such as "how to sleep with a stranger" and "how to convince her that anal is the way to go." That unfortunate individual was Marcus Plum, a sorry-looking, sweaty, and awkward man who had no charm, no confidence, and very little else going for him.

"He reminds me of you," Matthew had said when he first introduced me to Marcus. We were both sitting in the corner booth of a club, watching Marcus stumble and bumble his way through a conversation with a fifty-year-old woman who looked like she chain-smoked children for breakfast.

"Oh," I said, feeling a little dejected and wondering if I had ever been as hopeless and charmless as that, and then realizing that yes, I had been, and I probably still was.

"He's a thirty-year-old virgin who has never had a girlfriend, never felt a tit, never stroked a pussy, and never plunged his—"

"—Please stop there."

Ben had grown out of one difficult stage and into another. We got more sleep, but the feedings had increased, and the pooping had increased with them. He was six months old, although I was pretty sure that he had taken six years to get to that point. The person I saw in the mirror looked more like my dad than me. I had a hard time believing I was twenty-five. As did everyone who saw me.

After a few months, Lizzie and I began alternating nights out, so one of us was always there to look after Ben while the other enjoyed some time with friends. We hadn't enjoyed a night out together, and when one went out and came back drunk and smiling, the other was always annoyed. But it was the only way we could inject a little sanity into the situation. She was also due to start work again soon, so she had allowed me a few more nights out. Even better, she hadn't insisted that I start looking for a new job. Not yet, anyway.

Matthew grimaced as Marcus tried to lean against the bar, playing it cool as he'd been taught, but not noticing the over-filled ashtray.

"And you think you can help him?" I asked as Marcus yelped, knocked the ashtray off the bar, and then nearly knocked the ashy cougar off her stool.

"I'm starting to have my doubts."

Marcus had straightened himself and was standing again, his arms by his side. He seemed to be attempting to get over the awkwardness by standing still, saying nothing, and waiting for it to pass, despite the fact that everyone was staring at him and the bartender was waiting for him to pay for the drinks he had seemingly forgotten about.

"Does he have a thing for older women?" I wondered.

"No." Matthew held up a pair of large-rimmed spectacles. "I told him he looked better without them."

"What's that got to do with anything?"

Matthew pointed to a young and beautiful woman who had been sitting next to the ash-lipped, leather-faced woman several moments ago, but had gradually backed away during Marcus's arrival and proceeding antics. She was now several feet away as she stared at Marcus, probably trying to remember her self-defense classes.

"I told him to go for her. He took a detour."

I twisted my face and then smiled. "You've got some work on your hands, mate."

Matthew shrugged, a gesture that said he was skilled enough to follow through. "I can do it. After all, I helped you, didn't I?"

"I think *help* is a strong word, isn't it?"

"Well, what would you call it?"

"'Made a fool out of me and nearly killed me' would be closer to the truth."

"But at least I got you laid."

"No. No you didn't."

"Really?"

I nodded slowly.

Matthew looked thoughtful for a moment and then he slowly leaned across the table, a sparkle in his eye and mischief on his mind.

I pressed my hand over his mouth before he could utter a word. "I'm a happily married man," I reminded him before his deviousness could find room to maneuver. "You concentrate on cyclops there and leave me out of it."

Matthew sat back, looking disappointed. "Fine," he said, following it with one long exhalation. "I guess Marcus will be fun enough."

Matthew told Marcus to be confident and to "play it cool." He gave him one of his best chat-up lines, a favorite "trick" he had utilized to win him countless dates and one night stands.

"This is what you do," he explained in his cocky, assured manner. "You need to approach her without looking at her, don't acknowledge that you want to be with her, don't even acknowledge that she's in the room. Then"—he pulled out a slip of paper—"you give her this."

Marcus frowned at the slip of paper. It said: WHAT DO YOU WANT ME TO DO? in large bold letters, with two small tick boxes underneath reading KISS YOU and TAKE YOU HOME.

He turned his eyes back to Matthew. "And this works?" he asked.

Matthew opened his arms and leaned back in a manner that said, "It hasn't failed *me*."

I had an inclination to stop him at that point, seeing my own past race before my eyes, but I decided to let this one play out. I knew what Marcus would be thinking, and I knew that if I stopped him, he wouldn't think I was helping him. I knew that because I had been there, and I had believed the same things he was believing at that moment. He believed that Matthew was better than him in every way, that it wasn't just that he was better looking (although he was) but that it was because he was more confident, funnier, and much more charming. Marcus no doubt knew, as I had known, that what worked for Matthew might not necessarily work for him, but he refused to let rational thought get in the way, a mistake that I had also made. Marcus wanted a girlfriend, he wanted a *woman*, and as Matthew had never failed in that department, he was happy to take his advice.

Marcus looked nervous when he first used the trick. He was shaking as he stumbled across the dance floor, ready to give it to the girl of his choosing—a pretty brunette with a timid smile and a vibrant dress. I could see that he tried not to look at her, but she was attractive and he was soon staring. When she turned and caught his eye, I think he nearly had a heart attack. He tried to avert his eyes and act nonchalant so quickly that he lost his footing and stumbled into a heavyset guy who was dancing like a drunken epileptic.

The big man wasn't very happy with the interruption and was spitting vulgarities and nonsensical obscenities at Marcus by the time we made our way over. I took Marcus to one side while Matthew dealt with the big man, cooling him off and calming him down in a way that only Matthew could, because although he had lost most of his touch with the females, he still had it with the males. That was probably the reason I was still friends with him, simply because I was under his spell.

The girl had stopped looking at Marcus by the time Matthew gave him another pep talk and sent him back on his way, literally guiding him to her as if directing a blindfolded kid in a game of Pin the Tail on the Donkey. Marcus stood behind her and smiled his warmest smile—looking like a constipated pervert—before tapping her gently on the shoulder. She glowered at him when she turned around, as did all her friends. They had all been talking merrily, but they stopped when they saw him. They looked at him like he was about to tell them they had to leave the premises.

His voice caught in his throat. He coughed to clear it and sprayed a wash of spittle over the pretty brunette. He stared at her in horror as she recoiled and wiped the spit from her face, then she turned to her friends, who seemed to be looking for an exit or a savior.

"I'm sorry," he mumbled. He extended his arm, which was trembling violently, and offered her the piece of paper.

He grinned at her as she looked at it, thanked her as she took it from his hand, and then frowned when he saw that the paper had been soaked and the words had been smudged. He had been sweating so profusely that most of the ink was now soaking into his palms.

"What does that say?" Her friends gathered around, peering over her shoulder. "*Want me to take you?*" one of them said, before turning her eyes away from the smudged paper and toward Marcus, who was also clearly looking for an exit and a savior.

That savior came in the form of Matthew, who had been on standby, almost expecting Marcus to mess it up. He explained the awkwardness away, using his charm and his confidence to stop them from calling the police and preventing Marcus from making his way onto the sex offenders' list. I watched the events unfold without flinching, because as cringeworthy as it was, I had seen worse. If anything, Marcus actually seemed a little more confident than I was.

The following week, I joined the pair of them in the bar again. Lizzie was having a few of her work colleagues round to catch up on gossip before she returned the following week. They would drown Ben in high-pitched gossip, innuendo, and the sort of cackling laughter that can only come from mothers drunk on cheap boxed wine. I worried what it would do to his psychology, but figured he would have to get used to it eventually. His mother would send him round the bend with all kinds of cackling, gossip, and drunkenness in years to come. It's what mothers did. So, it's best that he got used to it.

Marcus was on the prowl again when I met him and Matthew in the bar. He was also still a virgin despite spending two weeks under Matthew's wing.

"What about the note?" I asked. "Are you not going to try that again? What are you, a Looney Toons cartoon?"

Matthew smiled softly, but the smile didn't seem to be directed at my joke and I sensed a story coming. "We *did* try it again," he said.

"Tell me about it," I said as Matthew fixed an accusing stare on Marcus. "What did you do to the poor man this time?"

"Me?" he said, looking incredulous.

"Yes, *you*, I've been down this road, I know what you're like."

Matthew held up his hands. "I'm not at fault here," he said. "I can get women. Most of the time I'm beating them away. You're the ones with the problem, you're the ones who can't follow instructions, you're the ones who—"

"So what happened? I asked, cutting him short and turning my attention toward Marcus.

Marcus sighed. "I figured I'd pick the girl who looked the most available," he said, trying to avoid using the word that was on his mind.

"The biggest slut in the bar," Matthew chimed in, feeling no need to avoid such a word. "Her pussy is so infamous they're thinking of naming a toilet stall after her."

Marcus sighed again. "Not strictly true, but anyway, she was drunk and I'd seen her write down her number for half a dozen men already—"

"—Although she could have been signing autographs."

"Will you shut up?" Marcus ordered.

Matthew held up his hands, his face alight with mischief.

"So I wrote the note, downed a few shots of vodka for Dutch courage, and then—"

"You didn't piss yourself again, did you?" I jumped in.

"He told you?" Marcus snapped. "And I mean no, that never happened." He cleared his throat and shifted uncomfortably in his seat. "And it wasn't piss, *the bathroom faucet burst.*"

Matthew took his cue to jump in again, "What were you doing with a bathroom faucet in your pants?"

"Do you want to hear this story or not?" Marcus asked, looking increasingly annoyed.

"Sorry, go on," I told him. "What happened with the note?"

"Okay, so I gave her the two options like Matthew suggested: 'kiss you' or 'take you home.' And I gave her the note."

"To be fair," Matthew jumped in again. "I blame your handwriting. You hold a pen like you're gonna use it to stab someone."

Marcus frowned at Matthew.

"And which one did she tick?" I asked.

"Well," Marcus said despondently. "She penciled her own option. She wrote 'fuck off,' gave it a big tick, and then gave it back."

"Ouch," I said.

Marcus gave me a pitiful smile and lowered his gaze to the table and to his drink. Matthew was grinning, but I felt bad for Marcus. I knew what it was like to be in his position and it wasn't pretty. Marcus was roughly the same age as I was, yet I felt like I had so much more experience than him. I'd been with the sort of crazy women that Matthew was trying to set him up with, I'd been with the quieter ones who turned out to be even crazier, and I'd also found a rose among all of those thorns. I didn't consider myself as experienced as Matthew, and I certainly didn't have his confidence, but I had a lot more than I used to have and I felt like I had enough to help Marcus out.

I finished what was left of my drink, stood, and asked Marcus to follow me.

"Where you going?" Matthew said. "Off to powder your noses?"

"I'm going to help him. I'm going to succeed where you failed."

He laughed so loudly that the women at the nearby table looked over. They noted Matthew with concern and then us with some degree of disgust. I mentally ticked them off our list and moved on.

Marcus didn't look as confident in me as he had been in Matthew, and I couldn't blame him for that. I took him to the bar and we both rested against it, with Marcus looking as cool as possible for a thirty-year-old virgin with glasses the size of wheel rims, and me trying my best to look remotely less awkward than him.

"You see, Marcus, it's not about the biggest slut or the drunkest girl." I surveyed the bar like a rancher checking his cattle, and Marcus followed suit. In truth, I had no idea what I was saying or doing, but I figured that if I at least looked like I did then I would instill some confidence. "You're a nice guy, and you need a nice girl. You need a girl that can make you feel good about yourself, a girl that can take away your self-pity and make you feel human, make you feel like a man."

I turned to him to see how I was doing and I was delighted to see that he was grinning and nodding. Before I could continue, my phone buzzed. I stopped, checked a message I had received from Lizzie, and then dropped in back in my pocket.

"Everything okay?"

"Just my wife reminding me that I'm lovely, she's very happy, and we have a great baby."

He looked confused. "What does that mean?"

"It means she's on her second glass. Give it a few hours and she'll start telling me how she suspects her work colleagues are evil and how they're all having affairs. Then she'll start getting inexplicably angry with me, before telling me she loves me."

"And then?"

"And then something amazing happens. She'll either fall asleep on a pillow that is half fabric and half drool, or she'll sober up and act confused when I tell her how drunk she was.

Marcus seemed both confused and impressed.

I patted him on the shoulder. "Anyway, as I was saying . . ." I surveyed the room as I continued with my speech. "You need a girl who won't care that you have glasses the size of small spaceships. A girl who can look beyond your puny bony and your oddly shaped face, one who doesn't see that your hair looks like it's been cut by your mother and your wardrobe looks like you've been forced to borrow clothes from your dad. A girl who doesn't detect that musty smell that you give off and doesn't notice that you walk like you're desperately searching for the nearest toilet. You need a girl who will love you, and that's what I'm going to help you find."

I turned to him again, smiling a smile that didn't stay for long. "What are you looking so fucking glum for?" I pushed him on the arm and he lifted his gaze up from his feet. "Come on. Stop feeling so sorry for yourself all the time. Let's find you a woman."

I was half right with Lizzie. Two hours later, she messaged me to say that her friends had left, but she didn't care because they were annoying her anyway. After another hour, she messaged me to tell me that Ben was asleep and there was no need to come home, but she was lonely and would love to spend some time with me. Early on in our relationship, I would have fallen for that, thanked her, and then stayed out. When I learned how much trouble that got me into, I began to read between the lines. But as much as I knew I would regret it, I decided to stay out. I felt a certain affinity with Marcus. It wasn't that I liked him. Or that I particularly respected him. If anything, he was a little too odd for me, and that's saying something. I just felt sorry for him. I saw a little of my younger self in him and I knew that leaving him with Matthew would be akin to throwing him to the lions.

So I turned off my phone, ready to pretend that the battery had died. My wife was no idiot, but I crossed my fingers, hoped she was still drinking, and let my own drunken mind convince my future self that it would be okay.

I stood with Marcus at the bar for a few moments. I let him buy me and himself a few shots for Dutch courage, and then I took him on a tour of the bar and its female attractions.

The first woman looked friendly enough, but there seemed like there could be an element of bitchiness about her. I took a chance, though; for the most part, she looked sweet and fairly innocuous. She wasn't traditionally beautiful, but had a certain quirky cuteness about her that Marcus liked. I told him to wait by the bar as I approached, tapping her on the shoulder. I had no idea what I was going to say, but I didn't intend to let myself think about it either. I knew that if I thought about it, then I would realize what I was doing, and if I realized then the panic would set in and I would stop doing it. I was just going to go for it and not think about anything. For the rest of the night, it would be as if I didn't have a brain at all, which was how Matthew did it.

She gave me an indifferent look, one that suggested that if I didn't impress her with the first words that came out of my mouth, then I wouldn't get a chance to impress her for the rest of the night.

"Hello there. I think I have something that you would like."

"Oh, really?"

I nodded and then looked alarmed. "I'm not talking about my penis."

"You're not?"

"No, no. I mean I'm sure you would lo—" I paused with my mouth open, she seemed amused. "Never mind."

"You're right, it's probably best to end it there." She giggled. "So, what's your name, and what do you have to show me?"

With my hand behind my back, I gestured for Marcus to come over. "It's my friend. He's had his eye on you all night, but he's too shy to come over and say anything. He was ready to leave, just walk right out of your life, but I told him that he couldn't do that, that for both of your sakes he had to give it a shot."

What do you know? I'm actually quite good at this.

The smile on her face suggested that she liked that as much as I did. "Okay, then bring him over. I'd love to meet him."

"He's here," I said, stepping aside.

I watched her face as Marcus approached, watched as the bright smile turned into an expectant grin, and watched as that expectant grin soured. By the time Marcus greeted her, she looked like she'd just found the rotten grape in an otherwise delectable bunch.

"*What. The. Fuck. Is. That?*" she said.

I turned to Marcus, whose chin had lowered to his chest once more, his eyes back on his feet. I felt so sorry for him, and at that moment I decided that I wasn't going to give up. I turned back to the woman to plead his case, but she had already turned her back on both of us.

"You're missing out," I told the back of her head. She didn't reply and didn't even turn around. "And your back fat looks like a small child is trying to escape out of your dress."

That was harsh. Very Matthew-like. I felt disgusted, ashamed, and happy with myself all at the same time.

This time she did turn around, but I stepped out of the way before she could slap me. "Get out of my face, creep!" she spat.

"Gladly." I gave her a bow for dramatic effect and to cheer up Marcus, who giggled like a schoolgirl. I wrapped my arm around him and led him away. "Don't despair, mate, we've got this, trust me."

The next girl was all by herself and looking just as lonely and as miserable as Marcus had been. She was sitting on a table in the corner, staring forlornly at her phone while twiddling the straw in a bottle of something unnaturally blue and probably unnervingly sweet. I told Marcus to loiter nearby and then I took a spare chair and plonked it down opposite her.

"Hello there," I said, sitting down. "How are you?"

Her eyes lit up when she saw me, which was always a plus, but this looked like more than just a friendly or even a flirty smile. She had an elongated face with a chin that seemed to be trying its best to escape and an underbite that you could hit a golf ball off, but I doubted that Marcus cared about either of those things. If she had a good personality and a vagina, then he was happy.

"You're looking a bit glum, anything I can do to help?"

"My boyfriend left me," she said, the smile still on her face, looking incredibly eerie considering the words coming out of her mouth. "Just walked out, said he wasn't interested. And we were supposed to get married and have kids."

"Shit, what a bastard."

She nodded, still smiling, a smile that was beginning to make my skin crawl. I wondered if her boyfriend really had left her, or if that's just what she told the police.

"You look like you're taking it well," I noted.

She nodded slowly, the porcelain smile still etched on her face. "Well, things are looking up now, aren't they? Now that you're here."

That's sweet.

"I mean, who needs him when I have you, right?" She broke her expression to giggle.

And that's kinda creepy.

"Yeah," I said, trying my best to join in, but secretly regretting sitting opposite her.

"So, are you married?"

"Am I *married?*"

She nodded. "You can't blame a girl for thinking about the future, can you?" She giggled again, an awkward giggle, a joking giggle, but her words seemed as sincere as they were psychotic.

"I think I should be going," I said, quickly standing up.

The smile broke instantly. "No, don't you leave me, as well." She also stood, and I was worried she would follow me.

"I'm sorry, I—"

"You're all just the fucking same!" she spat, slamming her fist down on the table, her face now looking like a rabid horse. She sat back down, buried her head in her hands, and began to cry.

"What was all that about?" Marcus asked as I grabbed him by the collar and quickly dragged him to the other side of the bar, as far away from Seabiscuit as possible.

"She's spoken for."

"Oh, that's a shame."

"Yes. Yes it is."

On our detour, we passed Matthew, who was sitting with his feet up on the table, a drink in one hand and his phone in the other. He gave us a cocky grin as we hurried by.

"Still no woman, I see."

"Fuck off."

I was at fault for the next two failures. Marcus picked them out and I zeroed in, but I fumbled my way through the conversations, losing their attention and any chance of getting them to meet Marcus, let alone take him home. My confidence was suffering, and Marcus was getting more and more dejected, but I was determined to continue.

Toward the end of the night, more drunk women were on the dance floor, and although I had told myself that I would avoid the drunk ones, I felt like I didn't have much choice. I went for a girl who had been quiet for most of the night, a shy and retiring type who had come alive thanks to several Jägerbombs and some neon cocktails. Her previously immaculate hair and dress was now all over the place and she was dancing and singing by herself, to a completely different song than the one everyone else was dancing and singing to.

I danced my way over to her. It took her a few moments before she realized that someone was in front of her, but as soon as she did, she began grinding up against me like a randy puppy—a two-hundred-pound puppy with no self-esteem, no inhibitions, and mascara all down its face. I managed to back off, at which point she called me a tease.

"I'm not here for me," I told her. "It's for a friend."

"Of course!" she yelled, "bring your friends along. The more the merrier."

"He's a nice guy and I think—"

"Do you want to do it here?" she slurred.

"Excuse me?"

"On the dance floor?" She looked around, sweeping her foot to make sure that it was sturdy ground, probably because she was sure it had been moving a few moments ago. "It's a little dusty, but it'll do, right?"

"I don't think—"

"No, no, you're right." She laughed and then burped, and then laughed some more *because* of the burp. I'd picked a winner here. "A bed would be better. Here—" she grabbed me and yanked me over to a table where she had spent the night with her friends. Most of those friends were now on the dance floor, doing their best to pretend they didn't know her, but one of them was still sitting at the table, looking grumpy as she sipped orange juice and most likely regretted ever agreeing to be the designated driver. I'd already hit on her earlier in the night without any success, otherwise I would have dumped the drunk one for her.

Before I knew what was happening, the drunk girl slapped a napkin in my hand. She had hastily scribbled an address, a phone number, and the words "me. you. fuck, tonight" in lipstick.

"Okay?" she shouted above the music, giving me the thumbs-up.

I nodded and put on my best smile as I watched her return to the dance floor. I was worried that I would have to leave there and then to avoid her trying to find me at the end of the night, but that worry faded when I watched her throw up all over herself and then slip and twist her ankle when she continued to dance.

The sober friend groaned and then reluctantly ran to help, while I stuffed the napkin in my pocket and made a sheepish getaway.

More drunk people followed, and I hoped that I could find someone for Marcus as the tiredness set in and everyone prepared to go home, but they were too drunk, too intelligible, and still not interested.

"I'm sorry," I told Marcus afterward, the energy completely drained out of me. "I tried my best."

I was so tired that I didn't realize he was smiling. "What about her?" he said, seemingly ignoring me and nodding toward a girl in the corner of the bar. I had missed her, but she looked like she was easy to miss. She was short, petite, timid. She had shoulder-length brunette hair, a cute smile, and two little dimples that were currently pointed rather shyly toward Marcus.

"I caught her eye," Marcus said. "I think she likes me."

She caught me staring and she turned away. "I don't think she's interested," I said, wiping the smile off his face and wrapping my arm around him again. "Sorry, it just wasn't your night. Or mine for that matter."

"You got a number, didn't you, on the napkin?"

I nodded. "The irony is that if she had kept it, she could have used it to wipe up the sick dripping down her legs when she left." I released an exhausted sigh. "Never mind, though. You live and you learn."

I left Marcus loitering by the bar and returned to the table where Matthew sat, a smug smile on his face. He still had his phone out, and as soon as I sat down, he threw his arm around me, leaned in close, and then took a selfie of the both of us.

"I had to get this on record," he told me when the picture was taken, his eyes beaming as he checked his handiwork. "The time that poor little Kieran tried to become a man and failed."

"You were right," I told him. "It was a bad idea."

"It's not your fault," he said. "It's Marcus. He's useless. I couldn't find him anyone, you couldn't find him—" He paused, his lower jaw almost hitting his chest. "You've got to be fucking kidding me."

I followed his gaze to the bar, where I saw Marcus locked in an embrace with the timid girl from the corner. He was so deep into her mouth, he looked like he was trying to eat her from the inside out.

"Holy shit," I said, laughing. "Way to go, Marcus."

The club was emptying, the lights turning on, and the music dying, and as everyone began to leave, stumbling over themselves and needing the support of their friends to remain upright, they all passed Marcus and the timid girl and they all cheered them and clapped them. The same girls that had turned their backs on him gave him catcalls, pats on the back, and as they departed, he looked like he was about to lose his virginity on the bar.

"Amazing," I said. "Just goes to show. Maybe he didn't need our help after all."

Matthew nodded, his shock turning into pride. "Do you think we should stop them?" he said. "Before they, you know . . ."

"Give him a few more minutes and—" Marcus stepped back and removed his pants, clearly lost in the moment. "—actually, yes, now's a good time."

It was a long night, but one that ended successfully, at least for one of us. Marcus went home with his new friend and couldn't keep his hands off her throughout the taxi ride. Matthew and I managed to stop them from going at it in the back of the taxi, but after we got off at our respective stops and left them to it, we knew there was a good chance Marcus wouldn't be a virgin by the time he made it home.

It was nearly three in the morning when I returned home, something that Lizzie was waiting to tell me. I'd been so caught up in getting Marcus laid that I had completely forgotten I'd told Lizzie I would be back by midnight. I'm sure it was in the back of my mind, just as I'm sure I had ignored it in favor of drinking and third-party flirting, but as I stood in my home, with an angry Lizzie in front of me, I remembered it all. I also remembered that I was a stupid idiot. Although Lizzie was keen to remind me of the fact just in case I'd forgotten.

She was wearing pajamas and a permanent scowl, and as soon as I stepped into the living room, she set about tearing me a new asshole. Ben was asleep upstairs, but Lizzie had mastered the art of shouting in whispers, so she could give me what for while ensuring that she didn't wake the baby.

"I'm sorry," I pleaded time and time again. "Things got away from me and—and—" I was tired and drawing a blank. I didn't want to tell her the truth, that I had spent the night hitting on women, and I was too tried to think up a decent lie.

"You're a married man, Kieran, and you're a father. You can't go gallivanting late at night anymore."

"I know, I'm sorry."

"I texted you. I asked you to come back."

That was the problem with her "Please don't, but if you don't mind" texts. It didn't matter which option I chose, it was always wrong.

"You mean the text about your friends?" I said. "I got that, but my phone died just as I was sending a reply."

Genius. I was impressed with myself. Something on her face suggested she knew I was lying, but that I was also too stupid to think of anything so believable so quickly.

Thinking I was on a roll, I decided to prove to her that my phone was dead. I pulled it out of my pocket and turned it so she could see, not willing to give it to her in case she tried to turn it on.

"I don't care," she said. "You said you would be back at midnight. What time do you call this?"

"Well, I don't know. My phone is dead and I don't have a watch."

Judging by the homicidal look on her face, I realized that that was one lie too far.

I made a move toward her, my arms outstretched in the pose of a hopeless and pleading husband who thinks kind words and cuddles can make everything okay.

"Get your hands off me," she said, slapping me away. "Take your coat off and get ready for bed. You stink of cheap booze and cheaper women."

I knew better than to respond to that remark, trying to defend myself at that moment would be suicide. It was what she wanted, and as soon as I did it, she would try to push me further, so instead I remained silent. Unfortunately, although my mouth was shut, there were other stupid parts of me that were very much active, and as I took my coat off, the napkin that the drunk women had given me fell out of my pocket.

I saw it out of the corner of my eye at first, a flash of white streaked with red, and when I realized what it was, my world fell still and silent. Time moved slowly. I grabbed at it, but it was already out of reach, already heading for the floor. My heart froze, and as Lizzie bent down to pick it up, I closed my eyes tightly. I knew in that instant that the whispers would stop and that I wouldn't be getting much sleep tonight.

"WHAT THE FUCK IS THIS?"

5

Mickey the Duck

"Kieran, for God's sake!" Lizzie yelled from the kitchen, her shrill shout cutting through the house and making me jump out of my skin. I was in the living room at the time, eyeing the patio door and trying to look as inconspicuous and unthreatening as possible. "I've told you before! Use a bloody coaster. You're leaving rings marks on the counter. I'm sick to death of—"

"*I've told you before. Blah blah blahblah.*" I mocked quietly in a childish voice, rocking my head from side to side.

She stopped yelling halfway through her rant, which was never a good sign. I felt a pang of dread in my chest, felt my eyes widen and my pulse quicken, as I heard her storm through the kitchen and into the living room, where she found me standing near the door pretending to admire the backyard.

Ever since the night after the club, she had been on edge, ready to destroy me for any minor mistake. I had told her the truth, but in the beginning, the only person I had to back me up was Matthew, and few people believed anything he said. Marcus had disappeared for the first few days, and we later found out that he had spent that time with his new girlfriend, catching up on all that he had missed.

He did help me settle Lizzie's anger in the end, but she was still annoyed. Lizzie wasn't the easiest person to reason with when she was in that state, and "that state" was heightened when she returned to work the following week.

It was hell. And it made me wonder just how annoyed she would have been if I actually had cheated on her.

"What did you say?" she said, thrusting her hands to her hips in a way that terrified me for reasons I couldn't understand.

I swallowed thickly and lowered my eyes from hers. It's amazing how she always heard me; through her own shouting, through her own anger, and through the living room walls, she could still hear my mumbling. I often wondered if she had actually heard anything or if she just *assumed*—correctly—that I was going to say something stupid. If that was the case, then that assumption formed the basis for much of our relationship and for nearly all of our arguments. But even armed with that knowledge, I still couldn't help myself.

"I didn't say anything." I was also a terrible liar, and she could see right through me.

She thrust a finger at me. "You're already in deep water, Kieran. You're treading on thin ice."

She always pulled out the idioms when she was annoyed. I raised my eyes, frowned at her. "I can't be—"

"Don't you dare fucking correct me."

"But—"

"You're digging your own grave."

"*Really?*"

Her nostrils flared and she looked like she was ready to attack.

"I'm sorry," I said, lowering my head again.

"You better be."

She turned around, ready to storm away, but she lingered for a moment, just long enough for me to contemplate saying something stupid and just long enough for her to expect me to. I did begin to say something, but my words were cut short by a snappy, hollow sound from behind me. I closed my mouth, silenced my attempted idiocy, and frowned in bemusement as Lizzie turned her Rottweiler-like features toward me, ready to tear me apart.

"What did you say?"

"I—I—"

I had no idea if I *had* said anything. It seemed like the sort of inopportune moment that I would see as an opportunity; self-sacrifice and pure stupidity were ripe for the plucking, but as sure as I was that I was about to say something stupid, and as sure as Lizzie was that I *had*, no words had left my lips.

"I didn't . . . I mean, I don't think . . ."

She stared at me, as if seeing through my soul and questioning my very existence. Then she turned around again, ready to set off, back into the kitchen to cook dinner and stew over my inadequacy. Then she heard the noise again.

She turned back toward me. "Was that a *quack*?" she asked, her eyes questioning my sanity as well as my stupidity.

I contemplated her question for a moment and then nodded. "Yes. I think it was."

She raised her head slowly, her eyebrows arched quizzically. I met her confusion with a smile and waited for her to turn around and march back into the kitchen, grumbling under her breath as she did so. I caught a few words, but none of them were worth repeating, and I prayed that most of them weren't aimed at me, but I suspected otherwise.

When she was out of sight, I turned toward the patio door and looked out onto the small backyard. Waiting patiently on the other side of the door, tilting its head to stare at me with one beady and expectant eye, was Mickey the Duck.

I had no idea why a duck had taken so well to my backyard, and I had no idea why I called him Mickey—at the time, Donald seemed too obvious and nothing else seemed appropriate. I had first seen him five or six days ago, straddling the fence at the end of the back-yard and staring at me with cute and suspicious eyes as I hung up the wet laundry. I fed him some bread, gave him some water, and then watched as he flew away, content with his small meal. He came back the next morning for the same ritual, only to repeat it every morning, afternoon, and evening since.

At first he was a little unsure and would only take the food when I put it on the ground and backed away, but gradually he had grown used to my presence. Eventually he was so accustomed to being waited on that he would happily take the bread from my hand and would get annoyed if he showed up and I wasn't there to feed him.

He quacked again and waddled away from the patio door, wait-ing for me to step out. There is something so hilariously sweet about ducks. About the way they stare, the way they walk, and the way they fly. They are the species that evolution forgot. They walk like they've only just learned how and they fly with the grace and style of drunken bumblebees. I had spent a few days learning about them and discovered that ducks prefer seeds to bread, which are a lot healthier for them. I also discovered that even though ducks really *should* eat seeds, no one has told them how. They take to a bowl of seeds like a limbless baby takes to a bowl of porridge—more of a violent, head-first smash-and-grab than a way to satisfy hunger.

But despite their lack of grace and their lack of style—despite the fact that they appear to be the byproduct of an obese bird and some giddy, alien toddler—I was enchanted by them. Although I had never really given them much thought until Mickey landed in my garden three times a day and demanded that I feed him. They were stupid and funny-looking creatures on the outside, but in a way they were also intelligent, and they were friendly, cute, and loving.

"Why is there never any fucking bread in this house?" Lizzie barked from the kitchen. "What the hell are you doing with the stuff?"

I looked at Mickey, who stared at me guiltily. I gave him as many seeds as I could, trying to balance his diet, but he had an insatiable appetite and preferred bread.

I bent down, pressed myself up against the screen door, and held a finger to my lips. Mickey waddled up to me and eyed me curiously as though contemplating what this invisible shield was, or why this stupid human was trying to communicate with him.

"Wait there," I told him softly.

He quacked a few times in reply. I have no idea what he was trying to say, but I had a feeling he understood.

I rushed upstairs to get Ben. He was asleep, but he slept for most of the day. One little adventure and a missed hour or two wasn't going to hurt him. I was also really excited to show him Mickey. I hadn't told Lizzie about the duck, but Ben had seen him on the first day and they seemed to have a friendship of sorts. It consisted of them staring at each other for many minutes at a time, before ending with one of them pooping themselves and creating a stink that I needed to quickly clean up. In many ways, it was like some of my very first relationships.

Ben loved Mickey. He either got his love of animals from me, or he treated him as a walking, quacking version of one of his fluffy toys.

Ben woke with a smile. He often did during the day, and it was that smile that reminded me I had done something amazing in bringing him into his world. It was that smile that gave me a reason to get up every day. I may not have had a job or any prospects, but I had a beautiful child who looked up to me and gave me more than a job, a career, and money ever could. Of course, he never woke up with a smile in the middle of the night. Because apparently he is a firm believer in Murphy's law, which dictates that he should be quiet when everyone in the house is awake, and noisy as hell when they're not.

I spoke softly to Ben as I carried him out of his crib and down the stairs, being careful to sprint past the kitchen door where an ill-tempered Lizzie awaited.

She didn't have anything against animals, but on the fourth day of Mickey's stay, she had noticed the mass of duck feces in the yard and I had listened to her yelling about how inconsiderate the neighbors were for letting their cat shit all over the place. She hadn't seen Mickey, but if she did, I was confident she would scare him away, and I didn't want him to leave. Not just for my sake, but for Ben's.

When I put him down in front of the window, he noticed the duck and giggled, and then the staring competition began. The first one to poop would be declared the loser.

There is never a good moment to bring up a strange topic. I tried to find one, waiting for the right TV program or the right conversation.

I even tried working my way up to it and then slipping it in, but as conversation so often does with me, I invariably took a detour and ended up in a more neutral position than I when I had begun. In the end, I decided to just go for it.

I stood and stretched to act nonchalant. I then remembered Lizzie telling me that every time I stood and stretched in such a manner, she knew I was up to something, so I quickly hid it with a succession of coughs, which made things weirder. She was watching me, staring at me in anticipation that I was going to ask something dumb. Her lack of trust in me and my intelligence was unfair and made me feel uneasy, so I moved away, out of sight. Then I said the stupid thing I had to say.

"I think we should buy a duck."

"A what?"

With the ice broken, I popped my head into the living room again. "A duck—you know, *quack, quack.*"

"I know what a fucking duck is."

I walked back into the room and picked up Ben, who had been playing with his toys on the floor. I knew she would be less inclined to swear at me or throw things at me if I was holding Ben. He didn't appreciate being a human shield and tried to wriggle free to get to his toys, but I held him tightly. He would thank me later, when Mickey was officially our pet and they could have their staring and pooping competitions out in the open.

"Well then," I said with a smug nod, "I think we should buy one."

She glared at me suspiciously. "Is this another one of your fads?"

"*Fads*?" I said with a preposterous shake of my head. "I don't have *fads.*"

"What about your stint as an aspiring professional musician?"

"Learning the guitar is not as easy as it looks." I was sure I heard a giggle from Ben at that one.

"What about the time you wanted to keep chickens in the spare room?"

"You're complaining now, but think of all the free eggs we'd get."

"What about the beer brewing, the Japanese cooking, the stargazing, the—"

"Okay, okay, I get the point," I said, feeling a little deflated.

"Or the time you wanted to start your own country?" she pushed on.

"That wasn't a fad. That was a dream that you had to go and spoil with your *rational thinking*. Most parents pass trust funds and old jewelry onto their kids. I would have made mine a king!" I held Ben up like Simba from the *Lion King*. He was impressed. Lizzie wasn't. He clearly took after his daddy, and I couldn't wait until he grew up and began defending my crazy schemes.

"It wasn't *rational thinking*," she parroted. "It just *wasn't* incredibly dumb thinking. You need more than a backyard and a flag to start your own country."

I shook my head. "I beg to differ, but that's beside the point."

"And what *is* the point?" she wondered. "The duck?"

I nodded firmly.

"You seriously want to buy a duck?"

I grinned at her hopefully. She didn't seem to be buying it. Even Ben—who had given up on his toys, seemingly finding more entertainment in his parents—didn't look convinced. But then she shrugged and her expression changed.

"You know what, I'm going to say yes. I've learned that disagreeing with you and these ideas of yours gets me nowhere. So, if it's what you want, and if you're actually going to go through with it, which I firmly do—" She paused and tilted her head to the side. "Did you hear that?" she asked.

"What?" I asked, although I had definitely heard it.

"It was a quack."

"I don't think so." I looked at Ben. "Did you hear a quack? No? I didn't think so."

"It was definitely a quack." She straightened her head, put her hands on her hips, and frowned at me. "You bought a duck, didn't you?"

I laughed at her. "No, don't be stupid."

"Thank God for—"

"He just sorta . . . *arrived.*"

Her jaw dropped open and for a moment her face was devoid of all emotion. I thought I had broken her, but then she erupted with the anger I had been expecting.

"Kieran, tell me what's going on right now before I get angry with you."

She had a way of getting angry and then warning me that she was going to get angry. I had always wondered if this was just stage 1 of her anger, a stage so vague and weak that she didn't even know it existed and was acting purely on a subconscious level. If that was the case, then I never wanted to see stage 2.

"There's not much to tell," I said with an apathetic shrug, doing little to calm her anger and avoid stage 2. "He just showed up one day."

"Where is he?" She stood and I automatically took a step backward. "You didn't let him in the house, did you?"

"No, no," I said dismissively. "Of course not."

She glared at me ferociously.

"I mean, I *invited* him, but he wasn't interested."

She heard the quack again and shoved straight past me, heading for the patio doors. She opened the blinds, and I saw Mickey get excited on the other side of the door. That excitement faded somewhat when he realized that I wasn't waiting for him with a handful of food and a mouthful of baby talk. But he didn't back away, so he clearly had high hopes for this new, smaller, prettier, redder human.

I expected Lizzie to shout or to try and shoo him away, and I cringed as I waited, but she didn't do anything at first. She stared at him for a moment, as if stuck in a trance, and then, after several seconds, realizing that this new human wasn't carrying any food, Mickey got impatient and quacked some more before tapping his beak on the glass.

"He's hungry," I said, sensing that Lizzie had softened.

She turned to me and I could see that the anger had gone. I wanted to jump up and down at that point, but I kept my cool and did everything I could to stop waving my arms about and squealing little a school girl at a One Direction concert. Ben couldn't hold back, though. As soon as he saw Mickey, he tried to squeeze out of my arms to get to him. I walked him over there and plopped him down in front of the glass, deciding not to tell Lizzie about the little competition they had going.

"What does he eat?"

"Bre—" I paused and then retracted my statement, realizing whose bread he had been eating. I cleared my throat and then said, "Seeds."

"Go get him some."

As I fetched a bag of hidden seeds, Lizzie slowly opened the door, making sure Ben didn't try to make a bolt for it. If you could call a sloppy, drunken crawl a "bolt." Mickey turned from Ben, ending the game, and as I prepared to be hit with a foul smell, he tilted his head to look at her. He then stared at her hands and at her face, as though asking where his food was. I gave her the bag of seeds, and she took out a handful that she then scattered on the ground beside a very excited and impatient duck.

"Who told you they like seeds?" she said as we both watched Mickey dig into them.

"I Binged it."

"You *Binged* it? Who uses Bing? What's wrong with Google?"

"I don't like saying *Google*. I 'Googled'—it sounds childish. Or worse, 'I Googled myself.'" I shook my head to indicate that I was above that. "It sounds like a kid explaining masturbation."

"And 'Binging' yourself sounds better?"

"I'd rather Bing myself than Google myself."

She stared at me for a moment and then shook her head. "Okay, so you 'Binged it' and it said—"

"Don't be stupid," I cut in with a smile, still watching Mickey make a mess of his seeds. "I Googled it. Who the fuck uses Bing?"

She glared at me and then nodded toward Ben. I put up a hand to apologize and silence her anger, but I could see the smile on her face.

"It said you're not supposed to feed them bread all the time. They need a little variety. So he's had white bread, brown bread, a bit of baguette—"

"He ate my baguette?"

"Just a little bit; I had to throw the rest out. Too much white bread isn't good for him."

"You're kidding me, right?"

I avoided that question. "He had a wild bird seed mix, as well, but he was very picky, so I bought some parrot seed for him instead. He preferred that. *This* stuff," I said, nodding toward the seeds now strewn around the patio, "is an organic fruit, nut, and seed mix from the health shop. The one that smells of sawdust and body odor. Apparently, the guy that works there doesn't use antiperspirant because it hurts the environment."

"*Organic?*"

"Maybe. Maybe he just rubs dog shit under his arms every morning. It certainly smells like it."

"No, I mean . . . you bought organic seeds for a *duck?*"

"Yes," I said simply, meeting her accusing stare. "If you insist on changing the subject."

"Why?"

"I told you," I explained slowly. "Because he needs a varied diet."

She nodded, opened her mouth to comment, and then shook it off. "You seem to be spending a lot of time with this duck. You realize we have a child, don't you?"

"I spend a lot of time on the toilet, as well. That doesn't mean I'm neglecting Ben for the bathroom."

"No, it means you should stop eating shit."

Both Lizzie and I tried to avoid swearing around Ben and we also made sure no one else did it. But somewhere along the line we came to an unspoken agreement that "shit" was perfectly acceptable.

"So, can we keep him?"

There were still some seeds remaining, but Mickey had stopped eating. His head was tilted to the side and one of his beady eyes was looking up at us, pleading with Lizzie, or at least that's probably what she thought. He actually just wanted a drink of water, but I didn't want to tell her and ruin the moment. Ben was trying to clamber toward the open door, either to make a break for freedom or to strangle Mickey like he strangles his toys. I picked him up to stop him, thankful that he hadn't ended his staring contest as the loser.

"He's staying in the yard, though," she said assuredly. "He's not coming in the house."

"Of course not."

Within two weeks, Mickey was a regular in the house. He became so fond of his morning feeds, and so impatient when they didn't come, that he often waddled inside and waited for them there. Once or twice, he even followed me through to the kitchen as I poured him a drink of water. I had never been one for indoor pets and the idea had never appealed to me, but Mickey changed that. He was very wary of Ben, but Ben found everything that Mickey did incredibly amusing. I'd never seen a baby laugh or giggle so much. One of our neighbors suggested that we shouldn't let a "dirty animal" in the house. I agreed, and then told her to get the hell out. No one insults Mickey. Lizzie was startled, but I suspect she was also a little impressed. She hated that woman.

Lizzie wasn't as worried about the whole situation as I thought she might be. She didn't like them getting too close and tried to stop Ben from touching Mickey when she was supervising him. I didn't mind so much, though. Kids are raised around cats and dogs all the time. The only difference between Mickey and a cat was that while Mickey was flying around, stealing bread, and taking a dip in the local lake, cats were killing anything they came across and picking up all kinds of diseases. As for dogs, they eat their own poop and hump anything that moves, while Mickey seemed to treat his poop as a by-product of walking.

I found Mickey hilarious. He often quacked when he walked, which amused me to no end. It reminded me of the old men I had seen tottering through the park. They had a similar way of walking—shifting their weight and taking small steps—and they often mumbled to themselves as they did. He also began to remind me of my dad, whose fashion sense—a mixture of bland and bright—wasn't too dissimilar from Mickey's gray coat and blue markings. My dad also spent his days walking around the house complaining about everything and making no sense.

This comparison was ruined somewhat when my father met Mickey.

"You realize he's a she, right?"

"What? No, don't say that."

"It's true," he said, grinning at my discomfort. "All ducks that color are females. The green ones are the male ones. That's why you'll often see one of each together."

My image of Mickey as a grumpy old man was ruined, but I was not deterred. Ben began picking up speed at that point, crawling less like a drunk amputee and more like a drunk. He began following Mickey around. At first she was a little freaked out by the drooling chubby human who wanted to follow her around and pull out her feathers, but eventually she seemed to settle into it. Ben looked like a little pink duckling as he waddled after her, and maybe she saw him as the same.

After a few weeks, she had become part of the family. She shit everywhere, she pissed everywhere, and she had a strange obsession with the TV remote. Take away the feathers, add some inappropriate flatulence, and she was Ben. Her shit wasn't unlike his either. It was just as widespread, just as colorful, and just as nasty, but at least I could wipe hers off the kitchen floor and didn't have to scrape it from her scrotum like day-old All Bran.

I got into a routine of getting up in the morning and then letting Mickey in through the patio doors, where she was usually waiting expectantly. She followed me through to the kitchen where we had bowls of food and water laid out for her, then for the next thirty minutes she would eat as I cleaned up the mess she inevitably created. Cuteness and random shitting isn't the only thing that ducks have in common with babies. They're also very lazy and have a habit of getting in the way. For the rest of the day, she would hover around the house, sitting on the furniture, shitting on the floor, playing with Ben, eating, and then flying away for the night. This continued for a few weeks, but then things changed when I opened the patio door one morning and saw two expectant duck-faces looking up at me.

"And who the fuck are you?" I asked the second duck. He was green, so I knew that he was a he, and he was also pretty protective of Mickey. He wasn't as forward as her and seemed ill at ease around me, but when she ventured into the house, he followed her, flapping at me as he passed.

I knew ducks were harmless so I wasn't worried about this new intruder; I figured the worst-case scenario was that he would eat all my food and then shit everywhere, but he'd have strict competition from Ben and Mickey if that's what he had planned.

As Mickey ate from her bowls, the new duck stood guard and I kept my distance.

"You do realize that this is my house, right?" I told him, feeling like I should point that out.

He didn't reply. He didn't even quack. Mickey was very vocal, but he was playing the role of the broken husband at a boring party, keeping his mouth shut and his eyes on his surroundings, waiting for his time to attack the free food before leaving when his wife got drunk and showed him up in front of strangers.

After she'd had her fill, Mickey left and he followed. They went straight out of the back door and, just before they left, he turned and gave me one last look. I wasn't sure if he was thanking me, warning me, or telling me to shut the door after him, I went straight upstairs and told my wife that we had been burgled and I had been violated.

After she stopped laughing, I told her the whole story, which set her off again.

"You're imagining things," she warned me several minutes later, the laughter now a distant memory, but something she ran through her mind over and over again so that she could recite it to her friends later. "Try to be friendly with him; he's probably just the same as her."

I believed her, but only because I *wanted* to believe her. The next day, when the troublesome pair showed up again, I did my best to politely welcome both of them. I offered Mickey's beau a piece of bread from my hand. He didn't take it, but he *did* try to snap my fingers off.

Surprised, I shouted and made a quick movement, nudging Mickey with my leg as I did so. The reaction was enough to send them rushing back out of the door in a flap. I yelled at them to stop, offering my apologies, but they flew away before my words were heeded.

I waited for them to return, hoping that Mickey would come back on her own, but happy to accept them both again if they showed up. They didn't make an appearance for the rest of the day. The following morning, I laid out a large spread of seeds and bread, my way of telling them I was sorry, but neither of the ducks showed up. Ben was just as disappointed as I was, and he spent a few days crawling around the house looking for her. Lizzie, although she wouldn't admit it, was also disappointed.

I waited weeks for them to show up again, checking the yard every morning and often several times throughout the day. I jumped to my feet and rushed to the patio door every time I heard anything that resembled a quack. I refused to let Ben watch Daffy Duck in case he had flashbacks. At around nine months, Ben began trying to walk, "trying" being the operative word. I couldn't help but notice that he walked with the lop-sided, bouncy gait of a duck. At first I worried that he had somehow been influenced by Mickey and that he was even doing it as a way of cheering me up. But Lizzie, as usual, pissed on my parade by telling me that's just how babies walk.

I stopped ordering duck from the Chinese take-away, instead turning my attentions almost exclusively to pork and praying that no cute piglets ever showed up at my back door asking for food and companionship.

As much as I waited, as much as I checked, Mickey and her companion didn't show up, and I never saw them again.

6

Teaching the Unteachable

Ben's diet, his poop, and his antics changed with each passing day. Or at least that's how it felt. The changes were actually more gradual than that, but in the haze that is early parenthood, when everything seems like a dream—because you're half-asleep all the way through it—it's hard to keep track. It did get easier, though. Half-asleep was better than the brain-death I felt during those first few weeks, and it was also great to see him age, to see him crawl, to see him attempt to walk, and to see him reach a point where he found everything funny. Not only was it comforting to see him laugh, but it was a great way to boost my ego. Most people don't laugh at my jokes, but Ben couldn't get enough of them.

At any point during the first month of Ben's life, someone could have swapped him with another baby and I'm not sure I would have noticed. That changed as I slept more and he grew more, but it was still a haze for the most part. Some people can function with little sleep, but I am not one of those people.

As a teenager, I treated sleep like I treated a bowel movement. It wasn't particularly fun or interesting, nor was it anything to talk about in polite conversation. It was something that could be suppressed if I tried hard enough, and something that was only interesting when I had suppressed it too long and the resulting release was something to be marveled at. As an adult, sleep was more like urination. It was short-lived, it quickly followed a pint of beer, and if it didn't happen at least a few times a day, then my body revolted.

Lizzie handled things a little better, despite the fact that she did most of the work with Ben and somehow managed to return to her job as a full-time teacher and a part-time art tutor. She bottled up her angst, her tiredness, and her stress and turned it into sporadic outbursts of neurosis. She'd had mood swings when she was pregnant, crying over insignificant things, but this was different. She once screamed at me for losing her sunglasses, not realizing that she had been wearing them the entire time. I could only assume that she blamed the change in color on a solar eclipse and was surprised she didn't blame me for that, as well. I had waited for the yelling to stop and the realization to kick in—which didn't happen in that order—and then calmly continued with my day.

I didn't get angry with her, I didn't blame her. I had it easy. I still wasn't working, and while that meant I was the one spending most of the time with Ben through the day, it was a job I wouldn't have sacrificed for anything.

Lizzie wasn't the only crazy one in the house either; it's a well-known fact that all humans are born manic depressive. One minute they're happy, smiling, and on top of the world, and the next they're screaming, crying, scowling, and secretly wishing you were dead.

Babies are also very much like old people, or maybe it's the other way around.

People get to a certain age and just think *fuck it, I've had it with this adult bullshit.* They eat tasteless food, bump into things, and feel the need to tell strangers about their day, even if those strangers have no idea what they're talking about. They nap constantly, are incredibly bitter to everyone and grumpy about everything, and they have a tendency to soil themselves and to fart inappropriately. Just before his first birthday, I took Ben to the supermarket. As I pushed him down the produce aisle, he proceeded to drop a series of bombs. It sounded like someone was slowly opening a zipper, leaving a trail of stink behind him like a B-2 bomber with a broken exhaust. I was hit with the full force of each and every one of his noxious ass-rockets, all escaping with a seemingly innocuous whiff of air, but creating a stink so strong that even the bananas clambered for an escape route.

After quickly ushering him away from the scene of the crime and down another aisle, I later returned—looking as nonchalant as possible—to find three shop assistants overturning handfuls of avocados, sniffing them and then shrugging to each other. I almost expected the supermarket to be on the nightly news following reports of a chemical attack—the beginnings of a new terrorist threat sweeping the supermarkets of England.

There's so much baby powder down there that every flatus should simply be a puff of flowery delight, but somehow the rot creeps through. The most amazing thing about a baby fart is, most of the time, they have no idea they're doing it. When he gets a whiff of one of his own farts, he give me a look that says, *What the fuck have you been eating?* In the beginning, I thought he was fucking with me, but then it occurred to me that he has no idea what a fart even is. He barely acknowledges his own shit. The only thing he is aware of is that every now and then, his diaper becomes somewhat uncomfortable, a strange man and a smiling woman expose his jiggly bits, slap some powder on his ass, and then give him a new one. I imagine that the day he discovers the power of his farts, he's going to have a lot of fun, dropping them in social situations and then merely pointing at me. I'm not sure if he gets that from me or his grandmother, but at some point, he's going to use that gift against us.

Bodily fluids are a weapon to him. He once got out of being held, poked, and prodded by a distant cousin by vomiting all over said cousin. She was a happy-go-lucky teenager who always saw the glass as half-full. But as soon as Ben filled that glass with white baby vomit, her outlook soured.

My mother once grinned her way through one of Ben's exorcist-style vomiting sessions, telling me that nothing disgusting could possibly come from a baby as cute as he was. She didn't have to change his diapers, so she could say that. The truth is that *everything* disgusting came from Ben. If there was anything off-color and off-scent in our house, there was a good chance he had been involved somewhere along the line. There were the vomit-stained clothes, which somehow tainted all the other clothes in the washing machine. The yellow stain on the carpet, from when he tried to mark his territory. And the black stains next to the couch, from when his markings failed him, he lost his bearings, and he shit everywhere.

"You'd think you do all of this alone," Lizzie had told me once, during one of my many rants. "I actually do a lot more than you do, and you never hear me complaining."

"That's because he's gotten to you," I told her. "It's like cats and toxoplasmosis, little parasites that they carry and pass on to you. And once you have them, you become their slave, unwittingly becoming subservient to them and—"

"Have you been watching the History Channel again?"

"That's not—"

"I told you to stop watching that shit. That's not really history, that's not real science. It's not real *anything*."

"That's beside the point," I told her, glossing over the History Channel marathon from two days previous. "The point is that he's gotten to you. He's planted his parasitic seed in you and now you only see the good in him. You don't see any of them bad. It's . . . it's—"

"Parenthood?"

"What?"

"That's what you're referring to. It's called being a mum."

I shook my head. "It's the poop. The stench. It's intoxicating, like a drug."

"A drug that makes me only see the good in him?"

I nodded vigorously, glad—and a little surprised—that she was getting it.

"Remind me, why did I let you father my child?"

I shrugged. "I think you were drunk at the time."

"That makes sense."

Lizzie, being the good, worn-down wife that she was, was happy to ignore those little rants and treat them with as much seriousness as she treated my biannual ambitions to start doing some gardening. The truth? I was just as intoxicated and just as affected as she was. The parasite of parenthood had gotten to me, as well.

We were the typical modern parents, worried about everything and following every piece of advice offered to us—except the ones

given out by those who actually had any experience in the matter. Rather than listening to Lizzie's parents, who had successfully
raised an intelligent, healthy, sane, and likable young woman, and
mine, who had succeeded in raising a young man, we followed
the advice given by soulless psychiatrists and "baby experts" with
no children of their own, obvious daddy issues, and accents that
couldn't be geo-located to any place within our solar system.

I had seen the same happen to a few friends of mine, and more
often than not it was the mother who led and the father who followed. But I had become just as absorbed in this pseudoscience
bullshit as Lizzie. During the pregnancy, it was me who suggested
we play Mozart to her bump, hoping the baby would be born with
an appreciation of the finer things in life. That turned out to nonsense, of course; babies were babies, they came out pooping and crying, not playing the violin and composing masterpieces. But even
after realizing I had been duped, I still fell for every other piece of
nonsense that came my way. If it was wrapped in a few big words
and delivered by someone with letters after their name, I believed it.

And that's how, at one year old, Ben ended up on a baby retreat.
It was hailed as an exclusive mental, emotional, and physical holiday for babies, one that could increase their awareness and their
understanding, turning them into brighter and more confident
individuals. It took me a day to realize that I would have been better off locking him in a cupboard with a print of the Mona Lisa and
a Mozart CD.

The retreat was located in a holiday spot by the coast. A series of
cozy log cabins for the parents and their offspring, and a few com-
munal areas where they played and where the "lessons" were taught.
These lessons generally involved some creepy old woman with a
voice like an uncoiled hinge pointing at colorful squares and asking

the babies to choose the right colors. As quick as I am to embrace even the most obviously bullshit schemes, I am equally quick at despising them. It wasn't that I expected overnight results, but I had been hoping that Ben would be doing something intellectual, rather than filling his diaper and emptying his nose.

Clearly the skepticism had been evident on my face from the beginning. During one of the many lessons, where the parents sat uncomfortably and impatiently while being patronized by someone who had just robbed them blind, the teacher was very quick to point out Ben's perceived success to me.

"See, see," the uncoiled hinge squealed. "He's pointing to the right one. I told you this would work."

"He's not pointing to anything," I told her. "He's showing you the snot on the end of his finger."

Ben wasn't very good at the tests she was putting in front of him, but that has less to do with his intellect and more to do with the fact that he was one year old. Despite her claims and despite the fact that she had duped so many parents into believing otherwise, she clearly had little experience with children. Or humans, for that matter.

The look that the half-cut cat-woman gave me was almost worth the three hundred we had thrown at her. Ben also saw it and seemed just as amused.

"He could be trying to tell you it's the green one," I offered.

She gave me a frustrated look and turned back to Ben just in time to see him eat the green slime on the end of his finger. She gagged and looked like she was about to throw up.

The other parents were all sitting in a semicircle around the teacher. It was supposed to be relaxed and cool, but it reminded me of school assemblies, of hardwood floors, hemorrhoids, and hungover teachers addressing disinterested children. They all saw Ben stick his finger in his mouth and lick it like it was a lollipop. A few of them laughed, mainly the ones who were just as fed up as I was, but the majority of them followed the teacher's lead and looked at him like he was a demon child. A look I had given him many times myself.

"That child will never learn." The teacher had lost her cutesy, grating baby-voice and was now using her actual voice, which was less cutesy, but equally grating. "He's not interested in what I have to say, he's not even listening to me, he's—"

"He's one," I told her. "What do you expect?"

"What about *these* children?" she asked, opening her arms to indicate the other kids, most of them ugly, all of them annoying. One of them had been labeled as "advanced for his age," because he apparently had the vocabulary of a kid much older. I had my doubts. He knew how to ask for things, he knew how to whine when he didn't get them, and he knew how to say "mummy," but only when it was preceded by a demand and only because he thought it was a synonym for *slave*.

The only thing worse than a whining child is a parent who will go out of their way to give that child exactly what he wants in order to stop the whine.

Oh, I'm sorry, here's your lollipop.

It's okay darling, here, have a hamburger.

I didn't mean to shout because you shat on the floor. I'm so sorry. How about next time I let you do it on my pillow?

Kids who get their own way turn into fat little sociopaths who think they rule the world just because no one has ever said no to them. That annoyed me. The one who kept picking his nose and wiping it on the trousers of passing adults annoyed me—at least Ben had the decency to eat his. The one with the twisted nose who whistled like a tea-kettle every time he talked annoyed me. The one who tried to hump my leg like a dog, all while hurling insults at me like I was a cheap whore with daddy issues, also annoyed the hell out of me. I'm a firm believer that you shouldn't do to others what you wouldn't like done to yourself. Yet if I had whacked the aspiring rapist-cum-wife-beater across the head and called him a cunt, I would be the one in the wrong. Sometimes life just isn't fair.

"The less said about them the better," I told her. It sounded like the right thing to say and I was glad I said it. But I sensed something was wrong when Lizzie, who had been surprisingly quiet until that point, sighed and shifted away from me. It was a combination of *I am so disappointed in you* and *him? No, I've never seen him before in my life.*

"What the hell is that supposed to mean?" one of the parents snapped. "Is there something wrong with my child?"

There were so many things wrong with her child that I didn't know where to begin. For one thing, despite the conversation going on around him, he was staring in the opposite direction, with his hand wedged down the back of his pants and a look of determination on his face. I had no idea what he was looking for, but I didn't want to be there when he found it.

"It's not just your child," I told her. "It's children in general. They're pointless little things who do nothing but eat, vomit, and then, if you're really unlucky, try to eat their vomit." They were shocked, but I wasn't finished. "It's not our goal as parents to teach them about these things; it's our goal to make sure they don't kill themselves. Babies are basically just stupid little humans. They don't even exist until they're five."

"How can you say that?" one incredulous parent muttered. "Of course they exist."

"Do you remember anything that happened before you were five?" I asked her.

She seemed to mull this over for a moment before shaking her head. "Well, no. But that doesn't mean I didn't exist."

"But it does mean that none of the shit you did was important. Yes, we need to teach them to be careful, but most of them will learn it themselves. We don't need to tell them when something is hot or sharp, because they'll learn when they get burned or cut. Don't get me wrong, I'm all for trying to manipulate his little brain into being smarter. I'm constantly falling for the shit spewed by crazy women with shrill voices, PhDs, and mustaches, but I'm starting to think that none of it matters." I heard the teacher gasp before mumbling under her breath as I continued. "They'll do their own thing and they'll figure the world out their own way. That's why kids go to school when they're five, and that's why the only ones telling you to teach your child in the womb are the ones who stand to make money from you doing just that."

I paused for breath. "I mean, look at him." I pointed to Ben. "He doesn't care about the shapes, he doesn't care that his daddy is currently digging himself a very big hole, and he doesn't care that he is surrounded by ugly babies and annoyed adults. The fact is that, for the second time this week, he's discovered his penis and he's going to sit there and play with it until he gets bored."

A few of the adults looked at him in disgust. One of them looked away when he realized that Ben was in fact so excited by his discovery that he was trying to pull down his pants so he could show everyone. Some of the men seemed to be suppressing a smile, and I for one was very proud.

"How many of you are first-time parents?" I asked.

Several hands went up. One reluctant woman kept hers down, even though her husband had already raised his. I frowned at her until something clicked. "Let's just imagine that I'm not insane for a moment and that by asking that question, I wasn't including puppies or kittens."

She raised her hand.

"That's the problem. We're so scared of messing up, so scared of failing where our parents obviously succeeded, that we go out of our way to listen to any quacks that try to sell us directions to the holy grail."

I noticed at that point that a number of people actually seemed to be listening to me, and not just waiting for me to finish so that they could beat me up or phone the police. That spurred me on as I endeavored to win over the others who *did* look like they were preparing to beat me up.

"Our parents didn't do anything special; there was none of this when we were born. They did what they felt was right and they didn't let some crazy woman with two degrees, no kids, and half a brain tell them what to do with their lives."

"Have you finished insulting me now?" the teacher asked, looking rather annoyed.

I looked at her, shook my head, and then addressed the class again. "Take this place for example," I said.

"What's wrong with it?" the teacher asked, preparing herself to be offended.

"A baby retreat?" I said, stressing every syllable. "Are you fucking kidding me?"

"Language!" one of the parents spat, almost instinctively.

I held up my hands in apology. It was her choice if she didn't want to expose a kid to bad language, just like it was her choice to expose that same kid to Happy Meals and chocolate milkshakes.

"These kids have no idea where they are. They have no idea what they're doing and they won't remember *any* of this."

The teacher jumped in again, keen to shoot down the dissenter. "It's not about what they will remember. It's about nurturing their development."

"With two hours of looking at colored squares?"

"And there's reading time, and TV time, and—"

"Oh, TV time, well of course there's *that*," I mocked. "I mean, thank God for that because it's not like I have a TV at home or anything."

She scrunched up her face. "I'll have you know that these events have been tailored around the baby's needs, ensuring they get optimum care and attention."

"Where's your proof?"

"Excuse me?"

"Your proof that this works, where is it?"

"I have degrees in social science and psychology."

"That means nothing, and you know it. This has nothing to do with psychology and everything to do with money. These people want nothing but the best for their kids and will do anything to get it. You have lied to them and tricked them so you can empty their wallets."

"How dare you!"

Her protestations were cut short by another parent, a downtrodden husband who had clearly had enough. He rose from his cross-legged position, groaned the pain out of his joints, and then joined me. "This man is right. This is all bullshit."

Another parent, this time a mother, stood with her ugly baby in tow. "I've got to agree with them. I fell for this in the beginning and I've been holding on to save face. But this is a load of shit."

"How can you say that?" the teacher said. "You don't know what you're talking about!"

"Have you seen the schedule for tomorrow?" she asked the other parents. "We have breakfast, nap time, and then, after taking the kids for a walk, we sit and watch a Disney movie." She turned back to the teacher. "This man is right. Is this a fucking joke?"

The bickering started and stirred a wave of chaos in the room. The whiny kid began to cry, a few of the ugly ones began to scream, but all of the parents ignored them and concentrated their anger on each other and on the teacher. Having started it, I managed to lose my grip on it and calmly backed away.

Lizzie was waiting for me at the back of the room, her hands folded across her torso. "Are you proud of yourself?"

I nodded. "A little, yes."

She shook her head in disbelief. You'd think she would have been used to this sort of behavior.

"Kind of ironic, isn't it?" I said as we watched the chaos. The parents looked like they were about to come to blows, with the teacher stuck in the middle of them. "They're all arguing about their kids' welfare and completely ignoring their crying children in the process." I laughed at that, enjoying the irony and the fact that I had been the one to notice it.

I turned to Lizzie, expecting some sort of recognition, but rather than pride, she had a stern expression on her face. "Is that like your permanent expression these days?" I wondered. "I mean, you know you can change it, right?"

"Did you forget something?" she interrupted.

I frowned at her, turned back to the melee, and then, between the warring parents—some arguing that they had been duped, some arguing that the retreat was helping, both prepared to fight for their stupidity—I saw Ben. I had left him on the floor in front of the teacher, which meant that he was now in the eye of the storm.

Shit.

I ran forward and barged through the crowd, catching some elbows and curses for my troubles, before scooping him into my arms. I expected him to be crying like the others, but he was loving the chaos and was annoyed at me for forcing him to beat a retreat.

"It's okay," I told Lizzie as I carried him back to her, struggling to keep him in my arms as he tried his best to wriggle free and get back to the front line. "He was actually having fun," I said. "I think he likes the shouting and the arguing. Just like his mother, eh?"

Again I smiled at her and again she gave me a stern grimace in reply. She propped open the door and nodded for me to walk through.

"You're really not in a smiley mood today, are you?" I asked on my way out.

"Can you blame me? Have you seen what you've done?"

I nodded and did my best to look ashamed, but I was still a little proud. I didn't like to cause chaos, but I'd had a chance to vent and to piss on that pseudo psychologist's little enterprise. There was a good chance that I had made a very angry enemy or two, but one or two more of those wasn't going to make much difference.

7

Matthew, Ben, and the Night to Forget

"Are you sure this is a good idea?"

Lizzie nodded. "Again, yes."

I sighed, still not convinced. We were going out for the night, and hiring our first babysitter had proved to be a traumatic experience. For me, anyway. Our options had been limited, and although it had been me who suggested the babysitter we eventually agreed upon, it wasn't a suggestion I fully intended or one I expected her to go with.

Ben was over a year old, and we had enjoyed nights out several times throughout that year, but we hadn't enjoyed a night out together in a long time. Not since before she was pregnant had we enjoyed a night where we could both eat, drink, and enjoy ourselves. Her moods, the occasional issues, and the fact that she couldn't drink had put a stop to that. After the birth, we had argued about letting our parents take control. I didn't want her parents anywhere near my child, worried that they would sell his soul to the devil or give him to a cult, and she insisted that if her parents couldn't babysit, then neither could mine.

It was a stalemate. And when we finally were ready to let parents take over, none of them were available. As a result, we were forced to go with someone I didn't really trust and someone who probably wouldn't sell my child's soul to the devil, but might do something just as bad.

"I'm going upstairs to get ready," Lizzie said. That was her signal that she didn't want to listen to me any longer.

I watched her go, leaving me standing in the hallway with Ben in my arms. Maybe I was projecting, maybe he had misunderstood and thought we were dumping him on his grandparents, but he looked as worried as I did. One of the few upsides to my chosen babysitter was that it *wasn't* Lizzie's parents. Even just five minutes with those crazy bastards could pollute his mind beyond repair. It's amazing Lizzie made it out with her sanity intact.

I heard the front door open, swing on its hinges, and then slam shut. The babysitter had arrived, and he seemingly wanted the entire street to know. Only three people walked into my house without ringing the doorbell. My parents didn't do it because they were worried they'd catch us having sex. My mother wouldn't even venture into the bedroom for fear we had turned it into a sex dungeon, after which she would have no option but to disown me. Lizzie's parents didn't do it either, presumably because they knew I'd feign a break-in, beat them to death, and then claim they were trespassing and I was acting in self-defense.

The only person other than myself and Lizzie who entered without knocking was Matthew, our babysitter for the night. I knew him well, of course, and that was a good thing, because when the police quizzed me at the end of the night, I would be able to tell them everything they needed to know.

Matthew strode past where I was standing, completely ignored me and the baby, and went straight into the kitchen. I heard him open the fridge, burp ceremoniously, and then groan at the lack of offerings. Moments later, he strode into the living room, plopped himself on the couch, popped open a can of beer, and turned on the television. The fact that I was standing in front of him holding Ben, the child he was supposed to be protecting and caring for, the very reason he was there to begin with, seemed to be nothing more than a minor inconvenience.

"Make yourself at home," I said.

Matthew turned to look at me, as though seeing me for the first time. "You're in the way."

I sighed but stepped aside—I was British, after all. We did annoyed and we did angry, but we didn't do rude. "Help yourself to some beer," I offered sarcastically, another thing we did very well.

"Will do."

"You're late."

He dragged his attention away from a re-run of a topical news show that hadn't been topical for three years. "I'm doing you a favor," he reminded me with the air of someone waiting for his medal. "The fact that I'm here at all should be enough. Who else would look after your dog for the night?"

"I don't have a—" I paused. "You're fucking with me, right?"

"Of course. So, what time are you getting back?"

"I don't know. Late. Ben will be asleep soon and he should sleep for the rest of the night."

Matthew looked disappointed. "But I have a full night planned," he argued. "There's a film on pay-per-view we were gonna watch, and I was gonna order a pizza."

"A pizza? You realize he's just a baby, right?"

He shrugged. "I'll get him an eight-inch."

I rolled my eyes and watched a grin spread across his face. "Don't fuck this up," I warned him, covering Ben's ears on cue. "This is the first night Lizzie and I will be alone together since before Ben was born. The first time, well, you know."

"The first time you can have sex without worrying that your dick's gonna give the baby brain damage?"

Matthew seemed amused with himself, but I was incredulous. "How did you—"

"I told him." Lizzie strode into the room, swinging her handbag and using it to smack Matthew over the head. "He's your best friend, he won't judge."

"No, that's exactly why he *will* judge."

"He has a point," Matthew conceded, rubbing his skull and flinching when Lizzie gave him the evil eye.

"Anyway, that's not what I meant, we're just going for a meal and a drink. I don't plan on having sex with my wife at a restaurant."

"Only because you're too boring and too scared to do it anywhere that isn't your bed."

I turned to Lizzie, shocked and appalled. She shrugged back. "I didn't tell him. He took a shot."

Matthew laughed. "And he scored. You're such a loser."

Lizzie tried to suppress a laugh. "Come on, let's get moving." She took Ben from me, gave him a kiss, and then lifted him into Matthew's arms. She made sure he was holding him properly before kissing Matthew on the side of the head and pointing a stern finger at him. "Don't mess this up."

He seemed appalled that we would even suggest such a thing, apparently forgetting that we knew him. "What is it with you two? I've got this, trust me."

In my worst nightmares, of which I'd had many since leaving the house, I imagined horrible things. I worried that Matthew would burn the house down, leaving nothing but crisp remains of where my livelihood used to be. I worried that in an effort to impress a kinky girl—his favorite type of girl—he would let her use Ben in a Satanic ritual and I would return to find him naked in the middle of a flaming pentagram with a dripping goat's heart in his hand. I worried that he would simply forget about Ben, lost in his own little world as he so often was, and my son, the light of my life, would choke to death on his own milky vomit.

I worried about so many things that I was forced to question my own motives for leaving my son with such a feckless deviant in the first place. Then I reminded myself that it was Lizzie's idea and that if anything *did* happen, at least I would be able to blame her for it. She had been the one who insisted that Matthew wasn't that bad deep down, that he was still a close friend and a good man, and that he, perhaps more than anyone, had something to prove and would go out of his way to be the good guy.

I didn't believe her, but we had no other choice. Her parents were in Australia, hopefully receiving several different shots of venom from several different murderous creatures, and my own parents had gone to spend two nights in Blackpool, where good fun, good manners, and great entertainment are always at least fifty miles away.

The differences in our parents were never more evident than when they went on vacation, but although Lizzie's mother and father had the money for lavish hotels and bucket list adventure vacations, I knew that my parents, stuck in a cold caravan while monsoon weather tore the shit out of the resort around them, would be the ones having the most fun. That was the problem with Lizzie's parents: they were so busy bragging about their experiences that they forgot to enjoy them.

Lizzie's friends refused. One was at a wedding, another had chlamydia—or it could have been a cold, I wasn't really paying attention. Sharon, Matthew's wife, was on a "business trip" to Birmingham, taking a rich businessman's respect, dignity, and money before he went home to a neglected wife who presumably did the same to him.

I would have asked Max, if I could find him, and I would have asked my other friends, if I had any. In fact, I would have asked *anyone* before I asked Matthew. Lizzie refused to use a paid babysitting service, insisting that she didn't want to leave her child with a stranger, even if that stranger was qualified, capable, sensible, and sane, and the person we chose in their place was none of those things.

During the car ride, I couldn't get Matthew's incompetence off my mind. I couldn't stop thinking of all the things he had done in the past and of all the things that could go wrong. At the theater, those thoughts faded slightly and they were completely gone by the time we sat down for a meal. I had allowed myself to listen to Lizzie's assurances. He was my friend, after all, and I knew in my heart that he wouldn't intentionally do anything to hurt Ben. I was being paranoid, stupid, irrational.

As we drove back home, with Lizzie concentrating on the dark roads, sticking her tongue out like a kid on an Etch-a-Sketch, the worries returned. And as we pulled into the street, I realized that, for once in my life, I had been right all along.

My fears were not unfounded, and Matthew really had fucked it up.

There was chaos in the street and most of it was focused on our house. There were police cars parked outside, their lights pulsating to the rhythm of my rapidly beating heart, the blue glow exposing ghostly expressions worn by a horde of shocked onlookers.

Of all the things I worried about, nothing came close to the scene that stretched out before me as I clambered out of the car and stood on weary legs. I was too shocked to speak. A small part of me hoped that this was a dream, or an elaborate joke. I had been incredibly tired of late, and it wouldn't be the first time Matthew had pulled such a dick move in the spirit of humor. But this wasn't a dream, and it didn't feel like a joke either.

I spotted police cars, an ambulance, a fire engine—and half of the neighborhood out to watch them. Mr. and Mrs. Andreasson, the quiet, middle-aged couple who lived in the house behind ours, were next to the ambulance. She was standing outside, fully exposed to the cold, and he was sitting down just inside the ambulance. They were dressed in their nightclothes, she in a satin nightdress hidden by a man's dressing gown, he in his pajamas. She seemed alert, but he wore a vacant expression as two paramedics saw to a nasty wound on his head.

She was more than alert; she was annoyed. I watched as she checked her watch several times and tapped her feet in irritation, seemingly oblivious to the cold wind that swept through her clothes and threatened to expose her. As much as she hated her current predicament, whatever it was, her husband seemed to be enjoying himself. The paramedics had placed a blanket over his lap, but his excitement had pushed on the fly of his pajamas and was pitching a little tent. He seemed oblivious to it, but the paramedics were doing their best to stay clear, keen not to overexcite him and give themselves more to clean at the end of their shift.

Next to one of the police cars, chewing the ear off a very bored-looking officer, was a young woman I recognized as one of Matthew's ex-girlfriends. She had a huge mouth on her, and she was incredibly annoying, but she had a huge pair of tits, and for Matthew, that made her a viable target. Seeing her again incensed me, and I had images of Matthew using my house to cheat on his wife—and doing so with a woman he had never really liked. He had once said that she could have a personality disorder, if only she had a personality.

She was smoking a cigarette that dipped in and out of her mouth, inhaling a toxic lungful between each erratic sentence.

Next to her, gathered around the front door of our house, were four young lads, all of them looking annoyed. They appeared to be in their late teens, early twenties at a push. They all looked fairly well-built, two of them in small T-shirts that exposed puffed-out chests and biceps as thick as my neck. Another—in attire more suited to the cold air—I recognized as one of the neighbor's sons. He was a rugby player, a mischievous and annoying little shit who was the apple of his mother's eye, but only because she was always too drunk to realize what a waste of space he was. His mother was also loitering nearby, her arms folded across her chest as she looked up at my house, next to the fourth boy whose shirt was wet through and whose expression was even more annoyed than the others'.

I was rooted to the spot. Only a few seconds had passed since getting out of the car, but it felt like hours. When I saw Ben, time reset and my entire being seemed to breathe a sigh of relief. He was being cradled by one of the many firefighters standing in front of the house. Lizzie also spotted Ben and ran up to him. I joined her and for a moment neither of us cared what was going on, neither of us cared what had happened. We had our son and he was healthy—that was all that mattered. Only when the relief died down and the curiosity peaked did we realize that the people in front of the house were looking up at the roof, and when we followed their gazes, we saw that Matthew was sitting on the top of it, beaming down with a sheepish expression and giving us a little wave.

"What the fuck did you do?" Lizzie barked.

The noise around us ceased and all eyes turned to her. Matthew had been sitting with his legs dangling off the edge, but when he heard her voice and saw the anger on her face, he shot to his feet and backed off, his hands held up submissively. He tried to defend himself, to explain himself, but Lizzie didn't let him speak.

"What did you do?" she demanded to know. "What are you doing on the roof, and what did you do to my baby?" She was breathing heavily, her face getting redder and redder. I thought about taking Ben from her, but I didn't want to do anything that might direct that anger toward me, so I remained passive. "And why is my front window smashed?"

I hadn't seen the window until she mentioned it. It looked like the entire sheet of glass had been removed, and if not for the broken pieces at the edges, and the fact that the curtains were billowing in the wind, it wouldn't have been visible.

"I'm afraid that was us." The firefighter who had cradled Ben stepped forward. "I'm assuming by the way you snatched him off me that this is your baby?"

Lizzie nodded, sensing some sarcasm in the firefighter's voice. I also sensed it, which is why I backed up another step. He was in trouble.

"Yes, he's my fucking baby," she spat. "What's going on, why did you break my window, why is that prick on the roof?" She turned around, gesturing to all the angry faces. "What are all these people doing here?"

"That's a long story." A policeman, previously idle by his car while he let his partner talk to Matthew's crazy ex, stepped forward. "Do you know the man on the roof?"

I nodded. "He's my friend. *Was*, my friend."

"Ouch!" I heard Matthew yell. "Nice to know that you have my back."

"Are you shitting me?" I shouted up at him. "I ask you for a small favor and I come back to this. What the fuck?"

He nodded, his hands on his hips. "Good point, you have me there. But I can explain."

"And I think he's the best one to do so," the firefighter said. "But he won't come down. We try, but he keeps kicking the ladder away. He's clearly a threat to himself and maybe to others. We have reason to believe that he was also going to harm the baby."

"*No!*" Matthew yelled. "I told you, that was bullshit. I'm not here to kill myself."

"Then why did you tell all of these people that you were?" the firefighter asked.

"I didn't!" Matthew barked. "They misheard!"

"All of these people misheard, did they?" he asked, the same condescending tone he had previously directed at Lizzie.

"Yes!" Matthew snapped. "Because they're all fucking useless, and it doesn't help that that stupid bitch is egging them on."

and then these dipshits came out from down the road." He nodded to the four young lads who all glared back, looking like they wanted to tear out his throat, and like they were capable of doing so.

"I tried to explain myself, but they were having none of it. They thought I was a burglar, a Peeping Tom, a fucking weirdo—they wouldn't listen to the truth."

"I don't know, that sounds spot-on to me."

"They started yelling abuse," he continued, ignoring me again. "And naturally, I started yelling some back."

"Naturally."

"And when they started throwing stuff at me, I threw some right back."

I shook my head in disbelief, imagining Matthew on the roof of my house throwing stones and hurling abuse at the neighborhood children. "Then the cheeky fuckers tried to climb up, that one—" he nodded to the odd-smelling one "—came straight for me. I had nothing to throw and nothing to stop him with so—" He shrugged and let his sentence trail off.

I stared at the boy with the wet T-shirt and the odd smile, seeing the anger in his eyes. After a few seconds, it hit me.

"You pissed on him?"

He shrugged. "What else could I have done?"

"Anything. You could have done *anything* that didn't involve pissing on someone. What is wrong with you?"

"I did what I had to do, and it worked. He stopped climbing after that."

I groaned and sank my head into my hands. "And then?" I asked, not sure I wanted to hear the rest. "How did little Miss Psycho get involved?"

"She came out during the commotion, with all the others. She must have friends or relatives here. I couldn't believe it. What are the odds?"

"That you would run into an ex-girlfriend that hates you?" I asked, raising my head to look him in the eye. "I'd say quite high."

"I tried telling them all the truth, but then one crazy prick said he thought I was trying to kill myself. I told them about the baby being alone. I said that if they didn't get me down then something was going to happen to him. But the wires crossed. They thought I was threatening to kill a baby and myself." He sighed heavily. "Before I could correct myself, that crazy slut started telling them that she knew me, that I had a few screws loose and always had."

"She has a point."

Matthew's eyes flared, moving from exhausted to annoyed in a blink. "Are you just going to sit there and make snide remarks?" he asked. "Can't you see what's happened? I fucked up. All those people, including your wife, are waiting for me so they can beat the shit out of me." He grabbed my arm tightly. "I need you. Help me. For fuck's sake, help me, and I swear I'll never watch porn again."

He was exasperated, but before I could speak, he corrected himself as I thought he might. "Okay, maybe not *never* again."

"You let me down," I told him.

He nodded and lowered his head. "I know."

"I trusted you. We both did."

No words escaped his lips this time, just a defeated nod.

"You put Ben's safety at risk and you went to war with the entire neighborhood. You nearly killed Mr. Andreasson, and everyone believes you're a lunatic on a mission to kill babies and piss on rugby players."

Again, he nodded and I let the shame sink in for a moment, I let the misery wash over him. He needed that, because he didn't get it enough. I turned to the crowd below, to the ambulance that was taking my happy and concussed neighbor and his wife away; to the police, who had sent the crazy chain-smoker away and were now there to keep the peace; and to my wife, who seemed to settle when she saw the peace on my face, the genuine regret on Matthew's, and when she realized that as long as Ben was okay, then the rest—the whys, the hows, and the what-ifs—didn't really matter.

I wrapped an arm around Matthew, causing him to lift his head in surprise, not sure if I was about to tell him that everything was okay or if I was about to toss him to the wolves. "But you're my friend, and as much as I hate you, I still love you."

He beamed a bright smile. "Thanks mate." He threw an arm around me and then we both turned to face the crowd. "Now what do we do?"

"Now we wait. They'll go home eventually."

"What about Fireman Sam down there?" he asked. "I think he wants to kill me for kicking his ladder and calling him a prick, but he's okay with you. You can talk to him."

I shook my head. "No. He's a dick."

"I heard that!" the firefighter called up.

"And now he wants to kill us both."

The Feline, the Fuckwit, and the Full-Blown War: Part One

I wasn't great with animals, but Mickey had softened me somewhat. I still wasn't ready to get a dog or a cat—that was a big leap and one I wasn't prepared for. I already had something small and cute destroying my house and shitting everywhere; I didn't need another. But despite my aversion to acquiring a house pet, one of them decided to acquire my house.

It was a cat, a species that somehow manages to be both adorable and arrogant, both loving and sociopathic. She wasn't as needy as Mickey the Duck, but she was just as cute. She began to appear at the front door every morning, and I had no idea why. Lizzie was equally clueless and happy for me to believe it was some kind of omen. I would later find out that she had actually been feeding the cat treats, and that the cat didn't even know where our front door was until Lizzie coaxed it in from the street with a slice of ham.

Cats like routine, and by the time I realized she existed, she had already established a routine of waiting by the front door until she was fed.

"Ah, it's so lovely." Lizzie was on her haunches by the open door, grinning at the cat as she caressed it. The cat was presumably wondering where the food was and how much more she had to tolerate before it arrived.

I put my foot down. "No, not in the house. Keep it away."

"But she's so cute."

"I don't like animals. They're dirty, they're devious, you never know where they've been and—"

"Mickey?"

My eyes opened wide, my head spinning in all directions. "Mickey?" I said. "Where?"

It took me a few moments before realization dawned. I reluctantly pulled my attention back to my wife and to the curious cat currently judging me from the doorway. "I see what you did there," I told her.

"I didn't do anything," Lizzie said, before shrugging and adding, "but I *did* make my point. And anyway, Ben loves her."

"Really, well . . ." I paused. Her words had worked; they softened me and made me think, but she hadn't counted on me not being oblivious. "How do you know? I haven't seen Ben anywhere near her." I should have figured it out then, but I wasn't as observant as I gave myself credit for.

She quickly changed the subject. "Ben has been lonely without Mickey. I think she would be good for him."

The cat's big eyes bore a pitiful, pleading hole right through me, and Lizzie's look wasn't too dissimilar. If I didn't know any better, I could have sworn they rehearsed this. "Okay," I said, relenting. "Just give it a saucer of milk. Leave it on the doorstep."

She gave me a look I had seen all too often. It was a look that said I was an idiot, and it always preceded an explanation of *why* I was an idiot. "You can't give cats milk. They're lactose intolerant."

I snorted with derision. "Nonsense, cats love milk."

"No, really. You can't give cats milk."

"Is this like when you tried to convince me that mice hate cheese?"

"Well yes, I mean, it should be common sense to anyone who doesn't acquire all of their animal knowledge from Disney cartoons."

"I think you're talking shit."

Walt wouldn't lie to me.

Her brow furrowed, her mouth twisted, and she gave me another look. This was the look she gave me when she was plotting to kill me, the same look she had given me when I laughed at her father's jokes—made at the expense of her mother—and when she caught me telling jokes to an air-headed, big-breasted shop assistant whose boobs jiggled every time she laughed.

"Okay then," she said slowly, making it sound like the prelude to a nefarious scheme. "You let her in and you give her some milk. If that's what you want."

"Her? How do you know it's a her?"

"She's intelligent," she sneered.

I frowned.

"She has no balls, okay?"

I invited the cat in and poured her a saucer of milk. She seemed to know what I was doing and followed me to the fridge, and to the counter. She dove in as soon as I put the saucer down, lapping it up. A smug grin spread across my face. I waited for her to finish, to lick the remnants of milk from her whiskers. I wore an *I told you so* expression and prepared a speech on the importance of humility.

The cat sat on my feet and Lizzie smiled at her as I gave her my speech. "I'm not going to say 'I told you so,' because that's not who I am. Many people—no doubt you included—would not let this opportunity pass them by, but I'm different. I'm *better* than that."

Lizzie was still staring at the cat, still grinning. It was as though she wasn't embarrassed at all, as though she hadn't just lost, as though I hadn't just been proved right.

"But I *knew* this was going to happen." I changed tack; her smile annoyed me. "I *knew* the cat would be okay, and I knew that because I do not get all of my animal knowledge from the Disney channel." I was on a high, but she still wasn't paying much attention to me. She was still grinning at the cat resting on my feet.

At that moment, I saw the cat walk up to Lizzie and brush past her. I stopped my lecture in its tracks, my finger still pointed at my wife like some fired-up dictator. The cat seemed happy, which was nice to see, but I could still feel her tail wrapped around my feet.

Lizzie was giggling. "You realize the cat threw up on your feet, right?"

I looked down to acknowledge the white vomit sprayed all over my socks and up my trousers. There were small chunks of half-digested meat mixed in with it, along with clumps of hair and other detritus that I had no inclination or desire to learn more about.

"I see that now, yes." At that moment, I knew that I had lost the battle and would need to regroup to reestablish my grip on the overall conflict.

"And as averse as you are to saying it, I'm perfectly fine with it," Lizzie said, giving me a cocky and assured grin. "I. Told. You. So." She paused for effect. "Now, clean up that mess."

The cat, who we named Ella, had no collar, and as far as we could tell, she was a stray. She was also very fat, which was odd. I didn't dwell on it, as I didn't want to make her self-conscious. She had a way of staring at me that suggested she knew exactly what I was thinking and what I was saying. I tried to think happy thoughts and told myself she was just big-boned.

Two weeks after she threw up on my feet, a trick she followed up by stealing my place on the sofa and then falling asleep on my pillow, we found a potential cause for her ample proportions.

Lizzie found it when she opened the patio door one morning. She was casual about it, and while there was a note of sarcasm, I didn't detect it initially. "Oh, look, a present!"

Feeling a little giddy, as if Santa had gotten his dates wrong and was too lazy to get down the chimney, I rushed out to see what it was.

It wasn't quite what I expected, and the shock forced me to release a sound that I would later—once the disgust faded—feel very embarrassed about. "What the hell is that?" I pointed, my voice a little higher than I would have liked.

"Ah, bless her. She brought you a present."

"A present?" I yelled. "What kind of sick animal are we dealing with here? I don't want it. I appreciate the sentiment, but it's not for me. Take it back. Exchange it for a living one."

"It's just a mouse," Lizzie said simply. "Well, it *was* just a mouse."

"Don't mice usually have heads?"

Lizzie disappeared into the house to retrieve something to pick it up with. I followed her, not wishing to be alone with it.

"She did this on purpose," I said.

"Of course she did."

"You knew!?"

"Kieran, that's what cats do. It's her way of saying she loves us."

"Remind me to pass that one on to Hallmark," I said. "What's wrong with a bouquet of flowers? I don't like mice and I like them even less when they're missing their heads." Something occurred to me. "I didn't see a head out there. Did you see a head out there?"

Lizzie retrieved the dustpan and brush. There was a muted expression on her face. She knew, but she didn't want to say.

"She ate the head, didn't she?"

She nodded. "I'm sorry."

"Not nearly as much as the fucking mouse."

"These things happen," she continued. "I didn't want to tell you before, but the other day I saw her eating a whole one."

"Another mouse?"

"I hope so."

"How many mice—What do you mean, 'you hope so'?"

"Well, I couldn't really see. It could have been a baby rabbit. Cats and rabbits in the wild, you know."

"The wild? *Baby* rabbits?" I stuttered, my head shaking as though trying to avoid the images it was processing. "There is just so much wrong with that. I don't know where to begin. I think I need to sit down."

She shrugged. For a woman who cried for three weeks after watching *Watership Down*, she was very nonchalant about this. "It was probably a mouse. Don't worry about it."

I chose to believe her. I wasn't sure I could live with the alternative. Next she'd be telling me that Ella had developed a taste for ducks.

"I'm sure it's not the first mouse," she said, "and it won't be the last."

"How many mice are out there?" I demanded. Having never seen one in my yard, I was now faced with the possibility that there were armies of them out there, hiding in the shadows and waiting for the right moment to pounce or to get eaten by a chubby feline.

"Well, there's two less now."

"That's it—she's not getting into the house again. We're not letting her. I don't want a murderer around my child, even if she is a cat." At that point, Ella walked into the kitchen and sat down next to my feet. She was doing this on purpose.

"I think she wants to be fed," Lizzie said.

"I think she's had enough," I told her.

I picked her up and, in my strictest voice I said, "That's it, I'm putting you outside and you're not coming back."

Ella had been in and out of the house every day, and I had enjoyed her company, but I was determined. I made it to the patio door before she made a noise that I could have sworn was an apology, or at least that's what I told myself. I gave her The Talk, making sure she understood that if she was going to kill and eat mice, she wasn't to do it in or around the house.

I also briefed her on my interests, in case she ever decided to bring me a present again.

The presents didn't stop. As well as headless, bodiless, and other limb-less mice, she also left a few butchered birds on our doorstep.

I warned her time and time again, but nothing I said stuck, and she continued to kill defenseless animals. The only other option was to lock her in the house—that would stop her from roaming the yard freely at night and from reducing the animal population of the entire county. Our next-door neighbor had recently bought two very cute little rabbits and I had images of waking up one morning to find them dead at my front door—Pebbles with a puncture wound to the neck, Fluffy's white fur dyed crimson red. That was an image that neither I nor the neighbor's children would be able to live with.

Lizzie was right about Ben. He did seem to like her. I wasn't sure that she felt the same way, as she seemed to spend half the time running away from him and half the time hiding. But Ben thought she was playing, and it was fun to watch his little pudgy legs waddle around the house and listen to his random screams as he found her, lost her, and chased after her. If not for Ben, and if not for the fact that she was a sweet cat, her "presents" would have been enough for me to kick her out of the house and stop her from entering again.

Instead, locking her in seemed like the best idea. Lizzie was against it, though. She said it was barbaric.

"Animals should be allowed to run free," she argued.

"I agree," I told her, looking rather smug. "And that's exactly why I'm doing it." I was convinced that I was doing my bit for the world, that I was saving all the poor little birds and mice and thus preserving the ecosystem of our home. As far as I was concerned, this made up for not recycling, something I'd never been able to get a grip on. Some bins are for one plastic, but not another, some are for paper, some are for cardboard; I get an impending sense of doom every time I drink a bottle of water, knowing that when I finish it, I'll have a conundrum on my hands.

It would also make up for the time I accidentally decimated our neighbor's flower bed and exacerbated their child's asthma. The box of weed killer didn't say anything about not using it on a windy day.

It seemed that whenever I tried to do something good, I always managed to do something bad, or to make life incredibly difficult for myself. When I gave some of my old books to the local school, I didn't realize that Matthew had crossed out all of the archaic curse words in one of them and replaced them with something modern before using his doodling skills to turn an illustrated edition of *Great Expectations* into the *Kama Sutra*. When I helped an old lady cross the road, I ended up being roped into a full day of shopping with her. I spent several hours holding her bag as she tried on cardigans before being labeled as a con man by her son when I walked her home.

I was confident this was going to be different, though. I was confident that nothing could go wrong. I had already accounted for some potential pitfalls. I had bought a litter box in case the cat decided to display her contempt in a symbolic form, I had bought a scratching post to save the furniture, and I had a two-month supply of cat food, none of which contained mice, rabbit, or poultry. I was fully prepared to turn this wild outdoor cat into a tame indoor cat that would be a great replacement for Mickey for both Ben and me.

What I hadn't prepared for, however, was that this one good-natured act would create a full-scale neighborhood war.

It began with a knock on the door, several actually. I don't know how many times exactly since I was asleep at the time, but when I opened my eyes, the impatient imbecile at the door had finally discovered the doorbell and was now hanging on it. It was a short and sharp ring, and that short and sharp noise was being repeated over and over.

Ella was on my chest, licking and pawing at my face, her subtle way of telling me to wake up and feed her. She had quickly grown accustomed to being an indoor cat, discovering the joys of being waited on paw and foot and becoming even more amply proportioned as a result.

"Do you not hear that?" I asked Ella, wondering when she was going to start pulling her weight and answering the door. Although I understood just how big of an ask that was—she had a lot of weight to pull.

As soon as she saw my eyes and my mouth open, she determined I was awake and she moved to wait by the open bedroom door. It was just after ten and Lizzie had already gone to work at her part-time job, the same one she had been working when I first met her. It was Saturday, and she only worked a few hours, but she wouldn't be back until later in the afternoon.

The doorbell was still ringing by the time I got up and dressed. I assumed the worst. What, aside from an emergency, could possibly compel someone to hang on my door at ten on a Saturday morning? I understand that not everyone sees ten as early, and for much of the week I would agree with them, but on Saturday, my day of rest, waking me up at ten in the morning was akin to taking a dump on my pillow.

I checked in on Ben before doing anything else. I had a two-way radio in my bedroom so that every cry, cough, and gurgle would be heard, but I was a heavy sleeper. And as I looked at his pudgy little face, and struggled to hear his breathing over the sound of the doorbell, I was thankful that he was, as well.

As I raced down stairs, twice stopping myself from falling ass-over-tit and creating another emergency, the questions raced through my sluggish mind.

Is my mother okay?

Is my father okay?

Has Sharon finally killed Matthew?

Is it a random caller seeking help after being shot?

Do I watch too many movies?

I hit the hallway running, shot a glance toward the front door, and was amazed to discover no one there. I stood there in silence for a moment, wondering if I had imagined everything. Maybe I had lost my mind. Lizzie had always said I was skating on thin ice in that department.

Then I saw a little head peek up and stare through the glass. I saw little beady eyes glimmer in the light as they saw me standing there. And all the while, the bell continued to ring.

Feeling less rushed, but still very keen to know just what the hell was going on, I ripped open the door. Standing before me, with large-rimmed spectacles, greasy hair, and a face that even a mother would struggle to love, was a small boy, aged no more than ten. He looked up at me, squinting. I looked at his hand, which was still outstretched, holding the bell.

"I'm sorry, did I interrupt something?" I asked.

He finally let go and put his hands by his side. He then paused to look me up and down before nudging his spectacles back onto the bridge of his nose.

"Do you know what time it is?" I asked him.

"Ten," he said simply.

I nodded.

You're not as stupid as you look.

"Do you know what day it is?" I asked, feeling that my point wasn't being made.

"It's Saturday," he said.

"Hmm. I don't think you unders—"

"Have you seen my cat?" he asked, cutting me off.

"Your cat?" I said. *"Have I seen your cat?"*

"Yes, have you seen my—"

"No I haven't," I butted in, enjoying myself.

How do you like it?

A thought occurred to me. "What does she look like?"

He went on to explain Ella to a T. He also called her fat, which was no way to boost her self-esteem.

"You hung on my doorbell and nearly knocked down my door— at ten on a Saturday morning, may I add—to ask me if I'd seen your cat?"

He nodded. "The neighbors said she stays here now." He pointed to the next-door neighbors' backyard, separated from ours by a short fence.

"What do they know?" I said. "Don't listen to them. For all I know, they could have been the ones feeding her the mice."

The little ugly kid looked confused. "Excuse me?"

"Never mind."

"So, have you seen my cat?"

"I don't know, where did you leave her?"

He seemed genuinely stumped by that one. "I want my cat back," he said eventually, looking annoyed.

"I don't have her."

"Don't lie."

I raised my eyebrows. "Excuse me?"

"You heard me. You're lying, and if you don't give me my cat back, I'll set my dad on you."

I laughed at that. "Look, kid, I don't have your cat. Now go away and don't ring this bell ever again."

"I'm not going until you give me my cat back," he said.

"Look, I don't have—" At that point, with impeccable timing, Ella strolled up alongside me and sat down, calmly watching the heated conversation as she cleaned herself. She was still hungry, but seemed satisfied to sate her hunger on neighborhood hostilities for now.

"That's her!"

"Her?" I chuckled, giving myself time to think of an excuse. "That's not a cat."

Clearly I didn't chuckle enough.

I shut the door without saying anything else, watching through the glass panel as the ugly kid's face twisted into something even uglier. He pointed a grubby little finger at me and, for the second time, warned me that he would "set his dad on me," a childish and empty threat that I responded to with the sophistication and maturity that it deserved, sticking my finger up at him and making a *nuh-nuh-na-na-nuh* sound.

I gave Ella her food and made breakfast for myself. It was only when the coffee kicked in and the fatigue departed that I realized what I had done: I had argued with a ten-year-old boy and then stolen his cat. The thought was enough to make me choke on my toast, but once I had forced it down, another thought occurred to me: So what? What kind of polluted, disrespectful, and screwed-up kid would hang on a stranger's doorbell on a Saturday morning? And for that matter, what kind of disrespectful, messed-up parents would let him?

I told myself that if the father came round, I would give him the talking-to that he needed, that I would teach him just how to be a father. I would tell him that you couldn't simply have children and then leave them to fend for themselves, that you actually had to look after them, to mold their minds and to teach them the ways of the world. I would tell him that you had to know where they were every minute of the day, because if you didn't then they could be under the wheels of a truck, locked up in some pervert's basement, or worse, they could be banging on my fucking door at ten o'clock on a Saturday morning.

I felt good about my lecture, about what I was going to tell the worthless father about his delinquent child if he did show up, but then I remembered that I had a child of my own and had completely forgotten about him. Swallowing my pride, and trying to look nonchalant in front of the cat, I took Ben out of his crib and carried him downstairs before plonking him in front of the television and giving him a toy to chew on.

That was parenting, and I was bloody good at it. My kid wouldn't be an ugly little deviant like that shit from across the road. God knew what sort of horrors they got up to in that house, god knew what they must have done to spawn such a feckless, ugly little deviant.

"Despicable," I said to myself, before switching on a recording of *The Walking Dead* when I realized the Cartoon Network was showing re-runs again.

The father of the greasy little kid with the oversized glasses and the undersized brain was much more respectful when it came to knocking on doors, but less so when it came to everything else. I thought it was the postman at first and got my hopes up that I had a package. I hadn't ordered anything, but I occasionally buy random crap when drunk that I forget about, making for a pleasant surprise a few days later.

The person who stood at my door did have something for me, but it wasn't a package. He looked as stereotypically thuggish as a stereotypical thug could look. He had a shaved head and a thick-set jaw, complete with several small scars. He was rather large and wore a tank top to show off the fact, but although he clearly thought of himself as some kind of bodybuilder, his muscles had sagged many years ago. He probably had a six-pack at some point, but now he looked six months pregnant.

"Did you steal my cat?" That was the first thing he asked me. My first instinct was to suggest that he might have eaten it, but I quickly fought that one.

"No," I told him, keeping it short and sweet, knowing that my mouth had a tendency to create problems for the rest of my body.

"My kid said he saw it in your house."

"Your kid was wrong."

"Are you calling my kid a liar?" he snapped, taking an aggressive step forward.

Of all the things I was thinking to call his kid, *liar* was at the bottom of the list, but I didn't elaborate the rest. "I'm just saying," I said, as innocently as I could. "Your cat isn't here."

I'm pretty sure that Ella would have used this opportunity to plonk herself alongside me if I hadn't locked her in the living room.

"I don't like you," he said, staring at me for some time.

I stared right back. "Ditto."

I enjoyed that, although probably a little too much. He seemed to be accepting of my lies and turned to walk away, but I felt a little giddy at what I perceived to be a victory, and I got a little carried away with myself. "And tell that kid of yours to stay away."

He turned around and stormed right back up to my door.

"What did you say?"

"You heard me."

"My kid was just looking for his cat."

"Your kid has no manners. Maybe he should search for them before he bothers looking for his cat."

He lifted a finger and pressed it into my chest, prodding me. "Do you have a problem with me and my family?"

"That depends," I said. I was annoyed, and his finger poking me in the chest didn't help matters. I felt the words coming out of my mouth. In hindsight, I would have stopped myself from saying them, but in the heat of the moment, nothing could have stopped me. "Are all of your family inbred, annoying little fuckwits?"

He hadn't expected me to say that and his shock was my get-out clause. Sensing that he was about to attack, I took a step back and slammed the door in his face. He was so close that the handle caught him on the hip and the frame of the door slapped him on the nose. I watched through the glass as he stumbled backward with holy hell spilling out of his mouth, then I locked the door. I wasn't a fighter and I wasn't a big fan of confrontation, even though my mouth seemed to love it.

"I'm going to fucking kill you!" he yelled at the door.

I wholeheartedly believed that he would do just that. And I probably deserved it. A rational person might have apologized or even backed away, but I gave him a cheeky little wave instead.

"You're dead!" he screamed, before spitting at his feet.

I was happy to see him leave and walk back to his house on the other side of the road. I rushed upstairs to get a better view, craning my neck to see out the window. My happiness faded when I saw him talking to his next-door neighbors, and when, before long, several others gathered on the front lawn. I had no idea what they were saying, but with the way they were pointing and thrusting, along with the less-than-neighborly looks on their faces, I had a feeling it was about me.

9

The Feline, the Fuckwit, and the Full-Blown War: Part Two

I wasn't exactly looking forward to telling Lizzie about the cold war I had started in our neighborhood. I hoped that I wouldn't need to—adhering to the typically male attitude that it would all blow over—but the neighbors remained gathered outside my house for most of the day. There were only a handful of them, lounging in the yard across the street, but they outnumbered me, even if I roped Ella in for support. Lizzie often said that when faced with adult situations, I reacted in childish ways. That was the main reason I didn't want to tell her, but the shouting—and the power she had over my sex life—were also valid reasons. I wasn't childish, of course; if anything, *they* were the childish ones. They started it.

As I watched from behind a twitching curtain, drinking a cup of tea and feeling like some noir detective as the steam shrouded my face, I realized what an ugly little bunch they were—devious and conniving like a villainous cluster of hideous imps. One of their children, who looked like he had been severely beaten with a tennis racket, saw me watching and called to the older freaks who all looked up. Realizing I was caught, I put down my cup of tea and pretended to clean the windowsills.

The bald thuggish one pointed and said something, then his deformed offspring decided to ring the bell again. They held onto it for a number of minutes as the others watched and laughed, but I ignored it and remained by the window, pretending to be admiring the view. After a while, and after thinking of something sufficiently cocky and amusing to say, I opened the window and prepared myself. What I hadn't prepared for, or even noticed, was that I had left my tea in the way, and when I moved to lean out of the open window, I knocked it out.

I cringed as I watched it fall, the front door and the imbecilic child directly beneath it. It was a heavy cup, and although there was little chance that the kid would receive any noticeable brain damage—on account of him being sufficiently damaged in that department already—I was still relieved when I heard it hit the ground. I was less relieved, however, when I heard the kid scream.

The tea was no longer hot, but the fact that half the street had just watched me "throw" a cup at a small child who was now in tears wasn't going to do me any favors. On the upside, he had stopped ringing the bell; on the downside, his father was preparing to take his place.

"I understand your anger!" I yelled as he tried to kick my door down. "But you're going about this the wrong way."

He took a step back and glared up at me. "Come down here, right now!" he ordered.

"Why?"

"So I can kill you, that's why."

"That's hardly an invitation I'm going to accept now, is it?"

"Down. Here. Now!" he yelled, as though spelling it out and using fewer words would make it a more tempting offer.

"I have a kid in here," I told him. "I suggest you be quiet. You're upsetting him." Ben was actually sitting behind me playing with one of his toys, completely oblivious to what was going on around him. The cat, the cause of all of this, was sitting next to him and watching his every move. "He's crying now," I added, turning back.

"And what about *my* boy?" he demanded. "He's crying."

"He'll be fine. It was a bit of warm tea, never hurt anyone."

"Do you think it's normal to throw tea at a child?"

"I don't know. Do *you* think it's normal to let your ugly little brat hang on someone's doorbell?"

"Come here now!"

"Fuck off!"

I slammed the window and went back to hiding behind the curtain while apologizing to Ben for swearing. He didn't seem to mind. He also didn't seem to mind the sound of the door being banged off its hinges downstairs, as the thug neighbor pounded his distaste and then went back to the yard across the street.

The boy had stopped crying, and his dad wasn't even paying attention to him, more concerned with his own anger. After a few minutes and many stares in my direction, the neighbors went to their respective homes, but I sensed that that wasn't the end of things.

Ben was asleep on the couch. He'd had a long day; not only had he managed to figure out a new puzzle, but he'd also learned how to undo the child catch on the stair gate just before I managed to catch him and stop him from bouncing to his death. I was asleep next to him. I'd also had a long day, but the less said about that the better. The cat was perched on the top of the sofa above us, purring like a mini-motorbike.

I awoke to the sound of shouts. I listened for a bit, still unsure if I was dreaming or not, and then I recognized one of the voices as Lizzie's. I ran to the door just as she walked through it. She looked annoyed and ready for a fight, so I shrank back immediately, wearing my most innocent expression and waiting for her to make the first move.

"That bald prick neighbor of ours has just confronted me outside," she said.

"Oh?"

"He told me everything."

"Oh."

"But I don't believe him," she added. "He said you called his kid ugly, threw tea on him, and then slammed the door in his face. Is that true?"

"No, of course not." I paused, decided that lying wouldn't do me any favors and then said, "I mean yes, but it didn't happen in that order."

Lizzie sighed. "Kieran?"

"Okay, I'll explain."

I told her everything, from the moment I woke up to the sound of the incessant bell, to the incident with the door, the neighbors, and the tea. I waited to be told that I was overreacting, that I was in the wrong, that I had acted childishly or stupidly—all things I would have gladly accepted. Instead she agreed with me.

"Who would let their kid do that?" She was appalled. "Which one was it?"

"It was the little kid with the wandering, twitching eyes and the vacant expression," I explained. "You can never quite tell if he's smiling at you or winking at the person next to you."

"That's horrible," she said uncertainly.

"But true," I was quick to add. "He's one daddy issue away from turning an AK-47 on all the classmates that have ever looked at him funny, which as far as he is concerned, is probably all of them."

Lizzy furrowed her eyebrows and frowned at me before saying, "I don't think that's how a lazy eye works. I'm sure he can see fine."

"You don't know that."

"The horrible little bastards," she said, shaking her head. "What kind of messed-up parents let their kid hang on someone's doorbell at eight o'clock on a Saturday morning?"

I had embellished the truth a little, but I didn't change the important parts.

"Exactly," I agreed. "But now they've created some sort of war out there. Them against us. And they outnumber us."

"But they don't outsmart us," she said, tapping her head and grinning. I grinned as well, although mainly because she thought that I could outsmart someone. "Most of them won't care; it's just the bald idiot that we have to worry about, but he's an easy target."

For the rest of the night, she wore a determined and somewhat evil expression on her face as she pondered a plan of action. I had never seen her in that state of mind before, but I liked it and I couldn't wait to see how things turned out.

The next morning, Lizzie got a taste of the kid's vile manners for herself when he hung on the doorbell again. It really was around eight o'clock this time, and the fact that it was Sunday drove both of us crazy with indignation. Lizzie was the one who answered it, and she did so just in time to see the little rascal running away, his high-pitched laughter echoing down the street. It stopped being about the cat, although I had my doubts that it ever was. We tried to encourage Ella to go outside at night, thinking she would go home, but whenever we left a door or window open, she would rush back in.

Lizzie tasked me with dealing with the buzzer issue. She told me to buy some equipment. She meant CCTV equipment, so we could catch the little devil, or his father, in the act. I went down another route, replacing the bell with one that would give anyone who touched it an electric shock. I even paid the man who installed it a little extra to increase the voltage. "Nothing deadly," I told him. "I just want to scare someone, not kill them."

Unfortunately, I didn't anticipate that the kid would be at school the following morning and that the first person to press the buzzer would be the postman with a package. He received such a shock that he dropped the parcel and nearly tripped over his own feet in an attempt to get away. I had been on my way to answer the door, but when I heard the buzz, the pop, and the scream, I ducked below the windowsill and watched as surreptitiously as I could. Lizzie hadn't seen it, so I quickly dragged the package indoors, disconnected the doorbell, and pretended nothing had happened.

She woke an hour later. The cat was in the yard by then, curled up in a ball by the fence, no doubt sleeping with one eye open so she could keep the other trained on any innocent animals that dared to cross her line of sight. Lizzie, who was wearing nothing but a nightdress, went straight to the kitchen and, after listening to her rummaging around in the fridge for a while, I heard her scream.

The kitchen door led out onto the side of the house, right next to a fence that stopped any intruders from sneaking around to the back door or the backyard itself. As I entered the kitchen, Lizzie was standing by that back door, in the process of shouting at our first intruder.

"What the hell do you think you're doing?" she barked.

I peeked over her shoulder to see Fuckwit, the small-minded, big-headed father of the inconsiderate child who had woken me up on Saturday morning, holding the cat in his arms and hurrying away. He had ducked in unannounced and taken the cat before trying to leave as quickly as possible.

"I'm taking my cat!" he yelled.

"Your cat? I said. "You mean the animal currently trying her best to get the hell away from you?"

He held Ella by the throat to stop her from squirming. She looked like she was ready to claw him, and he was aware of the fact, tilting his head back and keeping her at a distance.

"You're hurting Ella," Lizzie squealed.

"Who the hell is Ella?"

"The cat!"

"The cat's name is Mr. Tibbles."

Lizzie and I looked at each other. It was an incredibly stupid name for a cat, there was no denying that, but unless it was also an ironic name, then it probably made much more sense than the one we had given her. Or him, as it turned out.

"You can't just waltz into someone's garden and steal stuff," I told him.

He looked confused. Whenever we spoke to him in long sentences, there seemed to be a delay. English was clearly his second language, but I didn't speak the Inaudible Grunt he was so fluent in.

"Just watch me!" he spat eventually, hurrying away.

"Now what?" I asked Lizzie.

I don't know what I expected of her. I knew she would be angry that this idiot had just walked onto her property and taken something she liked, and I also knew she would be angry about the way he had treated the cat. What I didn't expect was what happened next: she ran after him.

He made it into the house before she got to him, her bare feet slapping the concrete violently and her nightdress blowing up and exposing things she didn't want to expose to people she didn't want to expose them to. She was a woman on a mission, and he was a little man two paces short of shitting himself.

I quickly climbed into my shoes and followed her, keen to stop her from killing him and equally keen to *watch* her kill him if I failed with my first mission. By the time I arrived at the house, she was banging on the front door, her hands balled into fists, her mouth open wide as a cacophony of hellfire spewed forth.

"He locked the fucking door!" she yelled. She was frothing at the mouth.

"I see that."

"What should we do?"

I had no idea. "Try reasoning with him?"

"Reasoning with him? Are you kidding? You can't reason with these people."

I shrugged again. "Maybe you should knock down the door and kill his entire family."

She liked that idea, and for a moment she actually contemplated it, but that moment quickly passed when she let her sanity do the thinking for her. "Middle ground, Kieran," she said.

"You could shit through his letterbox."

She didn't have time to contemplate my proposal because as soon as it left my mouth, Fuckwit shouted through the door. "I've called the police, they're on their way."

"He called the police!" Lizzie spat.

"So I heard."

"Can you believe that?"

"To be honest, I'm a little surprised he knew the number."

"What are we going to do?"

"We could go home and have some breakfast. Oh, and a package came for you this morning. I also made tea."

She glared at me. "What is wrong with you?"

How long have you got?

"Nothing," I said. "My wife is standing in the middle of the street on a Monday morning, barefoot, half naked, and with a police car on the way. If there was ever a time to retire, collect ourselves, and plan our next move, this is it."

She looked down at herself, as though only just realizing that a brisk breeze had been sporadically exposing her bare backside to the neighbors for the last few minutes. "Maybe you're right."

Back in our house, she finally dressed, looking a little brighter as she sipped her morning coffee before opening the parcel that had been somewhat haphazardly delivered.

"On the plus side," I said, making conversation, worried about both the cat and the police, "the kid wasn't hanging on the doorbell this morning."

"Did you order the CCTV equipment?" she asked.

"No."

She paused to stare at me. "I thought you said you'd sorted it?"

I had. But I wasn't talking about the CCTV.

"My mistake. I'll order it la—"

"What's happened to my vase?" Her hand was in the box that the postman had dropped, her eyes wide with horror as she picked up broken pieces of glass.

That was my chance to come clean, to fess up and to save the poor postman's job. "The feckless little prick," I said, shaking my head in disbelief, and also in an effort to rid myself of all right-eous thoughts. "You should phone them up and complain. The cheeky bastards were probably playing soccer with it back at the post office."

"You're right," she said. "I'll get straight onto them."

"Actually, why don't you let me do it?" I jumped in, worried they would tell her that their driver had been assaulted by our doorbell.

She kissed me on the forehead. "Thanks."

"It's the least I could do."

She stared at me curiously. "Why did you say that?"

Yes, Kieran, why did you say that?

"No reason."

Idiot.

She weighed me up for interminable seconds. I felt sure I was going to crack. "You're a weird one, but I love you for it." She gave me another kiss and then asked, "Should we wait for the police or not?"

"Do you think he honestly called them?"

She shrugged.

"I think he's probably had a few run-ins with them before and might not want to draw attention to himself."

"And why do you think that?" she asked, an eyebrow arched. She hated it when I stereotyped people, she hated my cynicism, and she hated that I often judged people who I didn't like. As far as I was concerned, if I didn't like someone then I was free to call them what I wanted, otherwise what would be the point in disliking someone?

I pretended that it wasn't because he talked like an extra from *Eastenders* and looked like he spent his nights hanging around bus shelters selling crack and murdering babies. "No reason."

"Anyway, you're probably right."

A knock at the door silenced the conversation. I could see a smeared silhouette of a tall person in dark clothes standing behind it. The dark shape knocked on the door again and then moved to ring the bell.

Shit.

I felt my heart hit the pit of my stomach. I heard the buzz of the doorbell and then—

"Did they just swear?" Lizzie asked.

"Yes. I think so."

I opened the door as nonchalantly as possible for a man who had technically assaulted two uniformed men in one morning.

"Your doorbell just attacked me," a waiting police offer said, a look on incredulity on his face.

I hooked my head around the corner to stare at the bell. "No, really?" I asked.

"Yes, really. You want to get that seen to."

"Maybe you should arrest it," I offered, chuckling softly.

He didn't find it funny.

I cleared my throat. "So, how can I help you, officer?"

He paused to look at his notepad. At that point, I noticed there was a short woman next to him, as wide as she was tall. She had her hair tied back in a ponytail, so tight that it looked like her eyes were about to pop out of her head. An expression on her face indicated she didn't like me or anyone else in this world.

"Are you Mr. GirlPants?" the male officer asked.

"Excuse me?"

"That's the name I have on my pad here. This is number 17, right?"

"Yes. But my name is McCall, Kieran McCall."

"Oh. I had a feeling it might have been a joke."

With deduction skills like that I'm surprised you haven't made detective.

"Can I come in?" he asked.

That depends, will you be bringing your Rottweiler with you?

"Of course."

I stepped back and allowed them both to enter. Lizzie had been standing next to the door when they rang but had disappeared into the living room when I opened it. She was now approaching them with the most insincere surprise I had ever seen. With acting skills like that, it was a good thing she went into teaching.

They sat down in the living room and explained that Fuckwit had phoned them and told them everything. They said they wanted our side of the story, which I was more than happy to give them. I saw the look on Lizzie's face that said *let me do the talking*, which preceded, as it so often did, the looks that said, *I don't trust you* and *please don't fuck this up*, but I was keen to offload.

"It all began with the little *kid*," I said, correcting myself just as I was about to refer to him by one of his many pet names. "I can admit that not all kids are perfect. I was a little shit myself as a kid and got into all sorts of mischief." I was smiling, hoping for some sort of reciprocated gesture, but there was none. "But he was ringing the bell at six o'clock on a Saturday morning." I avoided eye contact in case they could read my lies. "And there is no excuse for that."

I stared at the officers and they stared back. I panicked and turned away again.

"And then, well, things kinda got heated with his father, as you probably know. If he had apologized, then things would be okay."

"But he didn't?"

"No. He just made things worse."

"He was very abusive to both my husband and me," Lizzie jumped in. "I mean, what sort of man shouts abuse at a woman in her own driveway?"

The police officer nodded and seemed to agree with her. I should have let Lizzie continue, he seemed to like her and listen to her, but I wanted the same sort of reaction so I chimed in. "He was a bully, a waste of space. And when he realized that his tactics weren't working, all of his idiot friends joined in, standing in their yards looking up at the house."

"Just looking?"

"Yeah, but they were *mean* looks."

"Uh-huh."

"I don't want to press charges against them, though," I assured him.

"You don't want to press charges against them for looking at you?"

"I mean, unless you can."

He shook his head slowly, not breaking eye contact. He then turned to his notes. "He says that you threw hot coffee on his child."

"It was tea," I corrected, hearing an audible sigh from Lizzie as she gave up hope that the police would be able to help us. "And it wasn't hot, it was tepid at best," I said, before adding, "there wasn't even any sugar in it."

The look Lizzie gave me at that point said *Really?* But in my defense, the officer was writing something down, so although it seemed trivial to her, it was probably noteworthy to him.

"And then, this morning, I caught him spying on my wife."

That seemed to get his attention. He raised his eyes from his pad and stopped doodling. "Please go on," he insisted, perhaps a little more perversely than I would have liked.

"She was in the kitchen, right next to the back door, and she was naked. I mean, she doesn't walk around the house naked all the time or anything—"

"That's a shame," the short and wide woman said, making everyone pause and stare.

"—But even if she does, no one can see unless they open the side gate and get into the back yard." I tried my best to ignore the policewoman, who seemed to be there for comic effect. "Which is what he did."

"He just stormed in?"

I nodded. "No reason. Just opened the gate and stormed in. She got the fright of her life when she saw him standing there."

"He was just standing there?"

I nodded. "With his hands down his pants and a weird look on his face. Creepy, if you ask me."

"I can imagine."

He took a few more notes, asked a few more questions, and then went on his way. I showed them out and then returned to the living room where Lizzie was sitting with her head in her hands.

"What the hell was all that about?" she asked, looking up.

"I told him the truth."

"You made him out to be a pervert."

"He is," I said, before adding, "probably."

In such a small community, one minor argument with the wrong person or the wrong family can leave you castigated, but at the same time, one accusation can save you and destroy them. When the police returned to Fuckwit's house, he had a few of the neighbors over. In his cockiness and his willingness to prove that they were all in it together, he asked that the neighbors stay while the police question him.

He was so shocked and embarrassed by the comments that followed that the defense he provided was pathetic, feeble, and about as believable as the accusations I made. They tried to calm him down, but when one of the other neighbors remembered that she had seen a man "about his size" loitering around the woods behind their house and staring into their daughter's room, the damage was done.

That night, he was a broken and beaten man. The strange thing about neighbors is that they are friends of convenience only. They are there to back you up only when it suits them, and because they don't know you as well as a friend would, they also don't trust you enough to believe your word over that of a stranger's.

After Fuckwit fought with the police, spent the night in jail, and then returned a bitter, angry, but ultimately defeated man, he promised to stop his kid from ringing the doorbell early in the morning and he promised he would never spy on any of the neighbors again. The following morning, Lizzie ran into a few of the neighbors on her way to work and they all rushed up to her, apologizing, hugging, kissing. Fuckwit and his ill-mannered offspring kept a low profile for a few weeks, but the less they were seen the more the rumors spread, and before long he was public enemy number one and was forced to leave.

Ella, on the other hand, stayed. She became part of the fixtures for a while, but as cats tend to do, she eventually tired of us and moved on to find a new family. She felt like our cat by then, and Ben had really taken a shine to her, but we decided not to chase her down, knowing what happened to the last owners who did.

10

Cockawhat?

"Hello, darling! How are you?"

I was greeted with a call from a Stepford wife, dressed in an apron and a smile, with the smell of freshly baked bread wafting from the kitchen. It was enough to make me stop in my tracks as soon as I walked through the front door, enough for me to double check that I had the right house.

And the right wife.

Ben, who's usually the source of all smells in our house, was asleep on the couch, a trickle of drool an inch from soaking into his collar. I kissed him on the forehead, wiped the drool from his chin, and ventured further into the house, which didn't feel or smell like my own.

"How was Matthew?" she asked politely, looking like she genuinely cared.

". . . okay," I said slowly.

How was your journey to the 1950s?

"Anything interesting?" she wondered.

I began to worry. My first thoughts were that she was high or drunk. I didn't smell alcohol on her breath, and if she was on drugs then I hoped she had a long-term supply. I could get used to this—as soon as I stopped being freaked out by it.

She guided me into the kitchen before handing me a beer from the fridge and a sandwich that she had ready.

"I made it with homemade bread," she told me. "Three layers, all toasted like a proper club sandwich. There's ham, two kinds of cheese, bacon, mustard, lettuce, and tomato. The perfect sandwich."

I nodded slowly, wondering if she had slipped any of her happy pills into the sandwich, as well.

She continued, the smile seemingly engraved on her face. "I also made you your favorite for dessert, rice pudding."

That's when it hit me, that's when I saw the glint in her eye, the one that said this was all a ruse, a trick. I had seen that glint before. I had fallen for it then, and it didn't end well for me. I rolled my eyes and then asked her, "What are you up to?"

"Excuse me?"

"All of this," I said, gesturing around to indicate her offerings. "You either did something or you want something."

"Can't I just make the man I love his favorite dessert without being up to something?"

"That depends on who the man you love is," I told her. "Because I fucking hate rice pudding."

"Oh." She stared abysmally into the pan of boiling rice. "Banoffee Pie?"

"Closer, but no."

"Okay."

And suddenly, we'd entered a stare-off. She was still grinning at me, and that grin seemed reluctant to break, but it was getting ready. I waited for the inevitable words, the ones that always followed moments like these, but when they didn't come, I shrugged, kicked off my shoes, and said, "So I'll just go into living room and watch TV, right?"

Then they came. "I could give you a blow job if you wanted."

That was the final straw. "Right, what is it, what do you want? You finally killed my mother, didn't you?"

Or yours?

She lowered her eyes to her hands as she twiddled her thumbs, looking like a lost child about to admit to breaking a priceless vase. "I was just thinking."

Please tell me it was yours.

"I don't like the sound of that, but continue."

". . . that we should get a dog."

"Really?"

She nodded, an expectant look on her face. I almost felt bad for destroying her hopes. Almost.

"There aren't enough blow jobs in the world."

"Oh come on, I'll look after it. I'll walk it; you don't need to do anything."

I paused to give it some thought. I really wasn't much of an animal lover, but Mickey and then Ella had softened me somewhat. I was actually quite happy to entertain the idea of a little puppy running around the house. I wasn't going to let it be that easy, though, otherwise she'd have me right where she wanted me and the war that is marriage would swing in her favor.

"I'll think about it."

"I think Ben would really love a dog."

That was low. And she knew it. But she was committed to the cause. She sat down next to Ben and began stroking his hair, drawing my attention to him and hoping that a combination of her puppy-dog eyes and his cute face would result in a dog.

"I think he really misses Mickey and Ella." He wasn't the only one, and she knew that. "Just think how much fun he had with them. And with a puppy, it's ours, so there will be no chance of it flying away or finding another owner."

That was more about me than Ben. She knew that would get to me. But I didn't let it show. "Like I said, I'll think about it," I told her again.

She seemed hopeful, but the vacant look I gave her told her not to be. I enjoyed complete silence and complete control of the television remote that night. She didn't follow through with any sexual favors, but I was happy to take the small victories when they came. After several hours of having beers handed to me and watching all the shows that she hated, she asked me again. She had been watching Ben throughout, no doubt keen for him to wake up so she could use him somehow. But as desperate as she was for his help, she wasn't evil enough to wake him up to get in.

"Can we discuss the dog some more?" she said eventually, deciding to go all-in one last time.

I held up the little white flag. "Okay. Let's go for it. What breed do you want? Big dog, small dog? Have you given it much thought?"

She clearly had given it some thought. She waited until I finished speaking, but I knew the words had been on her lips since I walked through the door. "I want a labradoodle."

"A labra . . . what?" Maybe she was on drugs after all.

"A labradoodle," she repeated, as though it were the most normal thing in the world. "Or a goldendoodle. Oh!" She raised her hands. She was either having a eureka moment or the second dose had just kicked in. "Or a pugapoo!"

I slowly shook my head, absorbing the simpleton smile that she directed my way. "Have you had a stroke?"

The smile turned into a glare. "They're dog breeds," she informed me. "A labradoodle is a cross between a Labrador and a poodle."

"Ah, right," I nodded, pretending I understood and doing my best not to imagine how that abomination had been conceived.

"I quite like cockapoos, as well."

"Now you're just pulling my leg."

She shook her head vehemently. "They're real, honestly."

"Bullshit."

"It's true! It's a cross between cocker spaniel and a poodle."

"Come on, no one's that cruel, no one's that childish."

She got that determined look on her face, the one that was invariably followed by an introduction of the iPad and a Google search. Within a couple of minutes, she was showing me pictures of animals clearly the result of a sordid affair between a pony and a mop.

"That's a labradoodle." She fired off another search, flashed me more pictures of dogs with interspecies parents. "And that's a cockapoo."

I was amazed. I had never known these things existed, and my eyes had been opened to a new and exciting world, namely one where people bred incompatible canines and then mocked them with stupid names.

As my intrigue grew, she showed me more alien breeds. They were cute, but imagining their parents going at it was equal parts terrifying, adorable, and hilarious. There were pure-bred monsters, half the size of humans and twice as thick, getting frisky with pocket puppies.

"But where does this end?" I asked as that intrigue and hilarity turned into something else. "What if someone breeds a shih tzu with a cocker spaniel?"

Lizzie shrugged nonchalantly. "I don't see why not."

"Really? Come on, no one wants a shitty cock."

She lowered her brow in a disapproving gesture, but I was dead serious. The line had clearly already been crossed, and someone needed to draw a new one before the world was awash with Martian beasts who couldn't recognize their parents.

"So, which one do you prefer?" she asked me.

I shrugged, and as if to tease an answer out of me, she began swiping through the pictures, showing me dog after dog—cute faces, ugly faces, squashed faces, scared faces. Half of them had an expression that suggested even they didn't know what the hell they were.

"That one," I said after a while, more as a way of ending the slide-show of misery than anything else.

"Perfect. That's a labradoodle. My favorite."

I gave her my best smile, telling her that I was committed to this bizarre new desire of hers and that I was prepared to go through with it—even though I would be sleeping with one eye open and wondering when the race of super intelligent, genetically superior canines was going to conquer the world in a revolution reminiscent of the *Planet of the Apes*, only with fewer bananas and a lot more incest.

"It just so happens that there's a breeder nearby who has a litter."

What a lucky coincidence.

By "it just so happens," what she meant was that she'd already been in touch with the breeder, she'd already arranged a deal, and she'd already had the puppy wrapped up in a bow and ready to go. The "discussion" we'd just had was a show put on for my benefit, tricking me into believing I had any say in the matter.

"I just need some cash and then he's all ours."

"Sure," I said, taking out my wallet and flicking through the meager sum of notes. "How much?"

I was ready to go along with it, ready to welcome a new alien life-form into our home at the cost of whatever was in my wallet, but I detected a wry grin on her face as she watched me take out a few dollars. Then she told me the price and my mind quickly changed.

"You're fucking kidding me."

At the sound of a swear word, we both instinctively turned to Ben, saw that he was still sleeping, and then continued.

"It's a designer dog," she said.

"Great, then he can do some freelancing and earn back some of his fee."

"Stop being facetious."

"Stop using big words."

She glared at me, her hands on her hips, a momentary silence in the air. "Are you going to continue being difficult?"

"That depends, is he going to continue being expensive?"

She rolled her eyes and then made to move away, excluding her-self from the conversation. "If you don't want a dog, then we don't get a dog," she said. "Simple as that." She sounded convincing, but there was an undercurrent to her words and the way she dismiss-ively waved her hand at me. That undercurrent said, "but no dog means no more sex for you, ever; it means that I will pester you until the day I die and that if you want anything *ever*, even if I want that same thing, you have no chance of getting it." We had only been married for a couple of years, but I could sniff out a declara-tion of war.

So I agreed to the dog, and I also agreed to pay for it. I was broke, but it made her smile so it was worth it. I knew that if she was smiling and if she was genuinely happy with me, then she wasn't plotting to kill me. Because she was the one working, she was also the one to pay the rent and the bills. In fact, she paid for all of the essentials and whatever money I had was used to pay for nonessentials. Although, since losing my last job and not returning to the job market, I didn't have much savings left and most of my cash came from my parents.

The breeder was about as insane as I would expect. She was the stereotype of a cat lady and she lived it to the letter, but with dogs. She hated me from the moment she saw me, glaring at me and saving all of her smiles for Lizzie. I wasn't sure if she could sense that I wasn't an animal person, or if she could sense my annoyance at spending my last penny on a freak show puppy that would eat me out of house and home and then defecate on said house and home. But there was definitely contempt behind her eyes.

As she looked from her pets to Ben to Lizzie and then to me, I noticed a declining interest and an increase of contempt. It seemed that the more responsive a living creature was, the less she liked it. And as Ben began wiggling around on his mother's knee, trying to grab the ears or tails of passing animals and spurting random noises, the look she gave him looked like the one she gave me.

"Don't you have something cheaper?" I asked her at one point. There were so many dogs around, living inside the house and in kennels out back, that it seemed like a logical question. "Something a little older, a little uglier maybe?"

Lizzie seemed caught in two moods, unsure whether she wanted to flee the house and her husband or wait for the ground to swallow her up. It was an expression I knew well.

"Are you serious?" the breeder asked.

"He is, unfortunately," Lizzie chimed as I grinned at them both. Ben seemed amused, possibly sensing the tension, possibly feeding off the smile on my face, or maybe just reacting to the fact that we had taken him to an interactive zoo.

"I only have labradoodle and cockapoo pups," she explained. "A few of them have homes lined up, and none of them are ugly or old. I'm sorry." She didn't look sorry at all.

"I saw an older one around here earlier," I told her. "A fat thing, bigger than the others. He looked like he was well past his prime. You know the one—bald, a little odd looking, he was lying down. Ben tried to pull his tail."

She had a stern look on her face. "That wasn't his tail," she said, going some way to explain her sudden contempt for my child.

"Wow," I said, genuinely impressed. I turned to Ben and cringed as I noticed he was sucking on his fingers.

"That's Freddy," she said.

"He didn't tell me his name."

She clearly wasn't one for jokes. "Freddy is the father," she said. "He's not for sale. He's my baby. I wouldn't sell him for all the money in the world." I'm not sure I wanted him anymore anyway. I could live with a bald dog and an old dog, but I'm not sure I could live with a bald and old dog that still managed to emasculate me.

"The same goes for his mother, Angie," she said. I hadn't seen her, but she was probably hiding. Or, if Freddy was anything to go by, maybe she was in recovery.

I was fairly sure she was lying. The fact that she was happy to keep them as breeding machines, constantly pregnant and churning out little half-breeds that she could sell for a profit, suggested she didn't love them as much as she pretended.

"Have you got any other animals?" I wondered.

"Any *other* animals?"

It's amazing how people turn to repetition when they're confused.

"Ducks, cats . . . I quite fancy a parrot."

Lizzie covered her face with her hands, seemingly of the belief that if she couldn't see it, then it wasn't happening.

"I have none of those, I'm sorry." Again, I didn't believe her. I was convinced that she had cats somewhere.

"Okay, then I'll guess we'll take the dog."

"You guess?" She didn't sound pleased.

"Yes." I took the money out of my wallet and handed it to her, rather reluctantly. "One dog please."

At that point, Lizzie spoke. I heard the words, "Oh my God," escape her lips and slip past her hand.

"Well, Ben certainly seems to like him," Lizzie announced proudly as he took to the puppy like, well, like a baby to a puppy.

"Of course he likes him. He's an animated, excitable, drooling ball of fur. Take away the fur and two of the legs and they're exactly the same."

"Did you just compare our baby to a dog?"

"Not just any dog, a dog that costs as much as you make in a month."

She nodded firmly. "Okay then."

Despite my unease at having spent so much money on him— money I could have used to buy a pool table, a new Xbox, or something else that brought me fun and relief and didn't shit on my floor and ruin my slippers—I found myself falling for the little bundle of excitement. He was hyperactive, but I was used to that with Ben. He was also lovable. We called him Eddie. I have no idea why and I played no part in the naming process, but the way

Lizzie told me what we were going to call him, she made it sound like I did.

There's a certain joy in something that loves you unconditionally and will always do so, something that will not grow into a nervous and nasty bundle of hormones, lust, and hate. One of the things I had insisted on if we got the dog was that Lizzie had to walk it, feed it, and generally look after it. I was already cleaning up after one family member; I wasn't going to volunteer for overtime. Lizzie agreed to that and she stuck to that agreement, but gradually, over the process of a few weeks, I began to fall for his charms.

When she was at work and he was getting agitated at home, the idea was to send him into the backyard and let him do his business there, but he had learned where his leash was, and whenever I opened the back door, he ran to it. I was a sucker for animals, always giving them what they wanted, and I knew I had to take him. In fairness to him, it wasn't much of a backyard, no more than a few square feet fenced in and surrounded by neighboring houses. I certainly wouldn't want to empty my bowels on a patch of dead grass while half a dozen neighbors watched me.

"Okay, I'll walk you," I told him. "But don't tell your mummy. I don't want to set a precedent here."

One bright day, with the sun belting down a ferocious heat, I felt content as I pushed the stroller with a smiling baby inside and an excited dog strapped to it. I took Eddie to the local park and let him off his leash, at which point he sat in front of me and wagged his tail. I had no idea what he wanted, and wasn't sure whether he was waiting for me to play with him or to give him permission, but I did neither.

I settled into a park bench with the sun searing above me. He was still hovering around my feet, which was a little creepy. Lizzie had said he was reluctant to go very far. He probably had abandonment issues, worried that if he let us out of his sight, he would end up back with the crazy woman who burned effigies of penises and smelled like feet.

I took Ben out of the stroller, rested him on my knee, and then leaned back, soaking up the sun.

"Ah, he's so lovely!"

I hadn't seen anyone approach, but when I snapped open my eyes, I saw a young blonde woman standing over me. Eddie was jumping up and down by her side, desperate to hump her leg.

"Is he yours?" she asked.

"The dog or the baby?"

"The dog."

"Yes, he's mine."

Eddie continued to jump, and when she reached down to stroke him, he licked her hand. She seemed to enjoy that and let him continue, but would have acted differently if I'd told her what he'd been licking moments earlier.

"And the baby?" she wondered.

"He's mine, as well."

She grinned and sat beside me. Eddie followed her and pestered her all the way, but when he realized that she was no longer paying attention to him, he wondered off to find someone else who would.

"What's his name?"

"Ben."

She reached forward and squeezed his cheeks, making the baby noises that everyone seems to think are compulsory. I try my best not to make them, worried that Ben will grow up thinking that's how people talk. It did occur to me that if I'm the only one not talking like that, then my son will grow up thinking I'm weird. But that ship has probably already sailed.

"He's so gorgeous," she announced.

In my pre-married years, I would have tried to hit on her. She was sweet, pretty, but I was taken and as a result I had excused myself from the dating game. Ironically, that had made me more confident around woman, so although I had more chance of success, I had no desire for it.

Relationships were hard work. I knew that better than anyone, and with Lizzie I had done all of that hard work. I had struggled through the heartbreak and the delight, and I had emerged with a happy marriage and a healthy kid. To risk that would be stupid and would mean having to start all over again. I also still thought that Lizzie was the most amazing woman I had ever known and struggled to see that perfection in anyone else. I had stopped telling her that since we'd married. It was okay when we were courting, but marriage was different—marriage was a battleground and you had save your ammunition for when it was needed the most.

"Aren't you lovely!" She pinched Ben's cheek. "Just like your daddy."

"Thank you."

"So how old is he?" she wanted to know.

"He's just over a year, coming on to fourteen months now."

A sympathetic look spread across her face and she stared deep into my eyes. "It must be so difficult doing what you do."

I had no idea what she was talking about so I just smiled. That usually gets me through.

"You're so brave." She looked like she wanted to reach forward and pinch my cheeks. "My name is Charlotte, by the way."

"Kieran."

"Well, it's nice to meet you, Kieran," she said with a bright smile. "Do you come here often?" She winked.

"I've actually only just started."

"Well, you should come more. Especially now that summer is here." She stood, stretched, and then checked her watch. As soon as he saw her active legs, Eddie came trotting over and tried to hump them. "I have some errands to run. Maybe I'll see you here tomorrow?"

"Maybe."

I stayed for another hour or so, letting Eddie pester every passer-by. He chased an unfortunate squirrel and then engaged in a shouting match with a tree when the squirrel scuttled hastily up it. He finally did his business, but he chose to do it in front of a woman with a stroller, presumably because she refused to pay attention to it.

During that time, I was visited by three more women. A couple of them were schoolgirls, no more than sixteen, but the attention was just as nice, and Eddie enjoyed wiping his groin on two more sets of legs. The third was an older woman with a cougar glint in her eye. She devoted more time to me than the others and sat closer than they did, but she didn't try anything.

I left when it started to get dark, and when I returned home Lizzie was waiting for me.

"So, you caved after all, eh?"

I was still smiling from my exploits in the park where I had inadvertently become somewhat of a local hunk. She didn't seem to notice.

"Well, I'm off work for a week now," she told me as Eddie jumped into her arms and threatened to lick her face off. "So I can take over the walking duties for a while."

"No, no," I jumped in quickly, *too* quickly.

She frowned at me suspiciously.

"I mean, it's okay. It was fun. He was no trouble."

"Really?"

I nodded.

"He didn't pester anyone, he didn't insist that you play with him, and he didn't try to shove his nose in every dog's asshole?"

"No," I lied. "He was fine. He seems more relaxed with me. Maybe I should walk him more often."

She put him down. She was suspicious, and I wasn't very good at hiding my guilt, but eventually she shrugged. "Okay, if that's what you want, then you can walk him from now on."

I walked Eddie and Ben in the park every day, sometimes more than once. They both became minor celebrities, doted upon by every woman who saw them.

"They're so cute, I want to eat them up."

"They're so cute, I'm going to die."

It's amazing how when women see something cute, their first reactions involve murder, cannibalism, or suicide. A man might nod, smile, and get on with his day, but if you catch a woman in her prime, when the hormones are kicking up a fuss, then cuteness can be deadly.

Simply being with two small and cute things made me adorable by association. Men tend not to enjoy being called adorable, but I loved it. I became just as popular as Ben and Eddie, with the difference being that I could take advantage of that popularity. I could chat, I could flirt. I had no intention of taking it further, but that didn't mean I couldn't have fun. Lizzie wouldn't agree, I was sure about that, but that would also make her a hypocrite.

One of my oldest friends, Max, threw regular parties for his fellow businessmen and rich neighbors and we had tagged along to one of them. Even the bathroom attendant was better dressed than I was, but Lizzie looked like a goddess. She was swamped by aging party-goers all night, bombarded with compliments, and flirted with in the only way that rich old men can flirt.

"Let's have dinner in Paris, feast on some fine cuisine, and then, maybe, on each other."

"Let's take a ride on the Orient Express, let's see as much of the world as we can before we do the same to one another."

"Let me just pop in my dentures, take my pill, and we can go at it like rabbits."

Not all of those chat-up lines were genuine, but that was the gist of it. They bothered her all night, not knowing or caring that I was with her. They probably didn't see me as a threat. Money was everything to them, and the person with the most money had the best chance. As I sipped from a glass of flat champagne, Lizzie flirted back, teasing, joking. When I pulled her up on it at the end of the night, she told me that she was just having fun, that it was harmless. And after all, that's all I was doing at the park.

One of the most regular visitors to the park were two teenage girls. They looked fifteen, but I told myself they were eighteen—it made me feel a little less like a pervert. But only a little. Their names were Eleanor and Pepsi. When it came to unusual names, I couldn't help but search for the meanings and came to the conclusion that Eleanor's parents thought they were giving birth to a ninety-year-old woman with gray hair, and that Pepsi's parents were really committed to the Coke Wars. Parents can be cruel and some shouldn't be allowed to name their children, referring to an advisory board or an Internet poll instead. But Pepsi could take solace in the fact she wasn't named after another giant corporation and didn't end up as Monsanto, Five Guys, or Virgin, although judging by the way she dressed and the way she flirted, at least one of those names would have been ironic.

"My friend just had a baby," Pepsi told me as she played with Ben's cheek. "How stupid is that?"

"I don't know."

"She's only fourteen."

"Oh, then very."

"I mean, she should have at least waited until she was sixteen."

"Yes, of course. And what about the dad?"

She gave me a bewildered look, as though that was the strangest thing she had ever heard.

"What do you mean?"

I wondered if she'd had the talk about the birds and the bees and if what I'd said was tantamount to letting slip that there was no Santa Claus. But this was clearly a girl that not only knew about the birds and the bees, but had humped a few of them in her time.

"Isn't the father on the scene?"

"No. Well, I mean, maybe, but how would she even know who he was?"

I stared at her for a few seconds, completely confused. Eventually she returned to pinching Ben's check and playing with Eddie.

They were two of the regulars, but not the two I liked the most. Just like the others, they assumed I was a single parent, and I let them assume that. I would have gladly—maybe—told them otherwise if they had actually asked, but they didn't. The teenagers were the most surprised by it, but the older women, the ones I imagined my single self really going for, thought it was sweet.

One of those was Charlotte, the sweet girl I had bumped into on the first day. She was an aspiring actress, a hard-working student who hadn't had much luck in life or in love. She confided in me with stories of both.

"First there was Neil," she had said. "He was sweet, but he had this weird thing with his sister."

"Oh," I said as that found its way into my head. I mulled it over for a few seconds, and by the end I was desperate to know, "What 'weird thing'?"

I wouldn't have blamed her for not divulging that information, but she felt so at ease with me that she was happy to. "Well, when they were kids they used to share a bath together."

"Okay, well, that's not—"

"And they haven't stopped."

"Oh, yes, definitely weird. Maybe they're just trying to save water?"

"You're so funny, Kieran, that's why I like you." She giggled and shoved me on the arm. "And then there was Chris," she continued.

"He sounds like a dick," I jumped in.

She gave me a confused look and then nodded. "He was. He was very kinky in bed, which I don't mind, but it got a little weird."

Again I decided to push my luck. "Weird how? He didn't ask you to share a bath with him and his sister, did he?"

She laughed and nudged me on the arm again. I laughed with her, even though the shoving was becoming a little annoying.

"He was into whips, studs, that sort of thing. And when I said that wasn't my style, he thought it was part of the game, that I was being submissive."

"That couldn't have ended well."

"For him, no it didn't. I gripped his balls and threatened to crush them if he didn't put the whip down."

"Always go for the weak spot," I said, instinctively folding my legs.

"And then there was Matthew." She sighed as she mentioned his name. "He was sweet and kind and, well, everything that I wanted at first, but it turned out to be a lie."

"Oh." That made me feel a little uncomfortable.

Could it be?

"He was a womanizer," she told me. "Only cared about sex, and with as many women as he could—" She paused and frowned at me. "Why are you looking like that?" she asked. "Do you know him?"

Probably.

I shook my head. "No, no, of course not. I was just worried for you. I was just thinking about what you must have been through."

Definitely.

"Thanks." She put her arms around me. "You're the best. Ben and Eddie have done well to find you; it's just a shame that their mother left and that there's no one else waiting for you at home." She pulled back and stared into my eyes. "A man like you should have women lining up."

As it happened, a man like me had exactly that, but only because this man was a liar. I broke eye contact—fearing that she might go in for the kiss—and then checked my watch. "Oh, would you look at that, I better get going. This little man needs his feed."

"That's a shame," she said, looking genuinely disappointed. "Will you be here tomorrow?"

I smiled back, ready to answer, but someone answered for me.

"No."

My smile turned into a frown. Unless my mouth was fucking with me, then I hadn't said that. I turned to look at Ben, wondering if he had just spoken his first word, if he was trying to tell me something, but he grinned back at me with the same vacant expression that he always had. "You can tell he's your child," my mother would say when she saw it. "He has that stupid look on his face."

I turned back to Charlotte to apologize for what must have been a minor stoke when I saw that her attention was aimed above me. That's when the realization hit, when I recognized the voice.

"Hi, what are you doing here?" I asked as I greeted my wife. I was smiling at her, hoping she would reciprocate, but she looked like she would sooner cut off my smile and wear it than commit to one of her own.

"I think you better go," I whispered to Charlotte, for her safety and for mine.

"Yes," Lizzie said, stepping around to the front of the bench so that we could both see her. Eddie also saw her and decided to break the tension by humping her leg. "I think you should leave."

"Who is this, Kieran?" Charlotte asked, giving me a look that asked if she should be worried, a look that speculated that the woman whose leg was being sexually assaulted might be an insane stalker.

"Yes, Kieran, who am I?" Lizzie asked.

"Well, if you don't know then—"

"This is no time for jokes. Tell her," Lizzie said.

I sighed, lowering my head into my chest. "It's my wife," I said feebly.

"Sorry?" Charlotte asked.

I looked at her and nodded. "Yes, she'll make sure of that."

"You're damn right I will." Lizzie reached down, took Ben away from me, strapped Eddie to his lead, and then kicked me in the shins, forcing me to spring to my feet.

"I didn't know you were married," Charlotte said.

I showed her the ring on my finger. I had never taken it off and had simply tried to keep the hand hidden. I felt like removing it would be breaking a cardinal sin, while if I just let them assume I wasn't married, and surreptitiously hid my hand, it would be okay.

"But I thought we had something," Charlotte said, sounding hurt. "I told you everything."

I shrugged. I was a little baffled as to why she thought that was relevant, as if the fact that I was married would have stopped her from telling me about her incestuous ex, but now wasn't the time for those sort of arguments. It was the time for other arguments, ones with more screaming and much less interactivity on my behalf.

We left Charlotte on the bench, but as we walked away, with Lizzie seemingly keen to drag me somewhere quiet before butchering me, another one of my fans was heading our way. She waved to me excitedly and I tried to ignore her, but that only made her more frantic and that's when she shouted my name.

Lizzie glared at me. "Be polite, wave back to your little whore."

I gave her a little wave and, just when I thought it was over, she blew a kiss. The kiss was probably intended for Ben or Eddie, but it didn't put me in the best light either way.

"How could you do this?" Lizzie said, finally snapping when we were on the road back to our house, with Eddie on his chain and Ben in his stroller.

"I'm sorry, nothing happened."

"And how can I be sure of that?"

I shrugged. "It was just a bit of mindless flirting. I got carried away. They were there to see Ben and Eddie, not me. I was just an added bonus. An idiot on the side who told stupid jokes and made them laugh."

Lizzie nodded. "Yes, an idiot, that explains you perfectly. This is why you were going on all those walks. I knew something was amiss, I knew you were up to something."

I nodded and hung my head. "It was harmless and nothing happened, honest."

"I would *never* do *anything* like this to you, so how—"

I saw my chance and decided to use it before it passed. I raised my head, suppressed a smile, and seized on her like a mongoose striking against a deadly cobra.

"What about Max's party?" I asked her. "When all those geriatrics were stumbling around you, offering to take you back to their retirement homes so you could suck their saggy scrotums and watch *Murder, She Wrote?*"

"That was different," she said.

"How, exactly?"

"Because I'm a woman. I was just having fun. That's the way it works. It's okay when women do it, but when men do it, they're after something."

"Bullshit. What makes you think I wasn't just having fun, as well?"

"Because you're a man, and you don't think with your brain, you think with your penis."

"I saw you that night. I saw you way you smiled, the way you played with your hair and rubbed your nipples. If men think with their penises, then you were definitely thinking with your vagina."

Her mouth gaped open and she looked incredulous, but when it sank in, she realized I was probably right, which made me happy for a brief moment and then incredibly worried for a longer one.

"And I wasn't rubbing my nipples," she told me.

"You may as well have been."

She nodded. "Okay," she said with a long sigh. "Maybe you're right, maybe it's not different. I just got carried away, and I'm willing to believe that you did the same."

I nodded. "Although I got carried away with attractive young women, you got carried away with men old enough to be your grandfather."

"Good point."

"I mean, one of them looked like he was going to have a stroke next to the buffet table when he saw you puff out your chest, and when I say stroke I mean—"

"Yes, yes, you mean his penis. I get it. Very funny."

She was humoring me, but I could take that as a win. I nodded proudly. "Thank you, although I'd appreciate it if you let me finish my jokes."

She slapped me on the arm, gave me a smile and a shake of her head. "Come on then, Mr. Funny Man. Let's get you home before you start screwing everything with a Justin Bieber backpack and a squeaky giggle."

"And let's get you home in time for bingo."

11

The Stoning: Part One

"I have nothing against drugs, and I'll be the first to admit to trying a few in my time, albeit inadvertently, but they don't work for me."

From the look that Matthew gave me, you'd think I'd dropped my pants and pissed on his shoes.

I shrugged in reply to his disgust. "They just turn me into an idiot." His distaste reverted to a smile, but I jumped in before he could reply. "*More* of an idiot," I added, doing the work for him.

He seemed disappointed.

"And since when have you been into drugs?" I asked.

"I'm not *into* drugs," he told me. "I smoke a bit of dope, that's all."

"You know that's a drug, right?"

He glared at me fiercely. "Out of the two of us, which one got high on prescription medication and insulted a room full of women at a speed-dating event?"

I hung my head in shame. It was a day I had tried to forget, but Matthew wouldn't let me. What was one of my biggest embarrassments was Matthew's wet dream. I was sure the only reason we were still friends was because he enjoyed reminding me of my embarrassing moments and then watching as I made more. Maybe that was what true friendship was all about.

"Yeah, I thought so. Keep your opinions to yourself, McCall."

Matthew had come over to watch the soccer game, but instead of bringing a few beers, he brought a small bag of cannabis. He bought it from one of his many dodgy friends, people he hung out with because they reminded him of his youth—mainly because they lived with their parents and spent their days masturbating and talking shit.

He used to spend all of his free time with me. This had its upsides, but there were many more downsides. In the last few weeks, he had spent more time with a new group of people.

"I've known them forever," he'd told me, which was a complete lie. He hadn't known anyone as long as me, and we didn't meet until I was seventeen. After meeting Matthew, very few people stuck around. All of the women in his life, minus his wife, rarely gave him more than a few months before disappearing off the face of the earth, and those were only the ones he *didn't* sleep with. For the ones he did sleep with, he was probably the one who disappeared off the face of the earth.

Matthew had a weird way of choosing friends. Basically, anyone who had enough self-loathing and enough of an inferiority complex to look up to him; anyone who wasn't offended by things that should offend everyone; and anyone who had so little luck with the opposite sex that they looked up to his misadventures as something to aspire to. That described my younger self perfectly, and it also described Marcus, but with these other "friends," the tables had turned somewhat. Matthew seemed to be the one who looked up to them, as though the fact that they sat around in their underpants all day, masturbating to *Game of Thrones* reruns and ordering around parents who had all but given up on retirement and life, was something to aspire to.

"I really don't know what you see in those guys," I said, for what must have been the hundredth time.

He shrugged and gave me the answer that he always gave me: "I guess they're just cool. You don't know them so you wouldn't know."

But what Matthew had yet to realize was that I did know his dimwitted friends, as I had gone to school with one of them. Chris Peterson was the laziest and most pathetic of Matthew's lazy and pathetic friends. He was the self-abuser who the other self-abusers looked up to, the one whose crude jokes and lewd come-ons had gotten them all barred from the local clubs and blacklisted by the female population.

I hated him and I always had. It was probably going a bit too far to say that he was my arch nemesis, but he was definitely my arch nemesis. If I was Superman then he would be an overweight and sweat-stained Lex Luthor. If I was Spiderman, then he would be whatever fat and sweaty adversary Spiderman had. He was one of the few people in the world who made me sick at the mere thought of him. And not just because he beat the crap out of me and locked me in the girls' changing rooms. Although that did help.

I thought that Chris would recognize me by name, just as I had done with him, but the fact that Matthew hadn't said anything led me to believe that Chris had either forgotten about me—losing my memory among the faces of the dozens of innocent kids he had tortured—or Matthew was so ashamed of me that he hadn't mentioned me. I didn't know which one I would have preferred the least, so I tried not to think about it. I didn't want Matthew knowing about my history with Chris anyway. I wasn't sure how that would be received, but I knew it wouldn't be comfortable.

"Do you want some?" Matthew asked. "The game is starting in an hour; it'll make it a lot more interesting."

"England is playing," I reminded him. "The only thing that would make it more interesting is if we changed the channel."

He shrugged. "Your loss. Mind if I smoke this outside?"

"Yes, actually, I do."

"What?" He looked baffled. He was already on his way to the back door, but he stopped and gave me a blank stare.

"I do mind. You're not smoking that outside my house."

"But—But—" He paused to stare at the bag of cannabis before moving his eyes back to me. "Are you kidding me?"

"You're not polluting my air."

"Kieran, we've had this discussion before. You don't own the air outside your house just like you didn't own that duck that you tried to kidnap."

"How dare you!" I said. "I loved that duck. And I did *not* try to kidnap it."

"Whatever you did, it was weird."

"There was nothing weird about it."

"Dude, it was a fucking duck."

I glared at him until he wiped the smile from his face and apologized. "Okay, I take it back, I'm sorry I said that about Donald—"

"—Mickey."

"—Mickey." He arched his eyebrows. "Mickey? Okay, anyway, can I smoke outside or what?"

"No."

"Please?"

"No. Not only are we adults, but I have a baby, for God's sake."

"He's asleep upstairs, he won't mind."

"It doesn't matter. It's irresponsible. I don't want you using drugs anywhere near my child."

He grunted, but gave in. I felt more responsible than I had ever done. It scared me a little.

He looked toward the front door, but I knew he wouldn't go out there and smoke. As much as he liked to put on an air of confidence, when it came to the police, he was scared shitless. He'd had a few run-ins with them before—as you would expect from a man who treated the female race like supermarket samples—and on every encounter he turned into a repenting, nervous little boy. I knew why, because I knew how his mind worked. He had convinced himself that he was too pretty for jail and that he would wind up as a sex slave, passed around the prison like a forbidden cigarette.

"Can I make some food then?" he asked, putting the bag back in his pocket. "I'm hungry."

He walked into the kitchen and I followed him. Matthew had always treated my home like his own. When we first moved in, I had made the mistake of telling him to make himself at home. Three weeks later, he had done just that, only stopping short of leaving his toothbrush on my sink and his porn mags under my bed.

"I thought we were going to get a pizza."

"I'll make one, how about that?"

Something was amiss. "You want to cook? You only ever cook when . . ." I trailed off as something dawned on me. "You're not trying to have sex with me, are you?"

He winked at me and I suddenly knew how all of his sexual conquests had felt. I wasn't sure if I wanted to vomit or swoon.

"You're not my type, trust me. Come on, it's a piece of cake. You have cheese and tomato sauce, right?"

I had no idea; Lizzie did the cooking and didn't let me anywhere near the oven. Or the fridge. In fact, the kitchen was pretty much out-of-bounds. She said I was a liability. In her words, "You're the only person I know that could burn the dinner while washing the dishes." She also said that if I had it my way, I would subsist on a diet of pork rinds, biscuits, and tea. I personally didn't see anything wrong with that.

"Of course," I said, not wanting to expose my cooking inadequacies to a man who already knew all of my other inadequacies.

"And the ingredients for dough?"

That one threw me. I did what I usually do when someone says something I don't understand. I just smiled until he clarified.

"Flour and water."

"Oh," I said, nodding, as if I knew all along. "Of course. The tap is there and the flour . . ." I mumbled and then left the kitchen.

Good luck with that.

I felt like I had won that little battle. I had escaped without looking like a complete simpleton who didn't know what dough—or pizza, for that matter— was made from. But the relief had clouded my judgement, and I had missed the fact that a friend who hated to cook and loved to get the better of me was doing both of those things in my kitchen.

I was shocked, and a little appalled, as I stared at the plate that Matthew handed me, wondering what sort of monster had used it as a toilet. "This is a pizza?" I didn't know a lot about food, but I could tell the difference between something edible and something that required a call to the emergency services and a hazmat suit.

"It tastes a lot better than it looks."

"It would fucking have to."

He gave me The Look, the one I had received from Lizzie on a number of occasions but never thought I would receive from Matthew. It was The Look that always preceded The Talk, the one that began, "I have slaved over that," and led to a barrage of noises that only dogs could hear and culminated with sleeping on the couch.

"It's lovely, though," I said quickly, almost instinctively. I hadn't even tasted it yet. "But why is mine different from yours?"

He studied my plate with a mouthful of pizza, chewing and chomping like an animal, his chin flecked with strands of warm cheese. "I made yours especially. It's ham, sweet corn, and pineapple—all that freaky shit that should never be allowed on a pizza, but that you insist on eating."

That cheered me up. I looked down at my plate to confirm what he had said. I could see the ham; it was a little blacker than I was used to but it was there. I could also see the pineapple and sweet-corn, looking somewhat shriveled next to the blackened pieces of ham. I had seen better, there was no doubt about that. Even without taking a bite, I could also tell that I had *tasted* better, but coming from someone who I wouldn't trust to pour me a pint without leaving me sick, maimed, or wet, I was quite impressed.

"And what's yours?" I asked.

"Just cheese and tomato."

"And what's the green stuff?" I asked, pointing to the substance that seemed to have leaked oil onto his plate.

He stared at it for a moment, slowly chewing. "Pepperoni?"

My eyebrows narrowed to a point. "What do you mean, *pepperoni*? Is that a question or are you suddenly a teenage girl from Australia?"

"It's pepperoni," he said with a slow nod, staring at me all the while.

"It doesn't look like pepperoni."

"What does it look like?"

I inspected it closely. "Herbs?"

"Ah, you're right," he said, his nod much quicker now.

"I'm right?"

"Yes. It's herbs."

"Really?"

He was grinning now, his mouth still working tirelessly as he chomped through the suspect pizza. "Yes."

"And why did you shut the kitchen door and open the back door? You weren't smoking in there were you?"

He looked incredulous that I would even suggest such a thing. "No. I promised I wouldn't smoke in your home and I didn't. It got a little steamy and hot in there, I was just letting all of that out."

"You sure? Because it smells funny in there."

He shrugged it off and took a bite before speaking to me between chews, "It's just the pizza. Your problem is you don't know what freshly cooked food smells like. You eat too much processed shit."

"Hm." I stared at him until he finished chewing. He seemed to swallow with great difficultly, after which he returned my stare.

"I'm watching you," I told him.

"Feel free, but the game is on in ten minutes and that might be a bit more interesting."

Ah, Matthew, ever the optimist.

Lizzie had intended to go out with her friends, but when they didn't show, she put Ben to bed and then came down to watch the game with us. She didn't know a lot about soccer, but she wasn't going to let that get in her way. And while Matthew and I discussed formations, tactical choices, and the inability of England's midfield to gel like the continental teams that often show us up, Lizzie's comments were a little less tactically minded and a little more one-sided.

"He just spat! Isn't the ref going to book him?"

"You think they'd be tempted to just pick up the ball, wouldn't you?"

"Only a straight man would wear bright orange boots with a white shirt."

There was also a lot of aggression involved. She was usually quiet, only releasing her inner demons when she was angry, but when it came to sports, she turned into a beast, even if she wasn't entirely sure what was happening.

I had called her on it before, but she didn't even know she was doing it. She suggested that it probably had something to do with her grandfather. I wasn't sure how to take that. I didn't know if he was just an angry sports fan, or if he was some kind of vicious hooligan. I decided not to ask too many questions. I reasoned that ignorance was bliss, and if it was the latter, she might punch me.

Her lack of knowledge had nothing to do with not knowing the offside rule and falling to grasp other minor rules, and everything to do with the fact that she genuinely didn't have a clue what was happening. It was half-time before she realized that the manager was not an overly enthusiastic fan, and when a player had his name taken for remonstrating with the ref, she thought the belligerent striker was giving the official his phone number.

Sports weren't her thing, but that didn't stop her from trying to understand them.

Matthew found her amusing and enjoyed it whenever she watched a game with us. To him, she was like the crazy old man that you find in every pub. The one who sits on his own at the edge of the bar, butting in on everyone's conversations, offering irrelevant advice, shouting random obscenities, and generally being bat-shit crazy.

"It's like she's channeling an aggressive imbecile," was how he put it, and I couldn't argue with that.

The last time we watched a game, he began to worry that she was actually beginning to understand what was going on and would therefore lose her appeal. She got excited over every attack, every half chance, and even every corner. She overdid it a bit, and at one point she seemed to get her sports mixed up, thinking they scored when the ball cleared the crossbar, but she was on the right track and that worried Matthew. After nearly ninety minutes of excitement from her and no goals, England scored a winner in the dying moments and while everyone cheered, she remained silent.

"What happened?" she said when the cheering died down and we sat back down. "What in hell are you getting so excited about?"

Matthew could have kissed her at that moment. "She's so adorable," he had declared. "Can I keep her?"

This time, England scored early on and Lizzie cheered. She was on time, and that depressed Matthew, but after the goal, she began to settle into her usual routine, complaining about the player's haircuts, the spitting, and the commentator's voice.

"And what's with the cameraman?" she asked, annoyed. "Doesn't he know that women watch this shit, as well?"

Matthew shrugged. "Do they? I mean, for one thing, you just called it shit, which—"

"Shut it, dickhead," Lizzie spat, definitely getting into the spirit. "If I wanted to listen to an asshole, I would have farted."

Matthew grinned. He was in love.

"I mean, he spends most of the time finding the pretty girls in the crowd."

"Which I am grateful for."

Lizzie stared at Matthew until his heart froze inside his chest. "Sorry," he squeaked.

"And when he does show the men, for the other ten percent of the time, it's always the fat, ugly tossers that, quite frankly, no one wants to see. First of all, what kind of idiot would get a tattoo of their team across their chest." I grinned as Matthew instinctively put a hand on his shoulder, where his sleeve covered the embarrassment of an England tattoo from when he thought his national side was good enough to warrant branding his flesh. "Secondly, why would they expose that chest to the entire world when they have bigger breasts than their wives?"

"Maybe they're caught up in the moment. It happens to the best of us," I offered, hoping she would take a hint, but knowing she wouldn't.

"Maybe, or maybe they're just fucking idiots."

"Yeah," Matthew chorused, keen to side with the woman who was quickly becoming the love of his life. "I agree. What she said."

"You're an idiot," I whispered to him.

"Shut up or I'll set your wife on you."

At that point, Lizzie stood and Matthew nearly shit himself. He looked very edgy, and as I stared at him, I noted that his eyes were glassy.

"I'm going to grab some food," she said. "You two want anything?"

"We're good," I said. "We just had pizza."

"Oh, pizza," she mumbled as she wandered into the kitchen.

I turned back to Matthew. "Although I should have asked *you*, shouldn't I?"

"Sorry?"

"If you were hungry."

"I'm not, we just ate, like you said."

"Are you sure? You don't have the munchies or anything?"

I saw him flinch. He was good at lying; that's how he managed to convince so many women to sleep with him. He had called it charm and charisma, but only because he smiled when he lied to them.

"I do not know what you are talking about."

"Oh God," I mumbled.

A stoned Matthew was like no Matthew I had ever encountered. He was slow and methodical, and when he was trying to hide it, he was even slower and even more methodical, probably because his brain was taking so long to process the information.

"How did you do it?" I asked.

He gave me a long and blank stare as his muddled brain tried to find a way out of this maze. "I honestly have no idea what you are talking about."

"Let's just watch the game."

I fired a few glances his way throughout the first half, but he was dead to the world, grinning and drooling like a baby staring at a bowl of candy. His brain had gone on vacation. He didn't speak a single word for the rest of the half, and I wasn't sure he moved either. I didn't know how he had done it, but I knew from the look on his near-comatose face he had taken most of the bag.

Lizzie joined us again for the final half hour of the game. She practically stumbled into the room and threw herself down on the sofa. I had managed to rouse Matthew at that point, dragging him out of his coma and forcing him to face reality. I knew I was ruining his buzz, but I didn't want Lizzie to think I was letting my friends get wasted in our house.

"You took your time," I told her.

She turned to me, stared for a moment, and then nodded before turning back to the television.

I swapped curious stares with Matthew, who shrugged his shoulders.

"Where did you go?" I asked her.

She turned back to me again. "I'm not sure," she said, her voice laborious. "I mean, I know I went upstairs for a bit, but then I kinda got sidetracked and . . ." she shrugged. "Now I'm here."

I gave Matthew another stare, this one more worried and annoyed than the last one.

"Did you find some food?" Matthew asked.

When she turned back and beamed at the both of us, I knew what had happened before she spoke. "Yes. I had some of your pizza. It was lovely."

"You've got to be kidding me," I hissed at him. "You drugged the fucking pizza, didn't you?"

He nodded.

"And then you left it in the kitchen, in full fucking view?"

He shrugged nonchalantly. "It was a big pizza, I wasn't that hungry."

"You're joking, right?"

"Don't get pissy with me, I also left some of yours in there!"

"Bah!" Lizzie cut in. "Fucking ham and pineapple, I ain't touching that shit. But the other one, with the, the, the . . . what was it, exactly?"

"Dope."

"Dope," she said, sounding it out. "Yes. That was very nice. We should get some of that."

"Well," Matthew sat forward, sensing his opportunity. "If it's dope you want, then—"

I grabbed him by the shoulder and yanked him back before leaning forward myself. "So, are you feeling okay, sweetie?"

The grin was still plastered across her face. I had never seen her happier, which delighted and terrified me in equal measures.

"I'm feeling great!" she announced.

Of course you are.

"You've got a lot to answer for," I whispered to Matthew. "Drugging my wife. This is Chris Peterson's fault. I told you he was a bad influence. He's nothing but a little prick. He was a little prick at school and he's a little prick now. Nothing's changed. He didn't mature. And if you don't stop hanging around with him then he'll drag you down to his level."

He gave me a long and thoughtful stare. I thought my words were getting through to him, that in the wilderness of his inebriated brain, I was finally going to convince him to do the right thing, but those weren't the thoughts his brain was processing.

"You knew Chris Peterson in school?"

I opened my mouth to fire a rebuttal and then promptly closed it again.

Shit.

12

The Stoning: Part Two

I didn't need to worry about Matthew's questions. I didn't need to explain my history with Chris Peterson and, thankfully, I didn't need to endure Matthew's laughing and perverted curiosity as I recalled the time he had pushed me into the girls' changing rooms. I didn't need to do any of that because within a few seconds of the revelation, Matthew had moved onto something else, his attention span shorter than the queue for a Mel Gibson documentary on Jewish history.

It wasn't the best when he was sober, but under the influence of dope, he was one sneeze, one overheard conversation, or one ringing telephone away from losing track. I'd been there before with him. I'd once accidentally blurted out his wife's surprise plans for an upcoming birthday party, and while his stoned brain had computed what I had said, trying to find the meaning in it, I switched on the Cartoon Network and never heard about it again.

This time there were two of them, and they both seemed to keep each other occupied with mundane chatter and theories that bordered on the psychotic, but were somehow admissible when stoned. She listened to his theory on how television had been brainwashing us for years and was preparing us for a final war, which all seemed like fairly straightforward psychosis until he explained that the final war would be fought between thin people and fat people, with those of a medium build forced to starve themselves, gorge themselves, or face a life of uncertainty. He listened to her theory that all cats were secretly preparing to declare war on the human race, that their pandering was merely just to win the trust of the humans and to make the final conquest that much easier. I listened to both of their theories while secretly wishing I was dead and wondering if there was any of his special pizza left.

Once they had finished, they celebrated their descent into insanity with a drink of whiskey. I tried to stop them, but by then they had already reverted to an adolescent state and any attempts to create order led to a fit of tantrums.

"You can't tell us what to do," Matthew told me, his hand thrown around my wife's shoulders like a pair of drunken rebels.

"We'll be fine," Lizzie assured me.

One drink led to two drinks, and before long I decided to join them. I didn't want to get drunk, though—God knows where the two of them would have ended up without a partially responsible adult to take care of them. And I needed to make sure that there was a sober, responsible adult on call in case anything happened to Ben. He was probably good for the night now, but I didn't want him to wake up to a house full of stoned, drunk people. I just wanted to take the edge off what was going to be a long night.

After the drinking, then the shouting, the laughing, and the joking started. I tried to join in, I really did, but I had no idea what was going on. I became a grumpy old party-pooper, a role that suited my mood perfectly, and one I had some experience in.

"You're going to wake the baby," I pleaded with them. They had ventured into the backyard, no doubt preparing to dance naked in the moonlight or set fire to the neighbors' shed.

Lizzie gave me a long and hard stare before she asked, "What baby?"

My face dropped, and both Lizzie and Matthew took note, immediately bursting into laughter.

"Look at his face!" Matthew yelled, before prodding Lizzie several times. "Say it again, go on, say it again!"

"Grow up," I spat.

Lizzie put her hands on her hips and mimicked me like a child, saying, "*Grow up*," before sticking out her tongue and rocking her head back and forth. The joke was on her, though—I didn't talk like that.

"I mean, seriously," I implored. "You're too old to be acting like this."

"*You're* too old," Lizzie said, thrusting her finger at me.

"Yeah, you tell him." Matthew nudged her again.

I had seen Matthew stoned many times, but this was new to me. He usually just sat there and kept quiet, occasionally talking absolute utter bullshit about something completely off-subject. In all honesty, it's not something I minded. It was somewhat annoying when I needed to get a straight answer or a clear conversation out of him, but if he was silent then it meant he wasn't being crude, rude, or incredibly sexist, so it had its upsides. This, however, I had never seen before and never wanted to see again. I didn't know whether it was the added effect of the alcohol, or the fact that he had someone to be mischievous with.

"Oh, oh!" Lizzie said, sounding suddenly excited. "Look, a ball, let's play!"

"Yes," Matthew chimed in, clearly enjoying that idea. "We can do much better than those overpaid tossers." He paused. "Are women allowed to play soccer?"

"Of course!" Lizzie said, surprising me by not kneeing him in the testicles and calling him a sexist pig. "There's a women's soccer league, World Cup and everything."

Matthew looked genuinely shocked. "You're shitting me." He turned to me. "Did you know about this?"

I nodded.

"Woman *and* soccer, and no one thought to tell me? I mean, I need to see that. Do they do it completely naked? Are they oiled up?" Matthew had a hard time understanding any sport involving women. For many years, he believed that synchronized swimming was akin to pole dancing and was amazed when he discovered it was a sport. He was equally surprised to learn that the winners of mud wrestling matches were not contented men with empty balls, but the wrestlers themselves.

"They wear clothes, just like the men do," Lizzie said.

Don't tell him that. Not when he's in this state. You'll kill him.

Matthew was struggling with this one, but as soon as he had an image in his head, there was little anyone could do to alter it. "Don't be stupid. How would we see their boobs juggle?"

Lizzie wasn't in the mood for the physics of naked female soccer and wanted some action of her own. The ball she had spotted was in the neighbor's garden, owned by a kid who had littered our garden with tennis balls and soccer balls plenty of times in the past. She headed straight for it, diving at the fence.

I tried to stop her, hissing at her as I tried to shout and whisper at the same time, but she was up and over before I could do anything.

Matthew looked at her and then back at me, the images of naked female soccer players put on the back burner for now. "Are you joining us?" he asked, a glint in his eye.

He didn't give me time to answer. He bolted over the fence before I could say anything. Within seconds, I heard them both giggling and whispering on the other side.

"There it is!"

"They have a net here, as well. Come on, you get in goal, let's play."

I turned back to the house, instinctively looking upstairs, toward Ben's room. I knew I couldn't leave him, but I also knew that I couldn't leave my wife and Matthew running riot around the neighborhood. While Ben was asleep, imprisoned by his crib and unlikely to do any harm, my wife and my best friend were free, trespassing and playing with stolen property.

Eddie, who had been sleeping on the bed upstairs last I'd seen him, came downstairs to see what the noise was all about. He stared at me, yawned, stared at the fence, and then waddled back into the house. That was enough excitement for one night.

"Look after Ben," I told him.

He gave me a blank stare in reply. I took that to mean he understood, and I shut the back door, leaving it unlocked, before hopping over the neighbor's fence.

Despite being the only sober one, I wasn't as agile as Matthew or Lizzie and was also more prone to making an idiot of myself. That curse struck me when I made it to the top of the fence. I looked at the ground beneath me, judged my fall, and then went for it, not realizing that the back of my pants had become entwined on a loose nail. As I went down, my pants stayed up.

At first I suffered what can only be described as a catastrophic wedgie, with many of my external parts trying their hardest to become internal parts, along with my boxer shorts and half of my trousers. As my pants became lodged in the fence, refusing to let me find my feet and relieve the agony, I remained hanging there, my feet kicking wildly at the ground, the seat of my pants halfway inside my colon.

I hadn't been able to stop a scream from leaving my lips. I also hadn't been able to stop the ripping noise that my pants made as they tried to join my breakfast. Or the thudding noise my legs made as they hit the fence. Those sounds alerted the occupants of the house.

A light in the upstairs window snapped on and I froze. Matthew and Lizzie also saw it, and while I remained hanging out in the open for all to see, they ducked into the shadows. Moments later, a grumpy, disheveled neighbor appeared at the window. His tired, groggy eyes scoured the yard as I remained motionless—if you ignored the gentle rocking—hoping that I could somehow blend into a fence that I had very nearly become a part of.

My attempts at camouflage didn't work and he spotted me. His eyes flared. He pointed a finger at me and yelled something that didn't make it through the glass. He moved away from the window, but I knew he wasn't going back to bed.

"He's coming!" I heard Matthew say, a whisper that had probably been heard by the entire street. "Fucking leg it!"

I watched as they both ran across the yard and then stopped in the middle of it when they saw me. The look they gave me suggested that they had initially toyed with the idea that I might have been some sort of BDSM statue. I stopped kicking and breathed a sigh of relief, waiting for them to help me down, but the house attracted their attention again and they turned to see another light snap on, this one in the upstairs hallway, visible through the small window in the middle of the staircase. They turned back to me, gave me approximately two seconds of their pity, and then ran in the other direction.

After the hallway light came the downstairs light, its murky yellow glow firing though the smeared glass panel in the back door and spreading ominous beams onto the lawn. I knew that I had to get away or face an incredibly embarrassing arrest, and not for the first time in my life. I did the only thing I could do: something that Lizzie and my future self would not thank me for, but something that had to be done. I turned around, twisting in my pants and bringing the wedgie to the front. The pain was enough to make my eyes water, but I managed to block it out.

I couldn't unhook my pants while I was putting so much weight on them, so I grabbed the side of the fence and pulled myself up. My old high school PE teacher once joked that I couldn't do a pull-up if my life depended on it, and at the time I had agreed with him, believing that death was an acceptable alternative to upper-body exercise. But I managed to surpass both of our expectations as I lifted myself, easing the weight on my snagged pants and my crushed testicles, and giving me a chance to wriggle free.

When I finally dropped and felt solid ground beneath my feet, I felt relief the likes of which I had never felt before. That relief faded like a fart in a storm when I heard the back door click, and it turned into panic when I realized that running wasn't going to be a completely painless procedure for me.

I hopped, jumped, and dragged my way across the yard and down the side of the house, wincing and grimacing with every yard I gained, but delighted nonetheless to get farther and farther away.

I heard the back door open and the neighbor shout. The noise and the curses that spilled out of his mouth made me smile. He was a dick and I had never liked him much. And even though I had severely damaged my chance of having another child or a successful bowel movement, part of me was happy to get one over on him. Hobbling away into the night also gave me a rush and made me feel like an expert criminal, albeit a severely disabled one.

Lizzie and Matthew had already moved on to bigger things. A group of youths were hanging around at the end of the street, using the perimeter wall and overgrown hedges of a derelict house as their meeting point. It was their headquarters, a place where the local delinquents gathered in full view of half the neighborhood and any passing cars.

There were four of them in total, three boys and one girl, the former doing their best to get into the pants of the latter. They all wore baggy trousers, showing off their underwear in a way that always made Lizzie twist her face.

"Someone should just yank them down," she had told me once. She was joking then, so I agreed and thought nothing of it, but as I hobbled out into the street and saw the youths ahead, with Lizzie and Matthew hiding around a nearby corner, I realized that they were about to move from trespassing and into sexual assault.

The kids were no more than fifteen or sixteen, and every other word that came out of their mouths was an obscenity— like listening to Matthew describe his sex life. They had been annoying the neighborhood for weeks, but Lizzie and Matthew were equally delinquent that night and keen to be just as annoying.

Lizzie was the first to react. She exploded out from the corner, throwing her arms into the air and yelling as she did so, "I am the Underpants Avenger!"

The kids were too shocked to do anything. The boy closest to her just stood there as she propelled herself forward and yanked his jeans down, taking down his boxer shorts in the process and exposing his boyhood to the girl he had been hitting on. The other boys laughed, relieved that the Underpants Avenger was skipping into the night, laughing hysterically like some pantomime villain. But they hadn't counted on the perky vigilante having a sidekick.

Matthew had used the distraction to sneak behind them and steal something from their pockets. I watched him do it. I saw him take something, look at it, pocket it, and then stand there with a *should I or shouldn't I?* expression his face. As I tried to speed up my hobbling, he made his choice, and in two quick movements, he exposed the backsides of two more teenage boys before running away.

Two of the boys tried to follow him, but one of them tripped over his own pants and fell face-first onto the pavement, while the other fell on top of him. The third boy was seemingly too embarrassed by the penis incident to do anything and just stood there, hoping the fact that his two friends were naked from the waist down and lying on top of each other would serve to deflect some of his embarrassment.

There was an awkward silence. A moment in which the penis boy tried to smile at the girl, and a moment in which the naked boys tried frantically to wriggle off each other, only making the scene even more traumatic for the both of them. That was also the point at which I hobbled by, breathing deeply, wincing in pain, and trying my best to smile at them and thus avoid absorbing any of their anger.

They all stopped what they were doing and stared as I plodded along.

I saw the penis boy slowly mouth, *"What the fuck?"* right after I greeted them with a polite nod and a call of, "Nice night, isn't it?"

I found Matthew and Lizzie hiding down an alleyway, giggling like school children. They paused when I stepped into the opening and blocked the fluorescent light from the streetlight above, casting a shadow down the alleyway.

"Shit, it's the fuzz," I heard Matthew say.

I rolled my eyes. He watched far too much television.

"It's not *the fuzz*, it's me."

"Who's me?"

"Your best friend?"

"Marcus?"

I stopped, feeling a little hurt.

"Bah, only kidding," he said, bringing a giggle from Lizzie. "Get over here, see what we've got."

What they had was a small bag of hash, a solid brown lump. Matthew was holding it up proudly.

"You stole that?" I asked, shocked, although not as much as I should have been in light of everything that had already happened.

"Cool, eh?"

"Are you fucking kidding me? You stole drugs from a teenage boy who you then assaulted?"

Matthew gave me a dismissive wave. "It wasn't assault."

"Yeah, we were just doing our bit for society," Lizzie offered.

"You're both out of your minds."

"We're having fun, and you can't stop us, no one can stop—"

He paused, looking very alert. We all listened to what sounded like heavy footsteps coming from the end of the alleyway, followed by hushed and angry whispers.

"Bastards took my fucking dope."

"They're down here."

"What was that?" Matthew asked, looking like he already knew the answer and hoping I would tell him that a gang of fairies were coming to fondle him and bake him cookies.

"Someone's coming to *stop* you." I was grinning, happy that he was going to be taught a lesson and that my concern was going to be proven right. My smile faded when I realized the implications for me. Not only was I with them and guilty by association, but I was also the only one incapable of running away. If they found me hobbling after the people that had assaulted them, I might never hobble again. Or breathe, for that matter.

"Run!" Matthew said, turning.

I grabbed him on the shoulder, refusing to let him get away from me again. "I'm injured, you have to help me."

He turned to Lizzie and the two exchanged a brief stare, one where he asked if he could leave me to die, and where she countered that although it would be a viable option, I was the father of her only child and might still serve a purpose.

They each grabbed an arm and escorted me down the alley-way. We had made it to the end by the time we heard them at the entranceway behind us. They paused for a moment, their voices silent, and then we heard them shout.

"There!"

"Get them!"

My anus felt even looser and we all quickened our steps. The fear helped me move faster than I had before, fighting through the pain. They were also partially carrying me, but it still didn't seem like enough, and with each step the teens seemed to be gaining on us.

We made it down another alleyway—the sound of angry teen-age feet slapping the tarmac behind us—and then out through an underpass and into a park. We made a detour at that point, hoping that we could throw them off and buy some time. Instead of going onto the street beyond, we hopped the short fence that led onto the park, with Lizzie and Matthew doing the hopping and me doing the flopping. They would realize where we were eventually, but it would give us a few more minutes in which we could hobble to safety.

"We have to keep going," Matthew said, hearing my agonized yelps as I fought for breath and struggled to move, every step sending painful vibrations through my body.

"I'm. Fucking. Trying!"

"Don't get—" Matthew paused. "Shit."

I had my head down, unable to find the energy to keep it up, but when we stopped moving I looked to see why. My heart sank to the pit of my stomach when I saw what they were looking at.

A dozen feet away, sitting on a set of rusted swings, were three men. It was clear they were drunk, and it was also clear they were meaner than the kids we were running from. They had been drinking cans of lager and chatting loudly, but they stopped when they saw us approach. They slowly climbed off the swings and made a move toward us.

I felt my sphincter relax and my muscles follow suit. My body was leaving me. It was giving up. I was on my own.

"Well then," Matthew said, releasing me from his grasp. "We're fucked."

The taller and bigger of the three came the closest, his friends on either side of him. He stank of beer and cologne, indicating he had been at the bars before stopping off for some casual drinking in the park, as seemed to be common in the area.

"Everything okay?" he asked.

The fact that he seemed genuinely concerned and wasn't slurring his words gave me hope, and it also seemed to give Matthew hope, as he abandoned his fear of impending death, wrapped his arm around me, and did his best to look concerned. I lowered my head into my chest, anticipating Matthew somehow managing to make this situation worse. Beside me, I knew Lizzie was thinking the same thing as I felt her hand clench around my waist.

"You've got to help us," he pleaded. "There are some lads chasing us, they—they—they *abused* our friend. They got a kick out of beating him to a pulp. It was like a game to them, and they did horrible, horrible things to him."

I looked up, out of breath, still in pain. I tried to object, but couldn't offer anything more than a pained expression, which only served to make matters worse.

"Oh, that's terrible," one of them said, looking me over. "Are you okay?"

I turned to Lizzie and to Matthew, seeing the pleading looks on their faces. This was their fault and I had been roped into it, but as much as I wanted to make them suffer, if I didn't go through with this then I knew then I would suffer anyway. And quite frankly, I had suffered enough for one night.

"I'll live," I said in a genuinely agonized voice. "Just a little tender."

"There they are, the fuckers!"

The kids were behind us now. The shout made me flinch, which in turn made my fear seem even more genuine. We all spun round. The three boys—the girl presumably deciding not to follow them, and perhaps never to talk to them again on account of their anger, their small penises, and their poor choice in pants—were angry, out of breath, and trying to hold up their pants as they ran. It didn't

paint a very innocent picture for them, and the men who had chosen to protect us were quick to notice this.

"The sick little fucks," the tall one said, shifting forward and
standing in front of us.

The three kids halted in front of our new saviors, trying to brush
the brick wall of cologne- and lager-scented flesh aside to get to us.

"Who the fuck are you?" one of the kids spat. "Let us through."

The men remained where they were, refusing to budge.

"He's got something that belongs to us," another kid argued.

"Really?" the man said, folding his thick arms. "*Belongs* to you
now, does it? Well then, why don't you describe this *thing* that
belongs to you and I'll see what I can do about it."

The kid looked unsure at first, worried about the legal status of the
little brown lump. But it soon dawned on him, perhaps a little later
than it should have done, that the three drunk men in a park in the
early hours of the morning were probably not police officers. "Well,"
the kid, clearly unsure and hesitant, looked at me, smirked and then
shrugged his shoulders, "It's —"

He didn't get to finish his description before the man, repulsed by
what he had misrepresented, swung for him. The punch nearly broke
the youngster's jaw, and as soon as it landed, melee ensued. The three
kids jumped on the adults, swinging, kicking, and giving it their all.

We could have joined in, coming to the aid of the men who had
come to our aid. This thought ran through my head as I watched,
and I knew it would be running through Lizzie's and Matthew's
head, as well. We all exchanged glances, and through those glances
we agreed that we *probably* would help if the fight looked like it was
getting out of hand and the three men were in trouble. But only
because we knew that that wouldn't happen.

The fight didn't last very long, and we were saved the ignominy of involvement when the youngsters were sent scrambling away, back into the shadows, back onto the streets. The three men turned to us, to *me* in particular. I gave them my best damsel-in-distress look, and if not for the severe rectal and testicular damage that made everything from bending to breathing a chore, I might have even curtsied for them.

"Thanks so much for that," Lizzie said, still clinging to me.

The men smiled proudly at her, turning on their heroic knight expressions. This was their moment in the sun, a chance to show some pride and absorb some respect for saving the damsel in distress. Even though that damsel was a scrawny man who had been sexually molested by a fence.

"We're glad to do our bit," the leader of the three said, nodding at Lizzie. He then turned to me, exchanging the heroism for pity. I did my best to smile. "You must have been through hell."

I nodded. That much was true. I averted my eyes shyly, suggesting that I didn't want to talk about it.

"Well, get yourself home, get some sleep. You just need a little rest."

I nodded in agreement, although in this instance I also needed a pair of tweezers, as I had a feeling that I would be using them to pick splinters out of my ass for the rest of the night.

"We'll tell everyone what you guys did," Matthew said as we prepared to leave. "You'll get the recognition that you deserve."

They seemed humbled by that, but proud nonetheless. As Matthew and Lizzie carted me away, taking a different route home in case the three boys were waiting for us, I whispered to Matthew, "You better not fucking tell anyone."

He seemed to find that amusing. "You're kidding, right? This is hilarious, how can I *not* tell anyone?"

"Because if you do then our friendship is over."

He stared at me for a moment, weighing up the pros and cons. On the down side, he wouldn't be able to see me anymore, but on the plus side, he would have a great story to tell to all of his new friends. And this was the sort of tale that Chris Peterson and his empty-headed cronies would love.

"I'll also tell your wife that you tried to score with a fifteen-year-old girl."

"But that's a lie," he said, appalled that I would do such a thing.

"But you're a creepy pervert, and she knows that. Who do you think she would believe?"

"But—but—"

Matthew turned to Lizzie, looking for guidance.

She shrugged. "I'm staying out of this."

"Fine," Matthew grumbled, holding onto me just a little bit harder and dragging me along just a little bit faster.

When we returned home, I smoked some of the stolen hash. I was happy for something to dull the pain and take away the memories of what had been a long night. Not only had I been forced to leave a baby alone in the house, but I had chased my best friend and my wife through the streets, been assaulted by a fence, nearly murdered by a gang of youths, and played party to the theft of illegal goods. For Matthew, it would just be another night, but for me it was one of those nights that was only possible when he was involved.

Lizzie had sobered up a little and she didn't smoke more, taking over the parental duties as I smoked and Matthew raided the fridge. Matthew then fell asleep on the couch while Lizzie and I retired to bed. She was feeling guilty by then, shocked at what she had allowed herself to do and appalled that she had left her child alone, albeit just for twenty minutes.

"I feel like a druggie," she had told me when the warmth and the sedation was beginning to fade, turning into paranoia, fatigue, and worry. "Abandoning my son because of some drugs."

"No, don't be stupid," I told her. "And if anything, it was me who abandoned him. I could have stayed, but instead I decided to follow you."

"That's right," she said, finding her scapegoat in the same place everyone else seemed to find theirs. "It's your fault, you should have stayed, you should—"

"But then again," I cut her short, realizing that now wasn't the time to make her feel better about herself. "You got high, forgot about him, and then ran away like some hippie teenager hellbent on anarchy."

She scrunched up her face and bit the end of her finger. "You're right," she said, nodding. "It was my fault."

That's better.

I listened to her blame herself, then I turned the lights out and she fell silent. The day was over, done; no more pain, no more blame, just sleep.

"Oh no, Kieran! Kieran! Something's wrong," Lizzie said, the fear evident in her grating voice.

I groaned in reply. "What is it?"

"I—I—" She stuttered and I expected her to break into another profound thought, but instead she finally said, "I think I'm blind."

I reached over and snapped on the bedside light, my eyes quickly adjusting to the flame of brightness that threatened to split my head in two. "Excuse me?"

"Oh," she said softly. "Actually, never mind."

You've got to be fucking kidding me.

She clearly wasn't as sober as I thought she was.

I turned off the light again and stayed awake for a few more minutes, expecting more complaints of blindness or something equally absurd, but they didn't come. Eventually I heard her snoring, followed by low grumblings as she argued with herself in her sleep. After she seemed to lose the argument, increasing her voice to regain the momentum, she let rip an almighty fart that threatened to blow the covers off her.

Content that things were back to normal, I rolled over, closed my eyes, and within seconds, I was asleep, happy to put a long day to rest.

13

The Last Supper

When Lizzie was happy on the phone, I was usually sad off of it. It wasn't entirely because she was loud, or because the endless *"Really? No, really?"* grated somewhat after a while, but because I had no way of joining in with that happiness. One of the first times I had heard her on the phone with her friends was just before we were married. I had watched as her tone changed from smiley, to unreasonably excited. I had watched the *"no, you don't say?"* suddenly become *"I don't believe it"* and *"that's amazing."* I was on the edge of my seat by the end of it, eager for her to finish so I could find out what this amazing news was, expecting to hear how a friend had won the lottery, borne three triplets to Johnny Depp, or bumped into Elvis Presley down the cash-and-carry.

I was so eager to share in her excitement that I almost squealed when she hung up, but as soon as her finger hit the little red button, the smile faded. She turned her attention back to the television and said nothing. It was as if nothing had happened. She didn't even look at me. If she had, she would have seen a wide-eyed, drooling idiot on the edge of his seat, his hands pressed to his mouth to suppress a girlish scream.

After several moments, she turned to me to ask me where the remote control was. She barely uttered a word before she cut herself short and remarked, "—what the fuck is wrong with *you?*"

In the excitement and the resulting embarrassment, I didn't get a chance to tell her how I had been eagerly waiting, how I had been practically following her around, jumping like a little boy being told all his enemies had turned into Skittles. I brushed it off, but the disappointment was evident.

That was my first taste of it, but there were many more. I came to realize that as surprised and excited as she sounded on the phone, there was usually no basis for it. It was an act that she put on for her female friends and family members. They all did it, and it was creepy as fuck.

So when she did it when she was talking to her mother, I didn't react. But this time, she did have something to tell me when she hung up. It wasn't as exciting as her mother giving birth to Depp's lovechild, but it was just as horrifying.

"My mother is getting all of the family together for a Christmas dinner!" she announced, the excitement still on her face. "Everyone. My granddad Herman, Sally, Edward, John, Uncle Pete, Auntie Aggie—everyone!"

"That's nice," I said with a smile, realizing I had no idea who any of those people were and was probably better off for it. "You'll enjoy that."

The smile faded somewhat and a flash of bemusement cut across her features. "We both will."

"You want me to go, as well?"

"Of course."

"But—but—" I was incredulous. I hated family gatherings, even when it wasn't my own. I also wasn't a big fan of her family. I had only met her parents so far and would struggle to find two people who hated me more in this world. "—I'm not your family."

"You are now."

Shit. I knew that certificate would come back to haunt me.

"But—but—"

"It'll be okay," she assured me as I tried and failed to find an excuse. If she had given me some warning then I might have been able to, but I wasn't good at thinking on my feet. "They're not as bad as you think they are."

If I wasn't so grief-stricken then I would have laughed at that one. It wasn't the first time Lizzie had tried to convince me that her parents didn't really hate me. She often told me that that was just "their way," but unless *their way* was the way of two stuck-up, pompous bigots who didn't think that anyone was right for their daughter, let alone a hopeless ingrate, then I was justified in my assumptions.

I'd once tried to get her dad drunk and loosened up. But although the night began well, with some friendly sporting banter and a few jokes, it ended with him calling me a loser and trying to drown me in a urinal. It was like high school all over again.

If I couldn't befriend the parents then what hope did I have with the rest of them?

In an effort to ease my fears, she tried to tell me all about her family, but that didn't help. She told me about her Uncle Pete, who she described as one of the nicest and most genuine people she'd ever known, and her twin cousins Adam and Arnold, who she used to play with when she was younger.

"Oh, I so hope they'll be there," she added fondly, as I somewhat relaxed into the idea of meeting her family.

Then she told me about her grandfather, who would be the oldest man there. "He is a lovely man," she began with a warm smile. "He always dotes on me, always buys me presents and has nice things to say. He's so sweet and gentle."

"Sounds nice."

"I mean, he's incredibly racist and he's as homophobic as they come, but aside from that, he's fine."

"Oh," I said, immediately taking back all of the nice thoughts I'd just had about her grandfather. "Well, aside from *that*, sure, I mean as long as I'm not gay or black."

"Exactly!"

"You are joking, right?"

She grinned. "Look, I know it's awful and I know there's nothing I can say to justify it. But he's really sweet, trust me."

"Okay." I shrugged. "I guess all families have a few racist homophobes in their closet. Anything else I should worry about? Any cousins in the KKK, any Nazi uncles, any suicide bombers?"

"No, no, of course not," she said unconvincingly.

"You're lying to me. I can tell, because you're not very good at it. What is it? Your Uncle Pete isn't really Osama Bin Laden, is he?"

"He's dead."

"Really? I'm sorry to hear that. So then why is he going—"

"Osama Bin Laden, I mean."

"Oh," I said, adding, "I knew that," even though I had no idea. The news had a way of passing me by, on account of my aversion to newspapers and any TV program that wasn't animated.

"So what is it then?" I wanted to know. "What are you hiding from me?"

Lizzie let out a long sigh. She looked at me, looked away, and then looked at me again. "It's my cousin."

"Is he—"

"No, Kieran!" she interjected. "And it's a *she*."

"Okay. So what's wrong with her?"

Lizzie pondered this for a while and then said, "She's a little—how can I put this—*overly friendly* with the male population."

"She's a whore?"

"Yes."

"Oh, well, I'm fine with that." The smile I finished with was probably a bad idea.

Lizzie glared at me.

Definitely a bad idea.

"I mean, as opposed to her being a bigot like your grandfather."

"My grandfather is not a bigot," she snapped, changing the subject so I didn't have to. "He's a lovely man, honestly. You'll see that for yourself when you meet him in a couple of weeks."

The get-together came quicker than I would have liked, but that always seemed to be the case. It might have something to do with the fact that I tried to ignore it, to erase my mind of the upcoming event and thus make life easier to live until then, but that only makes the surprise and the dread even greater when it finally arrives.

We arranged to drop Ben off at my parents. The issues we had with letting the grandparents babysit seemed like a distant memory, and they weren't as relevant now that we had sampled the alternative. My mother was so excited about the prospect that she arrived first thing in the morning to pick him up, negating the plan to take him to her later in the day. The sound of her eagerly pressing the doorbell gave me flashbacks of the inbred delinquent neighbor-child, and I thought he had returned for his revenge. When I let her in and was subjected to an assault of fast-paced conversation, fueled by a morning spent drinking coffee and getting excited, I began to wish it had been the little shit.

In ten minutes she told me everything that had happened to her over the last few weeks. She told me of all of her and my father's medical problems, and she also ensured I was caught up on all of the illnesses and deaths that her friends and family members had been subjected to. I began to worry that she'd drive Ben around the bend, but remembered that this crazy person had raised me, and I'd turned out fine. Well, for the most part.

I said my goodbyes to Ben—waking him up to do so—and reminded him that as difficult as his night with my parents would be, my night with his mother's parents would be worse. I had actually entertained the idea of taking him with us and using him to deflect the attention away from me. But it would be a huge family gathering, and I couldn't put him through that amount of cheek-pinching.

I dressed up in my most uncomfortable clothes, gelled and styled my hair so I looked sufficiently like the sort of cock that her parents and the rest of her family would appreciate, and then plastered on my best smile. We bought them a bottle of wine on the way over, and although Lizzie rejected my idea of pissing in it, she did insist that I be the one to give it to them when we arrived.

"Do we really want to be getting your dad drunk after what happened last time?"

"You mean with my mum? No, that was a one-off." She seemed confused for a moment. "I didn't know I told you about that."

I nearly threw a fit in the taxi. "No, you did *not* tell me. I was referring to the time he tried to drown me in three inches of stale piss, *actually*. But perhaps there something else I should know about?"

"He's under a lot of stress, that's all."

"Your family is a regular bunch of fucking saints, aren't they? Remind me again why I married you?"

"Because you didn't meet them first."

That was true. But even after I had met them, I knew they were nothing like her. I still had my suspicions, of course. Every time she drank, I expected her to turn into a violent psychopath like her dad. And I knew there was still a chance she could mature into being a pompous bitch like her mother.

When we arrived, we let ourselves in. Lizzie practically jogged into the kitchen to follow the noise and the smell of cooking. I dragged my feet behind her, already watching the clock and counting the minutes until the night was over.

I gave her parents my fake smile and the bottle of wine. I hugged her mum and shook her dad's hand, knowing that regardless of how disgusted it made me feel, it would get me brownie points later. Lizzie's parents were both very friendly to me, though it was clear they were just being hospitable for Lizzie's sake and would probably sprinkle anthrax on my chips.

Her grandfather, Herman, was standing at the back of the kitchen during the introductions, and as Lizzie reacquainted herself with the parents from hell, he approached me. His face held no emotion at first, and if not for the fact that I was in my in-laws' kitchen, I might have been worried. In hindsight, that probably should have given me more reason to worry. For all I knew, he could have been an assassin they hired to kill me, talking about the "good old days" to lure me into a false sense of security before beating me to a pulp with his cane.

"And you must be the famous Kieran," he said, extending a hand.

"I don't know about famous, but yes." I shook his hand and he stared into my eyes. His hand felt frail and weak, but the handshake was strong. It went on for longer than was necessary or comfortable, but when I tried to break it, I realized that as weak as his hand felt, it was still stronger than mine.

After finally releasing his hand and his stare, he gave Lizzie a warmer greeting and then turned back to me. He put an arm on my shoulder and guided me into the living room. I tried to catch Lizzie's eye, to ask for her help or to at least to let her know my last whereabouts in case anything happened, but she was too busy attending to a boiled potato and a beer-battered chicken, or Mum and Dad, as she preferred to call them.

Herman immediately took me to the living room where I waited as he poured me a significant measure of scotch and sat me down in the corner, tucked away in a section of the living room that I had only ever seen Lizzie's father in—reading his paper and drinking his whiskey. It pleased me to know that not only was I in his spot, but I was also probably drinking his whiskey, which made it taste infinitely better.

I was worried that Herman would begin to ask me awkward questions, or even that he would follow his son's lead and turn inexplicably violent, but he didn't. He started by telling me war stories, and although I had no interest in them, they were notably better than being forced to drink someone else's urine.

I was relaxed, and I actually began to think that the night wouldn't be so bad after all, that I might actually enjoy myself. Lizzie was right; her grandfather was sweet. He was a humble, quiet, and respectable man, and upon meeting him and talking to him, I completely forgot all the bad things that Lizzie had said about him. But then things took an ugly turn, and they did so very quickly.

It began with some travel stories, and then, like a bout of gastroenteritis diarrhea, once things turned ugly, there was no way of stopping it. They say that travel broadens the mind, but for Lizzie's grandfather, it had just broadened his lexicon of racist terms. The world is a big place with a lot of people, cultures, and traditions, but the only thing he'd learned from his experiences was that the world was full of people who weren't white.

"You wouldn't believe it if I told you," he said, shaking his head in disbelief but looking content nonetheless, seemingly enthusiastic about his racism.

Then please don't.

"*Everywhere* they were."

Oh God no.

"I mean, how do they spread so quickly?"

He paused to stare at me, as if waiting for an answer. I had no idea how to respond to any of what he was saying, and every word sent me further and further into myself as I waited for the ground to open up and swallow us both.

Or him, yes, just him, that'll do.

"I don't know." I shrugged. My face was red with embarrassment and I knew he noticed it. I could see him eyeing me up, wondering what kind of race I was turning into and judging just how much he should hate me.

"So, you had fun on your travels then?" I said, hoping to change the subject.

"It was war, son, war is never fun."

"Clearly you've never played *Call of Duty*."

The stare he gave me suggested that he didn't get the joke, or that he was about to kill me. Or both.

"War isn't very funny either, son."

He had the demeanor of a principal, the sort of person who took things too seriously and was impossible to break down. Once you crossed the line, there was no way of stepping back, no way to bring them to your side. You just had to wait for the stern lectures to pass and try your best to avoid that line in the future.

I gave him a meek and apologetic smile, wondering just when the sweet old racist had turned into an intimidating one. He was a ninety-year-old man who had seen the world, hated every bit of it, and tried to kill most of it. He had served in both World War II and the Korean War, which was something I was eager to learn about but scared to ask about. At that moment, Lizzie, who had been setting the table and gossiping about promiscuous neighbors, came over to see how we were getting on, and the insane old racist reverted back to a cute grandfather. He gave her a kiss on the forehead, pinched her cheek, and told her that she was getting prettier every day. When she went away, I hoped that the friendliness would remain. When he turned back to me, I had a smile waiting for him, but that smile soon faded.

"I hope you're keeping it clean with my granddaughter, young man."

I nodded slowly as I tried to understand what he was asking me.

"Strictly vaginal sex, you understand," he said after a while.

Oh sweet Jesus, no.

"The other way is neither Godly nor sanitary."

I felt myself getting even redder and redder, while craning my neck to see where Lizzie was in the hope she could save me from a man who was one segue away from asking me about my masturbation habits and demanding I tell him about any homosexual fantasies I'd had.

"Well, you know what they say, cleanness is next to godliness," I said, for want of anything better to say.

"Exactly," he agreed. "There are other things to try, of course. All sexual relationships need a bit of variety. For instance, there's nothing wrong with letting her suck your pecker every now and then, but only if you return the favor."

I quickly turned back to him. "You mean . . . ?"

"I mean going down on her."

"Oh, thank God. I thought you were going to tell me she was born with a penis."

I seemed to have stumped him and cut short his awkward line of conversation. "You're a strange one."

I nodded.

He opened his mouth and then closed it again. I thought I had baffled him into silence, but he continued, his mind floating away to a dark place where only memories of murder and bigotry lay. "I remember once doing the dirty on a Korean girl."

I cringed. "And by that, you don't mean that you slept with her and then never rang her back the next day?

"Get with it, boy!" He reached over and slapped me on the cheek. The slap was audible, as was my gasp. I looked up to see who had heard it and when they were going to take this crazy old bastard away from me, but they were all continuing about their business as if nothing had happened, as if I hadn't just been assaulted by a nonagenarian Nazi in slippers. "I fucked her up the ass."

"Oh, and . . ." I shrugged. He seemed to be waiting for a response. "Was it nice?"

"Nice? Nice!" I flinched, worried he was about to slap me again, but he seemed to have gotten it out of his system. "My pecker looked like a melted Snickers bar afterward."

I considered myself to be a fairly immature adult, ignorant to many ways of the world and content in my own childish bliss, but at that moment, all of my innocence died, along with a large portion of my sex drive.

He seemed to be waiting for another response, as though he thought that this was a two-way conversation and not a one-way assault. But I was dead inside, incapable of responding. I simply stared at him, at the curious and sly smile that curled the corners of his wrinkled mouth. If I didn't know better, I'd think he was doing it on purpose, just to fuck with me.

"Anyway," he said eventually. "That's enough sex talk. Too much of that and it'll put me off my dinner. It's never polite to have an erection at the dinner table."

I should have been amazed that a man of his age was still capable of having erections, and even more amazed that they would come so easily, but at that point, nothing about him amazed me.

The others began arriving and I became trapped in a procession of greetings, of handshakes, hugs, smiles, and—in the case of a very bubbly great aunt who smelled like peppermint and tasted like death—a big sloppy kiss. There was an assault of names and titles, far too many for me to remember, and after the procession stopped, after the greetings had turned into excitable and then polite conversation, there were around twenty people all crammed into the small house, including a cluster of kids.

The kids grouped together early on and began running around the house, up and down the stairs, generally making a nuisance of themselves as kids do. Many times Lizzie's parents insisted that we should have brought Ben and that he was missing out on the fun. But he was barely fifteen months old. He couldn't walk in a straight line, he couldn't converse with the other kids, and he couldn't tell interfering adults to leave him the hell alone when they decided to bother him. Contrary to what they wanted to guilt us into believing, it would not have been fun for him.

I decided to join the kid's games at one point, but a stern look from Lizzie steered me back toward the adult conversation, which seemed to be entirely about people I had never met and places I had never been.

"Now then, that's a name I haven't heard in a long time. I hated her, right nosy cow she was. Does she still have that stupid perm?"

"Maybe. She's dead now."

"Oh no, what a shame. Well, may she rest in peace."

I got the obligatory travel talk from Lizzie's father, uncle, and cousin, all asking which route I had taken; all telling me how bad the traffic was and which route I *should* have taken. If not for that and sports, I wouldn't have had a single word to say to them. Although the conversation was tedious and repetitive, it was preferable to what had happened moments earlier with Satan's grandfather.

The drinks began to flow and the noise levels increase. I had my cheeks pinched by at least three different old women, who may have been aunties, grandmothers, or cousins, but could have also been random strangers off the street. After a couple of hours in a whirlwind of familial comfort, with me standing out like a soccer hooligan at a chess game, the food was served and the rush was on.

It was a buffet, which saved me the awkwardness of having to sit next to and across from people who would insist on talking to me. But during an attempt to sneak a go at the buffet table, after everyone had grabbed their first platefuls and were content with stuffing their faces until they needed seconds, I bumped into a timid young woman who had attempted the same move.

She was around my age, give or take a few years, and she was very pretty in a nervous sort of way. The first thing she said to me, as I was staring at a suspicious plate of what I assumed were pork pies, was, "You might want to avoid them."

"Oh?"

She nodded and laughed softly. "Aunty Aggie made them."

"Which one is Aunty Aggie?"

She pointed to the blushing great aunt who had previously tried to lick my face off.

"Oh. Her."

"Yes, she's not the best cook." She had a way of averting her eyes when I spoke to her, and playing with her hair when she spoke to me. She also had a sporadic giggle, which I instantly loved. "When he was alive, my uncle always said she was trying to poison him. He refused to eat anything she cooked."

"When he was alive? He didn't—"

She giggled again. "She didn't poison him, no. He was hit by a car ordering take-out from McDonald's."

"You're shitting me."

"Yes, yes I am."

She was amusing, and I found myself wondering why I hadn't been introduced to her. She seemed just the sort of person I would get along with. It also occurred to me that I *might* have been introduced to her during the initial melee and had just forgotten her name. As if reading my mind, she reached forward and held out her hand.

"I'm Laura," she said.

I shook her hand. "Kieran. I'm—"

"Lizzie's husband, I know."

"It seems my reputation precedes me."

"No, we met half an hour ago."

"Oh."

"I'm just joking." She tapped me on the arm. "I saw the look you gave me, the one that said, '*Do I know her, did I introduce myself to her?*'"

"Ah, I'm that transparent, am I?"

She shrugged noncommittally. "That and the fact that I saw how bemused you looked when everyone entered. You looked like you were ready to run home."

I nodded. She was right, I was. "To be fair, I had just spoken to Lizzie's granddad, which might have had something to do with it. That guy is—wait, is he related to you, as well?"

"He's my granddad, too."

"Oh, then never mind."

She giggled again, "It's okay, I know what he's like, but he's sweet. You just have to take the good with the bad."

I nodded, although I wondered if, like Lizzie, he hid the majority of that bad side from her and saved it up to use on any unfortunate men who married into the family.

"So," I said, perusing the food table. "Is there anything here you recommend, anything that isn't potentially lethal?

"Hmm." She put a finger to her lips and moved around the table, pointing out the dishes. "My uncle's curry, you definitely want to avoid that."

"Bad?"

"Strong. He has no tastebuds and I think he buys his chilies wholesale."

"Ah."

"My granddad's bread. A little stale, bland, chewy,"

"That's enough about your granddad, what about the bread?" I laughed and expected my new friend to join in. Instead she had a look of complete horror on her face and was staring over my shoulder.

"Shit," I mumbled under my breath. "He's not—"

"—Oh, hey, Granddad!"

My heart sank and I immediately spun round. I expected to see a wrinkled fist greeting me. I probably deserved it. It wouldn't be the first time I had put my foot in it, and it probably wouldn't be the first time the old man had floored someone a fraction of his age and twice his size. But there was no one standing behind me, and when I turned back around, my new friend was laughing at me, covering her hand with her mouth as she did so.

"You bitch," I hissed.

"I'm sorry," she said, still laughing.

"No you're not."

"You're right," she said. "I'm not."

I laughed with her, more through relief of not being beaten up by a decrepit bigot than anything else.

"What are you two laughing at?"

This time her granddad really was standing behind me. He gave me such a fright that a small and instinctive yelp escaped my lips. He stared at me like I had just asked him out on a date.

"What the hell is wrong with you?" he demanded to know.

"Nothing. Honestly."

Please don't hit me.

"Okay then." He turned his evil expression away from me and then smiled at Laura. "So, what was so funny?"

"Kieran here was just telling me a joke."

I felt my insides freeze in anticipation of what was coming next. Laura, the funny, awkward girl I had just met and immediately liked, gave me a sly grin as her granddad turned his deviant eyes on me and said the words that I knew were coming. "Well then, tell me. I want to hear this joke."

"You don't really, it's too rude."

He didn't say a word, but his expression did all the talking for him.

"Good point," I said in agreement. "Okay, here it is . . ." I was terrible at telling jokes and even worse at remembering them. The only ones that had stuck were the ones I had heard as a child, which were far too innocent. "I—I—" I shrugged. "You know what, I've forgotten already."

Laura gave me a puppy-dog expression that suggested I had disappointed her. Herman picked up a handful of chips from the table and stuffed them into his mouth. He was a sloppy and noisy eater, and he also didn't let eating get in the way of conversation. "What a surprise," he said, spraying me with chunks of potato. "I'll tell you a joke that will really get your pulses going, how about that?"

"I don't think—"

"Sure!" Laura jumped in, seeing how awkward this was making me and eager for it to continue.

The next few minutes were some of the most awkward minutes of my life, which is saying a lot. I wasn't sure if he told the joke right, as he seemed to stumble over a few of his lines and missed the punchline entirely, but extreme vulgarity and racism was the ultimate punchline on this occasion. When he had finished, he was in stitches, laughing and punching me on the arm. At one point, I thought—hoped—he was going to run out of breath or choke on some undigested potato, but he managed to get through it in one piece. I tried my best to laugh along while staying out of his reach, but when he finished, he didn't seem impressed by the fact that I wasn't rolling on the floor laughing.

"I don't think you got it," he said.

"Oh, I did, believe me. Hilarious."

"Maybe I told it wrong. Here, I'll tell it again."

"No, no, you told it great. Please, my stomach can't take any more laughing."

He glared at me for indeterminable seconds and then smiled. "Yeah, it was a funny one. So, what do you recommend?" he asked, pointing to the food.

"You have to try the pork pies," I told him. "They're simply divine."

"So, how did you two meet?"

The question came from an uncle who had, until that point, been incredibly quiet. He had a nice smile and, due to his silence in the face of all the banal chatter, I was actually beginning to like him. I had been asked about my sex life by drunken cousins, had my face pinched and my hair pulled from great aunts, and I had suffered several menacing stares from the grandfather from hell, so it was nice that at least one person kept his opinions and his hands to himself. That is, until he spoiled it by asking the one question I hated more than any other.

Mine and Lizzie's story is long and somewhat romantic, albeit in a haphazard way. Some have said it was worthy of being made into a book, but I wouldn't go that far. We met when we were young—fleeting glances and awkward conversations across a small playground in the middle of a drenched and desolate caravan park. I adored her from the first moment, and that adoration increased when I met her in my teenage years. We dated and we departed, although through error rather than anything else. It was tragic and I was heartbroken, but we met again as adults and fell in love for the second time, without even realizing it.

That was the story that I often told, but toward the end, I had a tendency to rush things and try my best to avoid the inevitable question. But it came, as it usually did.

"That sounds so sweet, so how *did* you meet as adults?"

I looked at Lizzie as the previously silent uncle opened his trap again. There were nearly two dozen people crammed into the living room, some on the floor, some standing, some sitting, and at no point had all of them been involved in one conversation. But now, thanks to the silent but deadly idiot in the corner, they were all focused on me. I felt my face turn red and I turned to Lizzie, whose expression suggested that I was on my own.

I was a terrible liar, so I decided to tell the truth. "We met in a psychiatric hospital."

The pause continued after I spoke. A few people smiled, thinking it was a joke but not committing themselves to a laugh just in case. I smiled as well, easing the tension, and for a moment I thought I was going to get away with it. I was hoping I could laugh, joke, and then promptly move on as though nothing had happened, but the uncle was preparing to piss on my parade.

"Lizzie worked in a psychiatric hospital, right?" he asked. "Did you work with her?"

The look I gave him could have penetrated steel. "I was a patient."

The smiles faded, swapped with awkward glances. Seeking solace, I searched out Laura, who had previously cheered me up and seemed to be the only person in the family, other than my wife, who I actually liked, especially now that the uncle had turned into a giant dick. She was standing at the back of the room near the door, an understanding and sympathetic smile on her face.

"I wasn't in there because I was mental," I added, laughing softly and trying to play it cool.

"Oh, really?" The uncle was waiting with another question. If I wasn't scared that he would kick the living shit out of me, I would have slapped him. "So, what happened?"

Do I tell them the truth?

What's the worst that could happen?

"Well, it began with this naked, one-legged woman who I got drunk and then slept with, she—"

"—I think that's enough," Lizzie said, jumping to her feet and tapping me heavily on the shoulder. "Can I speak to you in the hallway for a moment?"

She phrased it like a question, but I knew better. I followed her into the hallway, brushing past Laura as I did so. She backed away to let us through, and when I passed, out of my wife's eye line, she gave me a sympathetic pat on the shoulder. She had freaked me out briefly when she put me in an awkward spot with her granddad, but at that moment, she felt like the only person in the room who didn't hate me.

Lizzie dragged me into the hallway and into the kitchen before saying, "What the fuck, Kieran?"

"Did I do something wrong?" I was playing the idiot, a role I knew well.

"My family doesn't need to hear your crazy stories."

"I agree," I said, nodding. "But they asked. It's that uncle of yours, Steve, Matt—"

"Uncle Martin."

"Yes, him. I think he's doing it on purpose."

"You mean being polite?"

I frowned at her. "That's not polite. He knew."

"He didn't know. No one knows."

I gave her a rush of exaggerated nods. "He knew, trust me. I don't know how he knew, but he knew, and he's using it to fuck with me."

Lizzie pressed a hand to her temple, lowered her head, and sighed. "Sometimes I wonder if I did the right thing taking you out of that mental hospital."

"*Psychiatric* hospital," I corrected. "And you didn't take me out. The doctor did."

She raised her head again. "Just stay quiet, would you? If anyone asks you a question, ignore them."

"If you're that worried about the answers I give, why didn't you step in to help me?"

"Well *excuse me* for thinking you could handle a few white lies. I apologize for thinking that you were an adult, that you knew how to react when people asked you awkward questions."

"Apology accepted."

"I was being sarcastic."

"No shit."

She sighed again. "Just keep your mouth shut for the rest of the night, okay?"

That annoyed me and pushed me over the edge. "I'll promise to keep my mouth shut if you keep your mental fucking family away from me!"

I had done nothing wrong. Yes, I had made a mistake, but only when I felt pressured by a bunch of people I didn't know. I had raised my voice a little louder than I should have to let her know how angry I was, and in the silence that followed, I realized that I had also let everyone in the living room—every last mental family member—know just how angry I was. The embarrassment and horror on Lizzie's face was evident, as were the mumblings of discontent and disbelief, and the awkward look that Laura gave me when I craned my neck to see back into the room.

Shit.

Lizzie's wide eyes, raised brow, and reddened features told me everything I needed to know. I slumped to one side as she stormed into the room, on a mission to reduce the damage that my words had caused.

After several minutes of standing around and waiting for the ground to swallow me up, which it seemed I had spent most of the night doing, someone opened the kitchen door and I heard Lizzie's raised voice say, "No, no, he wasn't talking about you."

"Do you have another mental family that we should know about?" her grandfather asked.

The door shut again, the noises reduced to mumblings, and I looked up to see Laura entering the kitchen. She had a restrained grin on her face and when she opened her mouth, it was to suck in a breath through clenched teeth. "Well," she announced. "That was awkward."

"Tell me about it."

"Do you need a shoulder to cry on?"

I shook my head. "I think I need to be alone."

"I understand," she said, sounding genuine. "It will probably be best if you lie low, but don't let them get to you. They'll all be drunk soon and they won't remember a thing. Hell, some of them are drink already."

"Thanks."

"Speaking of being drunk, do you want me to fetch you another drink? I'm prepared to cross enemy lines if you want some whiskey or beer or . . ."

"I'm good. I've put my foot it in enough times tonight; getting drunk won't help that."

She nodded and gave me an awkward but pleasant smile. "For the record, if it helps: you're right, my family is mental."

"That does help."

"They're also very annoying."

I nodded vigorously. "Definitely."

She giggled and before I knew it, she was right next to me and we were laughing together, inches apart. I could feel the heat given off by her body; I could smell the wine on her breath. When I looked into her eyes I felt a connection. I saw her face change, and I knew what was coming next. Only then did it occur to me that I might have given her the wrong impression and I quickly jumped back, awkwardly ruining the moment but doing so with good intentions.

"This is not—"

"Oh, I know."

"Oh, so you weren't?"

"No, no." She shook her head several times. "Of course not. Not here."

Not here? What's that supposed to mean?

There was still something on her face, a wry smile, a confident flicker. I couldn't decipher it but it was as though what she was telling me was for the benefit of someone who wasn't involved in the conversation. I gave her a long and hard stare, trying to figure her out. At one point, I could have sworn she was giving me the come-on, but those thoughts were tossed out when she picked up her glass from the counter and turned around slowly, looking at me over her shoulder.

"Back into the breach I go. Wish me luck."

I didn't wish her anything, and instead I followed her out of the kitchen, although I had no intention of going with her into the living room. When she opened the door, about to reenter, I heard that the conversation had returned to a cacophony of random chatter, dozens of voices all clamoring to be heard. I was no longer the topic of choice for any of them, but I still didn't feel very sociable.

"You going to join me after all?" Laura said, waiting by the open door.

"Maybe later," I told her, although there was no indecision about it. "I'm going upstairs to lie down, get some alone time."

She smiled in reply, and I waited for her to return to the melee before I ascended the stairs. The thought that I was technically in someone else's house and would be crossing a number of boundaries didn't occur to me. They were throwing a party, opening their house to everyone inside it; they were begging me to dig through their medicine cabinet and bedside tables. They had also pissed me off, so I saw my rudeness as an act of defiance and vengeance.

This was the house Lizzie had grown up in, the house she had spent the majority of her teenage years inside. She had lived here when we fell in love for the second time all those years ago. As those memories swam through my mind, I felt the bitterness and resentment that typically follows any argument. I still loved her, but in those few moments, I also hated her.

Lizzie's room was located at the back of the house and had been kept exactly the same as she had left it, complete with Take That posters and a sickly sweet pink wallpaper. There was a desk along one side of the room that had been covered in scribbles, and I was disappointed to learn that none of them mentioned me, just as disappointed as I was to learn of her infatuation with Gary Barlow. She'd certainly kept that well hidden, but I couldn't blame her.

The bed was the only thing I imagined to be different. I pictured her as having some sort of pink duvet set, or even a Take That one, but the duvet was a bland brown and had been covered in guests' coats. I lay on the bed, on top of the coats, and stared at the ceiling

as I listened to the mumbling from the living room, directly underneath me.

I imagined Lizzie doing the same years ago, possibly as she shied
away from a family gathering; unwilling to dip her face in the saliva
bath that greeting her aunts involved; unwilling to listen to her
grandfather's rants about the "good old days" of his youth, when
half the world was at war but at least England was still white.

Then I realized that Lizzie would have done none of those things.
She loved those people and they loved her. They were her family;
that's the way it worked. It was me they hated, it was *me* that her
grandfather saved his most gruesome sexual references and most
twisted racist comments for. It was *me* that her mother avoided eye
contact with. I didn't have those issues with my family, but only
because a "family gathering" consisted of a prolonged phone call
on my birthday, when my dad said all he needed to say with two
words and my mother kept me up to date with all the friends and
neighbors that were either diseased, divorced, or dead. I didn't have
a racist grandfather, a watery aunt, or a dickhead uncle, and I certainly didn't have a sweet cousin who—

At that point, I heard someone walking up the stairs and I felt
my heart kick against my chest. There was a toilet downstairs so no
one needed to be upstairs. I had no idea what they were doing, but
when they made it upstairs, they would be asking the same thing
of me. They hadn't caught me when I had been fruitlessly searching
for a dildo in Lizzie's mother's bedroom, and they hadn't caught
me when I had been contemplating mixing up her father's Viagra
and sleeping tablets in the bathroom. But I was alone in what was
technically a teenage girl's bedroom, which was just as bad. There
were a few things that made it less weird, of course, but there was
still something innately creepy about it.

I reasoned that if they weren't going to the bathroom then they were going to get their coat, and if they were going to get their coat then they heading straight for me.

I did the first thing that came to mind. That has very rarely done me any favors in the past, but I didn't have time to think and had nowhere else to turn but toward my own common sense. I slipped underneath the coats and underneath the blankets. It was already dark in her room, lit only by the moonlight and a few distant street-lights, so I was confident I wouldn't be seen as I flattened myself as much as possible.

I waited and listened, the sound of my own heart heavy in my ears. I heard the footsteps pause at the top of the stairs. I heard them walk across the creaky floorboards that led to the spare room, and then to the master bedroom, stopping at the doorways both times. Then I heard the door to Lizzie's bedroom open and I nearly wet myself. It wouldn't be the first time I'd wet the bed, but it would be the first time I'd wet someone else's bed.

The footsteps stopped in the doorway and then I heard the door close. I allowed myself to breathe and prepared to throw the covers and coats from me, but when I heard the footsteps again, I realized they were in the room with me.

I felt hands on the coats, pressing down. I felt one of those hands slide underneath the coats and touch my thigh. I didn't know what to do so I did nothing. The hand moved up and then I heard a female's voice whisper, "Is it just my imagination or is there a sexy man hiding underneath there?"

It's definitely your imagination.

It was Lizzie, and the relief I felt couldn't have been greater. As soon as that relief came, it was quickly followed by lust. I was in the bedroom of a sexy teenage girl, a girl who I had lusted after for years. I felt like I was a hapless teen all over again and was finally living out a scene I had dreamed about many times, albeit without the arguments, awkwardness, casual racism, and coats.

She crept under the covers with me and I felt that desire intensify. "I'm so so—"

She put a finger to my lips to stop me from apologizing, which, admittedly, is not a great aphrodisiac. Then she kissed me. She was a little sloppy and she tasted heavily of wine, but I accepted that the latter probably had something to do with the former.

She used her free hand to grope me and strip me. I waited eagerly as she peeled my shirt and pants off before removing her top—her warm naked skin pressing against me. I wanted to see her, but the fact that we were in complete darkness, hidden from view, somehow made it even sexier and more risqué. It was certainly as risqué as I was ever going to get when it came to sex.

When things heated up, with us both writhing around naked, the heat and the constant activity became too much and the coats began to fall onto the floor. At one point, there was succession of bangs, most likely caused by keys, coins, or phones in pockets, but in the heat of the moment, we didn't notice them.

We also didn't notice when several people began to rush up the stairs, their footfalls a little more urgent than Lizzie's had been. I only knew of their impending arrival when the door flung open and the light snapped on.

I heard a gasp and I turned to greet the source, shielding my eyes from the light that threatened to scorch my retinas. Lizzie's mother was standing in the doorway with an appalled look on her face as her half-naked daughter sat on top of me, about to do all the things that not only gave her a grandchild, but also gave her nightmares.

Her mouth hung open and a single word escaped. It confused me at first, and I assumed I had misheard, but when she said it again, I knew otherwise.

"*Laura.*"

Lizzie's mother wasn't staring at me. I thought she had been staring at Lizzie, but then I saw Lizzie nudge her mother aside and enter the room. I felt sick. Dizzy. I didn't want to turn and look, as if by not seeing who was on top of me, I would be avoiding the charge of adultery.

Lizzie clarified things for me. "Laura, Kieran! Are you fucking kidding me!?"

I tried to speak, to defend myself, but I was too shocked and my words caught in my throat.

"You know, now it all makes sense. You never wanted to marry me; you've wanted out of this relationship from the beginning. All those inklings, all those times I've suspected something was amiss and let you off because you're an idiot and get into those situations by default. It's true. You have been cheating on me from the beginning, haven't you?"

Reality snapped into place with a sickening shudder, exposing the brightly lit hell in front of me and the shimmering, sweaty girl on top of me. I grabbed Laura by the waist, feeling her soft and warm flesh on my palms flesh I had thought belonged to my wife. I moved her aside, practically tossing her off me. She complained, grumbling, as if she expected me to finish what I had started.

I remained in bed but did little to cover my dignity. Exposing my bits to a family of psychopaths and pricks concerned me considerably less than losing the woman I loved. "What? No, that's not true, how can you say that?"

"It all fits into place," she continued, tears running down her face one by one. "Taking Eddie and Ben for walks so you could flirt with all those young girls, *teenage* girls for fuck's sake. The telephone number in your pocket, on the lipstick-stained napkin."

Lizzie's mother dropped her jaw in disbelief, turning her horrified expression to Lizzie and then back to me. That was the sort of gossip that people like her thrived on, and she seemed insulted that she had never been told anything about it. It was fuel for a fire that had been raging since our marriage, and I knew that if I managed to get out of this with my marriage, then Lizzie's mother would use that against me until the day I died.

"No, no," I said desperately, shaking my head. These were the sort of things I knew would be brought up and used against me, but I had always hoped it would be innocent, that she would use them to make me put the trash out or to give her the remote. "We've been through this," I told her, begging her. "They were misunderstandings, you've got it all wrong."

"Of course I got it wrong," she said sarcastically. "Because I'm just some silly little idiot, aren't I?"

"What? No, don't—"

"Some silly little idiot who couldn't see that her husband was trying his best to sleep around, couldn't see her marriage was over as soon as it began."

I stuttered and stammered, trying my best to come up with a reply, but she turned away and left. Her mother remained in the doorway berating me, but nothing that she said sank in. I felt vulnerable, exposed, stupid. There I was, half-naked and in bed with my wife's cousin, while a room full of racists, bigots, and twats stood over me and gave me their fiercest expressions. I knew that

I deserved it for what I had done, or for what they thought I had done, but that didn't make me feel any better.

The next few hours felt like a dream, and a surreal one at that. I went from having a wife and an accidental lover to having neither. Once Laura was exposed, she tried to push the blame onto me, saying that I led her on, that I got her drunk and took advantage of her. It didn't matter about her reputation as a whore, or anything that had gone before. I was the outsider, I was the bad guy. On the journey over, Lizzie had described her family as a busy household: her grandfather was the television, the one they all loved even though they knew they shouldn't, and the one that kept them entertained; her father was the liquor cabinet, the stash of expensive booze that everyone had forgotten about, which was her way of saying that he was a secret alcoholic; her mother was the hearth, essential, posh, and archaic; and her cousin was the remote control, because she was very rarely where she should have been and everyone had had a play at one time or another. It was common knowledge that she was loose, but they didn't want to let that get in the way of besmirching me.

I tried my best to ignore the busybody matriarch, to ignore all of them and to get to Lizzie, but she was nowhere to be seen and getting to her involved running through an obstacle of old men who wanted to prove themselves. On my way out of the bedroom and out of the house, I had two offers to "take things outside" from men who still referred to fighting as "fisticuffs," along with an invitation from Herman to see his gun collection, which was what convinced me to get as far away from the house as possible.

14

The Fallout

"Well, what did she say?"

My mother was waiting outside the psychiatrist's office with an expectant smile on her face. I had only been in there for an hour—although it had felt like much longer—and she had seemingly pored her way through every single magazine on offer, most of which sat on her lap. On the seat next to her was a pair of scissors and several coupons that she had cut out of the magazines.

"Are you allowed to do that?" I asked, pointing to the coupons and ignoring her questions.

"They're coupons, dear, of course you're allowed to do that. That's what they're for."

I let that one hang. The look I received from the woman at the reception desk suggested that she wasn't allowed to do that, but it also said that she'd already had that conversation with her and had only stopped because she valued her sanity too much.

"Did she fix you then?" she asked as we left the clinic.

I groaned in reply.

"Is everything okay now?" she pushed.

It was sweet that she was so concerned, but it was also annoying. Since the night at the party, my head had been all over the place. Weeks of nothing but frustration, doubt, and regret. I hadn't spoken to Lizzie, at least not in the way that I wanted, and it was killing me.

"No, everything is not okay," I told her.

"Oh, so you're still mental then?"

The worst thing about that question was the honest grin on her face when she asked it. She wasn't joking, and she expected an equally serious reply. We were at the car waiting to climb in, her at the driver's side and me at the passenger's side. I was watching her little face over the roof, her judging eyes quizzing me as they had done since that regretful night.

"I'm not mental."

"You're seeing a psychiatrist," she reminded me. "That doesn't sound like the actions of a sane man."

My jaw dropped and then I heard my dad, waiting in the back of the car with a window cranked open like a loyal dog. "Your mother has a point."

"But *you* sent me here."

"And why do you think we did that?" she asked.

"I—I—" I honestly had no idea, but the absurdity of the situation was robbing me of all coherent thought.

"Exactly," she said with a firm nod.

I turned to my dad and he also gave me a firm nod, although he wasn't able to hide his smile.

"You're crazy," I told them both.

"Now, now," my dad chimed in. "I don't want to have to tell you the story about the pot and the kettle."

"Shut up!" I barked before flopping into the passenger's seat, folding my arms, and plastering a discontented pout on my face.

"There's plenty more fish in the sea."

"That's what they all say."

"But it's true. And if you don't live by the sea, well, that's what escorts are for."

"Good point. What was your wife's number again?"

The look Matthew gave me suggested that I had gone too far. The barrier that would have stopped me from saying such things in the past had broken down. I no longer cared.

"Mate, that was below the belt."

That was rich coming from Matthew, a man for whom there was no belt. Everything and everyone was fair game in his universe, but that was the sort of person he was and always had been. It was different for me, because I wasn't a careless bastard.

"I'm sorry," I said. "I didn't mean it."

I expected him to tell me that it was okay and that he didn't take offense, but in expecting such things, I was forgetting who I was dealing with.

"But if you do want her number, I'm happy to give it to you. I think she could teach you a thing or two."

"You're joking, right?"

He shrugged. "I'm just saying, it's not about sex, remember, it's strictly no contact. It's all about dominance. Maybe she could help you get over Lizzie."

I merely stared at him, waiting for him to find my reply himself.

"Fine, if that's the way you're going to be . . . just don't say I didn't try to help you."

"I won't. You have my word."

Even if I did want to take Matthew up on his offer to let his wife spank me and call me names, I doubted she would agree to it. She had taken Lizzie's side. It wasn't that they were great friends, or that they had taken a vow of solidarity on account of them both being mature women married to immature children, but rather that my version of events was hard to believe. The only one to believe me was Matthew, who was so used to my reckless fuckery that he didn't need to question it to believe it.

Sharon had been at my house when I tried to pack some clothes and reason with my wife while she was in an unreasonable state. Sharon sat on the sofa listening to our conversation, nodding and agreeing with Lizzie, and heckling me like a one-woman talk show audience.

For most of the visit, Lizzie wasn't interested in what I had to say. She didn't want to hear my side of the story. When I eventually ground her down, she stood in the middle of the room with her hands on her hips and a stern look on her face. It suggested that whatever I had to say wasn't going to be believed or well received, and that even if I dropped my pants and began to defecate rainbows, she still wouldn't be impressed.

"Well then," she had hissed. "What is it, what is your side of the story? What excuse could you *possibly* have?"

I contemplated whether I should lie. It had been a week since the incident. A week that I had spent trying to get hold of her and a week she had spent avoiding me. She had changed the locks, turned off the phone, and emailed all of our mutual friends to tell them that I was scum and was not to be trusted. After all that, and after finally getting my foot in the door, I knew I needed to lie, but nothing came to me.

Instead I told her the truth and then, when I had finished, I waited to be embraced. I waited for the nightmare to be over, or for her to slap me and kick me out. What I didn't expect was for them both to laugh, which is exactly what happened.

"That's the best you can come up with?" Sharon said, offering her two cents where it wasn't welcome. "You've had all this time and that's all you have?"

"In my defense it was a week, and stop laughing. I'm not one of your clients, I don't enjoy being humiliated."

Sharon's mouth fell open and I felt a little rush of delight. I liked her and I certainly didn't have an issue with what she did. In fact, my only issue was that I couldn't do it myself. But she had annoyed me, so that felt good.

"Pack your suitcase, Kieran." Lizzie's laughter didn't seem genuine. It was tired, maniacal, and in that moment, I saw what I had done to her, and I realized that as much as she hated me for what had happened, I hated myself even more. She still had Ben and Eddie to look after—our child, our dog, our family. I had made her life, and by association theirs, much more difficult.

"I'm so sorry," I had told her.

"I don't believe you."

Two weeks had passed since that conversation, and I hadn't spoken a word to her. I had sent many messages and emails, but had only received a handful in return, and most of them told me to give up. It got to the point where that was exactly what I felt like doing, because no matter how hard I tried, nothing seemed to work and Lizzie wasn't willing to listen. I had no proof, nothing but my word, and even when I had been allowed to express that word, it hadn't been believed.

"One of my exes is available."

"Sorry?"

Matthew was still persisting. The compassionate friend in him, which occupied a very small space, was telling him that he needed to help me, that he needed to cheer me up. The rest of him, the smaller parts that held his reasoning, his logic, and his common sense, was what he used to find that help for me.

"You can hook up with them. One of them, Cheryl, or Cherrie, or—" he paused, looking confused for a moment before shaking it off, "her name is not important, but she can *definitely* help you to forget. Trust me."

"I don't want your sloppy seconds."

"I was with her years ago. She's probably been with dozens of guys since. You'd be lucky if it was just seconds."

"You disgust me."

"I'm trying to help you."

It also hurt me that I hadn't seen Ben in over three weeks. I could have gone through the courts, taken the legal route, but I didn't want to cause Lizzie any more stress. Hope was quickly fading, but I still believed that we could get back together and I felt that taking legal action would make the split official.

After our conversation at the house, I got very drunk and phoned her. The house phone had been cut off and eventually she turned off her cell, so I phoned her parents instead. I was too drunk and too upset to care, and even though they hated me, and even though Lizzie wasn't with them, I saw them as a link to her and demanded that they listened to me as I explained myself. It didn't go as well as I had hoped.

"Just please, listen to me. No one will, no one gives me a chance," I had begged, beginning as I intended to go on by sounding like a depressed teenager.

"Kieran, you cheated on my daughter. I have nothing to say to you."

"Then put your wife on."

There was a groan as the phone changed hands. Lizzie's mother was stuck up, but she was also reserved and much too polite to hang up on me. She was the sort of woman who would give up her morning to talk to someone selling door-to-door vacuum cleaners or salvation. It wasn't because she was a people person or because she loved to talk, far from it—she was just worried that the image of the polite and upper-class woman that she had worked so hard to achieve would crumble if she told someone to fuck off.

"Please, listen to me," I said as soon as I heard her breathe, one that turned into a sigh. "You have to let me explain myself."

"I don't *have* to do anything."

She had a point, but I wasn't prepared to back away. "That night didn't happen the way you think it did. I went to Lizzie's room to get away from the noise and—"

"The *noise?*" she said. "What do you mean, *the noise?*"

"That's not important."

"I think it is. I think you just described my family as, and I quote, 'the noise.'"

I had done just that. But it could have been worse. In fact, of all the things I could have said about her family, that was the least offensive.

"It was noisy, that's all," I said, keen to push on. "Anyway, Laura spoke to me, she was friendly, but I think she got the wrong idea and thought I was coming onto her."

"From what we saw, it very much looked like a mutual decision."

"No, no, it's not like that, listen to me . . ." I paused. There was a gap where her name should have gone, but—

"You don't know my name, do you?"

"I—I . . ." I finished with a grumble. I was sure it had come up before, but it hadn't stuck.

"You don't know your own mother-in-law's name?" I sensed the anger in her voice. The veil was shifting and her emotions were finally showing through. I hoped she wasn't as needlessly aggressive and violent as her husband was. I had been innocent when he beat me up, and now that I was guilty, I dreaded to think what would happen to me.

"In my defense . . ." My mother had once told me that whenever I used those words to begin a sentence, I very rarely actually had a justifiable defense, and although she was right, I was too drunk to realize it. "It's not like Lizzie calls you by your first name or anything. She calls you mum, mother, or she-devil."

Again, I attributed the last bit to the alcohol, and although I regretted it as soon as I said it, I also enjoyed it.

"How dare you speak to me like that?"

"How dare I?" I spat back, feeling my own anger increase. "How dare you treat me like you've always treated me. How dare you drag *my name* through the mud. How dare you think less of me or my family just because we weren't raised on a diet of caviar, Queen's English, and fucking incest?"

She gasped. "You can't speak to me like that!" She was annoyed, surprised, but she didn't hang up, and I wasn't finished.

"How dare you stand there and treat your son-in-law like a rotten vegetable, something to be pushed away, discarded, and grimaced at if it ever gets too close; how dare you look down your nose at my family, at a mother who has been nothing but polite and accommodating to you, a mother who has shown her child and grandchild nothing but love, and a mother who is respectful of everyone that her child dates because she is a *human fucking being*. And that goes for my father as well, a man who—who—" I felt my argument drying up. "—*how dare you?*"

"You can't speak to me like that."

"Yes I can. But if you don't want to hear any more then put your husband back on. That is, if he isn't drowning his misery in a bottle of whiskey, or drowning some poor sucker who did nothing but try to befriend him in his own piss."

She gasped again. "You can't speak to me like that!"

"Oh, get a fucking thesaurus. And quit the posh bullshit while you're at it. I know you're from *Hull*."

That was when I hung up on her. I had sobered up by then, the anger and the adrenaline seemingly boiling the alcohol out of my blood, but after suffering through that conversation, I needed another drink.

I sighed heavily and slumped back on my bed. I felt a horrible nagging migraine creep up on me as I remembered the phone call with Lizzie's mother. I had enjoyed it, but I still regretted it. Lizzie didn't like the way her mother treated me and was often on my side when I bitched about her, but this was different. This time I had done it to her face, and I had done it during a tense time, a time when I should have been trying to make peace.

I rested back on my hands, staring at the ceiling and the poster of Kate Moss in her prime. My father had bought it for me when I was sixteen. He thought it would make me see him as the cool father, when it fact it made me think he was kinda creepy. I wasn't even a big fan of Kate Moss, but I didn't want to disappoint him so I had agreed to let him put it in my room. The fact that he put it above my bed and then winked when he told me reminded me—as if I needed reminding—just how disturbed he was.

"What about that Sally chick?"

I groaned. Matthew was still at it. He'd arrived a few hours ago and had been trying to cheer me up ever since. Most of his methods involved ex-girlfriends, escorts, and even hardcore pornography, and the Sally in question was just as unlikely to cheer me up as all of those things were.

"She's sixty, Matthew."

"She's a cougar."

"Have you seen her skin? She's more like an elephant. What could you possibly see in her?"

"She has huge tits."

"Of course. I should have known." I sighed, closing my eyes and not for the first time wishing that when I opened them, all this would be over. "She won't do. No one will."

"What about Erica?"

I rolled over and wrapped the pillow around my head, hoping it would drown him out. Sharon was out of town, so a small part of me was happy that Matthew had given up masturbation time to come and help me, but I needed silence, peace, time to think things through. I had done very little else over the past couple weeks. Except drinking, that is. I had done a lot of that.

The night after the phone call to Lizzie's parents, I got drunk again and decided that I would go straight to the source, so that I could make an idiot of myself there, as well. It was late, I didn't have a key, and I didn't want to wake Ben, so rather than holding up a stereo that played our favorite song, or singing her a melody myself, I tried to climb in through an open window.

It seemed like a sensible idea at the time, but that's the problem with alcohol: dumb things begin to make sense. It took me ten minutes and a very sore backside before I scrambled up the drain pipe; ten minutes and five steps before I remembered I was terrified of heights; and ten minutes and thirty seconds before the police van arrived.

One of the neighbors had phoned them. Lizzie didn't even know I was there until the van pulled up and the two officers stood at her front window, looking up.

It was the same guy who had visited during our tiff with the neighbors, but this time he didn't have his little sidekick with him. I hoped he wouldn't remember me, and although he didn't mention the previous incident and seemed not to recollect it, I had a feeling he knew.

"Can you come down now please, sir?" he had asked in a calm and relaxed voice that didn't match the situation or the grin on his face.

The window to the spare bedroom was open, but not by much. It was also a very small window and as I stood on the ledge, I began to question my logic for ever climbing up there in the first place.

"I can't," I shouted back.

"Yes, you can. You climbed up and now you can climb back down."

"I really can't. I'm scared of heights."

He raised an eyebrow and then looked at his colleague, who did the same.

"I know this might sound crazy, but this is my house."

"You're right, sir, that does indeed sound crazy."

"But you've been here before. You recognize me, surely?"

He stared at me for a moment and then shook his head. "I don't recollect such an event, sir."

"It's true, trust me."

"I make it my business not to trust drunken men on window ledges."

I groaned in frustration and watched as Lizzie came outside, dressed in a gown and looking shell-shocked. She raised her eyes to look at me before shaking her head in disbelief.

"See," I barked quickly. "That's my wife, you can ask her."

"Is this true, Miss?" the officer asked, still acting like this was a regular occurrence for him. "Is this your husband?"

I did my best to smile at her while pressing myself as tightly to the window as I could, but she didn't return the smile.

"No, that's not true."

The officer turned back to me. I heard him sigh and then saw him take out a notepad and pencil. "Now then, I suggest you tell me what's really going on here. First, let's start with your name."

I looked at Lizzie, pleading, begging, but she merely shook her head.

"I'm sorry, Lizzie, for everything. But please, you need to listen to me. I just need to explain myself."

"I think you already have explained yourself."

"Well, yes, but—but."

"And you also explained yourself to my mother," she added.

"Oh, she told you that." I deflated so much I nearly fell off the ledge. I could have sworn there was a glint in the officer's eye as he saw my foot slip and waited for me to hit the ground and save him the trouble of a negotiation.

Lizzie stared at me for a moment longer and then turned to the police officers. "Can I leave you two to it?" she asked. "I have a baby in there and it is rather chilly out here."

"Of course, go ahead, we'll try not to disturb you."

I watched in open-mouthed disbelief as Lizzie reentered the house, closed the front door, and then locked it. Once she was back inside the warmth, the police officer turned to me, his pen hovering in wait. "So, what did you say your name was?"

I fell asleep listening to Matthew as he offered me every girl he had been with, and every girl he hadn't. He didn't stop when I drifted off to sleep, and as a result, I had nightmares about the sort of things that Matthew often dreamed about, and I woke up feeling even worse than when I had gone to sleep.

Matthew had gone, but as I ventured downstairs to drown my sorrows in as much alcohol as I could find, my parents assumed the role of trying to make me feel better. My father was as distant and as vague as he always was, and my mother was full of her usual blend of peppy optimism.

"I don't think you should worry too much," she told me. "I have a good feeling that this will turn out okay."

"I'm glad you think so, but I don't. There's nothing I can do to make it better. Everything I try only seems to make things worse."

"Trust me," she said. "It will be okay."

I stared at her for a moment. I saw through the eternal optimism that all mothers are blessed with, and I saw something else. She was assured, almost cocky. "Why do you say that?" I asked suspiciously.

She tapped her nose. "Let's just say that a mother knows best and leave it at that, shall we?"

I couldn't help but roll my eyes at that one. She saw me and didn't look very impressed.

"I'm sorry for not having much faith in you—"

"And so you should be," she cut in.

"But," I said firmly, continuing, "this seems like a lost cause and I'm not sure there's anything you can do to help. I'm sure you would if you could but . . ." I trailed off and finished with a hopeless shrug. There was something comforting about opening up in front of my mother, because I knew that the more hopeless and pathetic I looked and sounded, the more she would try to convince me that that wasn't the case. And I needed all of the cheering up I could get.

"Don't be so down on yourself," she said, taking me by surprise with her lack of sympathy and pity cuddles.

"You seem very upbeat about this."

She grinned and shrugged. She looked like she had something that she was itching to tell me and yet was refusing to talk about at the same time.

"What is it?" I asked, feeling very curious. "What's going on?"

"As I said." She tapped her nose again. "Mother knows best, let's leave it at that."

I turned to my father, allowing him to see the bemused look on my face. He averted his eyes from the television. "What she means is that this is all part of her game," he said, before turning back to the game and leaving my mother's eyes to burn holes in the back of his head.

"What's he talking about?" I asked her.

"It was a setup," he said, this time not looking away. "The psychiatrist—your mother planned it all."

"I don't understand. What's going on?"

She sighed, slapped her hands on her thighs, and then began with a long and drawn out, "Welllll," which usually indicated that she had been up to no good. "You know that Lizzie works in the hospital, the one where you . . . you know."

"Yes, mother, I remember."

"Well, I happen to know that she happens to know a few psychiatrists that work at the clinic where I took you today." She had been staring into her lap, but now she raised her eyes to mine. "Including the one you saw."

It took a moment to sink in, but when it did, and when I saw through my mother's mischievous smile, I asked, "You got me an appointment with one of Lizzie's friends?"

She nodded. "Genius, eh?"

"What?" I said, struggling to believe what I was hearing. "No, no it's not. Don't you think Lizzie will get suspicious? She'll think I'm up to something, she'll—"

She held up a hand to silence me. "All sorted, dear."

"Excuse me?"

"You see, I phoned up in advance, several times actually, to book fake appointments under fake names."

"She even did the voices," Dad chimed in.

I turned to look at my father who was still engrossed in the soccer game, and then turned back to my mother, unable to suppress a smile when I saw that she was nodding happily, incredibly proud of herself.

"I found out what days her friend would be working by herself, and what time slots she had free. Then I phoned up for you on one of those days, pretending that it was an emergency appointment and saying we would take anyone who was available. You see, there are ten other doctors there, and as far as I know, Lizzie doesn't know any of them. They'll think of it as nothing more than coincidence."

My mouth was open by the time she finished. I struggled to come to terms with my mother being so devious and so smart.

"And thanks to my actions at the clinic, and no doubt what you told the doctor, they'll think it was all my idea. Just some crazy, overprotective mother who went too far." She finished with a smile. The last time I had seen her looking so pleased for herself was when they announced that she had won the pub quiz, which was right before they announced that they were reading the list from back to front.

"But . . . I never knew, I mean, I've never even heard of her. How did you know?"

"I listen," she said. "And as she's your wife, it would pay you to listen to her as well once in a while."

I nodded. "Fair enough."

"So," she said, shifting in her seat and looking like she was ready to be hoisted on my shoulders as I sang her praises. "What do you think?"

I didn't reply. I stood up, planted my hands on her cheeks, and then landed a big kiss on her forehead. "I think you're a fucking genius."

"Language!" she said, her face instantly changing one way and then the other. "But I'm glad you think so."

The next few days were hard, because with each passing hour I began to believe that my mother's plan, and my only chance at redemption, was slipping further and further away. I had all but given up when my chance finally came.

I was upstairs at the time, wallowing in my own misery. I heard the doorbell ring and thought nothing of it until my mother raced up to my room, threw open the door, and then whispered, *"It's for you."* She'd made an obscene amount of noise to get there, and as she stood in front of be, smiling proudly, I wondered why she hadn't just shouted in the first place.

"Who is it?"

"It's—"

"Stop whispering."

"Sorry, it's Lizzie."

That was enough to get my attention, and I nearly tripped over myself as I raced out of my bedroom and down the stairs, slowing my pace and keeping my cool as I hit the bottom. I tried my best to look as nonchalant as was possible for a breathless man who had seemingly been sleeping on a pile of Lego bricks to look.

Lizzie and Ben were in the living room talking to my dad, or doing my father's version of a conversation, which was to say hello, make a joke, squeeze his grandchild's face, and then sit down and read the newspaper.

I spoke to Lizzie first, but in my excitement I wanted to pick up both of them, to squeeze them, to apologize.

"We need to talk," Lizzie said.

"It's okay, you can leave the baby with me," my father offered politely. "Why are you staring at me like that? I'm being serious." He glared at us for a moment longer. "Seriously," he pushed, "stop it. I'm beginning to take offense."

I took Lizzie gently by the arm and felt like doing a little jig when she didn't push me away. "Come on, he's fine, my mother will be down in a minute."

"Charming!" I heard my dad say as I took Lizzie into the dining room.

My heart was beating like crazy as I tried to read every half-smile, every movement, every time she played with her hair, looked at me, or looked away. "Listen, Kieran, I know what really happened," she said eventually.

"And by that you mean what *really* really happened, or what you *think* really happened?"

"What really really happened," she said, before adding, "at least I think that's what I mean."

I nodded and then changed my mind. "I'm lost."

She laughed softly, "Okay, maybe this will help." She leaned forward and kissed me. I probably tasted like dirt, a cross between stale Cheetos, ice cream, and armpits, but she didn't mind. She kissed me like she had kissed me the first time we fell in love, when life was easier, simpler, much more exciting, and much less scary. She kissed me like she did on our wedding day, when we had our whole lives ahead of us and I had yet to risk everything by sleeping with her promiscuous cousin while Gary Barlow watched from all angles. It felt like our first kiss, and once it was over I was no longer worried that it would be our last.

"I'm so sorry," she said.

"But why the sudden change of heart?"

She shrugged. "It's a long story."

I nodded. Not only was it a long story but it involved breaking patient-doctor confidentiality. She didn't want to admit the truth because she didn't want to expose her friend as being unprofessional. I didn't want to admit the truth to expose my mother as being right. Neither of us would live it down, so instead there was a general air of vague acceptance.

"So, you'll take me back?"

She nodded. "I was never happy about leaving you in the first place. The house seemed empty without you. No one there to make a mess and not clean up."

"Well, there's Ben."

She nodded. "Good point . . . He's lost without you. Refusing to eat, pouring perfume into the fish tank, peeing on the floor."

"I promise to never do any of that ever again."

She grinned and shoved me lightly. "I was talking about Ben, but you're right, like father like son, I guess. I really am sorry. For everything. For not believing you and taking the word of my bitch cousin, for humiliating you like that, for—"

"It's okay," I jumped in. "You caught me in bed with a family member, inches and seconds away from—" I paused when I saw the flame reigniting in her eyes. "But like I said, I forgive you."

She laughed and shook her head. As she did so, Ben crawled into the dining room and sat in between us both. We both looked down at him and he giggled up at us.

"Dad," I called into the next room, keeping an eye on Ben. "Is Ben okay?"

He replied without hesitation. "Yep, he's—" I heard him shuffle his newspaper, lowering it to peek over the top. I then heard him clear his throat, panic setting in. "He's . . . ermm."

"It's okay, he's here," Lizzie said, sparing his blushes.

"Well . . ." The paper ruffled again as he sat back down and righted himself. "That's okay then."

I picked up Ben. He hadn't seen me for a few weeks, but he wasn't in the mood for reconciliation and tried to wriggle free as soon as he was in my arms, seemingly more interested in a collection of ornaments on the table beside me. "And what about your parents?"

Lizzie shrugged. "None of their business."

I put Ben down and he soon forgot about the ornaments, choosing to aim his curiosity elsewhere. "What did your mother say about the phone call?"

"What do you expect? She said you were a horrible, disgusting little man and she was glad I had finally seen sense and gotten rid of you."

I giggled, sounding a little more sinister than I had hoped. Lizzie raised an eyebrow and I immediately apologized.

"It's okay," she said. "I'm actually looking forward to bumping into her again. All throughout this, she has staunchly defended Laura. She has spent the better part of a decade calling her a slut, and now she hasn't got a bad word to say about her. She's practically a nun."

"She's definitely not a nun," I said. "I can tell you that much."

Lizzie put her hands on her hips. "This is not going to work if you keep reminding me how close you were to sleeping with my cousin."

"You're right." I nodded. "I'll stop."

I picked up Ben again, held him tighter than I had ever held him. "I missed you so much, little dude."

Lizzie smiled at us, content that we were back together, clearly missing the image of father and son in her household. "You missed him more than you know," she said. "He spoke his first word while you were away."

The delight that had gripped my face burst like an overinflated balloon. "Oh," I said, physically sinking as I stared at my son. A smile curled the corner of my lips when I noticed that he was grinning at me and trying to lick my forehead like an affectionate cat. "And what was it?"

Lizzie looked momentarily embarrassed, so much so that she turned away, unable to look me in the eye. "Well, about that," she said slowly. "It was a little more than just one word and, well, I can only apologize."

I lowered Ben, resting him on the floor as he tried, and failed, to stand upright. He fell on his backside, giggled, and then began playing with my shoe, finding contentment in whatever was right in front of him as always.

"Well, that's the thing," she said. "It wasn't a one-time thing, he's said it again. In fact—" She bent down and tried to get his attention. When he finally looked up at her, he had my shoelaces in his mouth and an expression on his face that said, *find your own food, this is mine.*

"Ben, sweetie, are you going to speak for mummy?"

She grinned. Ben spat out the laces and returned her grin. When he opened his mouth, I held my breath, only to breathe again when he vomited on my shoes.

"If that's it, then I've heard it before."

She frowned at me before using a baby wipe to clean my shoes.

Baby wipes are amazing things. They clean things up quickly and without a trace, barring the eternal smell of stale vomit that never goes away but is generally accepted as a fact of life by everyone who has kids.

She picked up Ben and then gave him to me, pointing his face, and the deadly weapon that was his mouth, directly at me. He grinned and I tilted my head back, doing my best to stay out of projectile range.

"Speak for mummy," she said again.

Still he said nothing; he didn't even look at her. She sighed and seemed to prepare for the inevitable. "Okay then, Ben, but you'll speak for Daddy, won't you?"

That seemed to hit a nerve, and I could sense that something was happening inside his little head. His smile vanished and a look of concentration spread over his face, the same look he has when he's filling his diaper.

"Daddy," he said.

I gasped. I was so taken aback that I nearly dropped him to raise my hands in celebration. Beside me, Lizzie's face changed. She didn't look as happy, and as soon as he said my name, she lowered her head into her hands and groaned. I ignored her, though, because whatever her issue was, I didn't—

That's when I realized that he wasn't finished, that he had more gurgled words to utter. It wasn't a word, it was a sentence, something he had heard time and time again and was repeating like an obedient parrot. He was grinning from ear to ear when he finished, but by that time, my own grin had vanished, replaced by a look of vacant bewilderment.

What did he just say?

What he said wasn't worth repeating, but it came suddenly and took me by surprise. So much so that I turned to Lizzie, my mouth open and a question on my lips that the expression on her face answered immediately.

"Did he just—"

"Yes," she cut in.

"But—"

"I know, I'm sorry."

I was shell-shocked, but I was dragged out of my trance by my father, who began laughing hysterically in the next room. He had been reading the paper, dead to the world as he usually was, but he had also been eavesdropping and Ben had just made his day. I heard my mother rush out of the kitchen to question him in a panic.

"It's Ben," he hissed, doing his best to whisper and failing miserably. "He just called Kieran a fucking idiot."

I rolled my eyes and turned back to Lizzie, who gave me an apologetic shrug. "That's my fault."

"No shit."

She looked like she was about to correct me for my language but quickly decided against it. "Sorry," she said.

I turned to Ben, who seemed proud of himself. After a while, with my father still stifling a laugh in the next room, I began to enjoy the funny side of it. To be fair to him, he didn't know what he was saying, or so I hoped, and at least I was his first word.

Ben laughed with me for a bit and then Lizzie joined in. After a few moments, Ben opened his mouth again, a string of drool hanging from his lips like crystal spaghetti.

"Daddy," he said.

I nodded, and when he opened his mouth again, preparing to follow it with the words he had heard his mother speak time and time again, I pressed my finger to his lips.

"Yes," I told him. "I'm your daddy, and let's leave it at that."

Acknowledgments

I wouldn't be where I am today if not for this series. *An Idiot in Love* was the first book I published, and because of its success, I was given a chance with a sequel and with several other books. So, thanks to everyone who purchased it the first time around, and indeed everyone reading this book now. I am eternally grateful, because without those sales and that support, *An Idiot in Marriage* would not have been published.

I would like to thank my partner, Yiota, to whom this book is dedicated. Eleven years ago, she left a life in the Greek sunshine to live with me in miserable, gloomy England. She has been my editor, my designer, my biggest fan, and my sternest critic. She helped me mature both as a person and as a writer, and I can't thank her enough for that.

I would also like to express my gratitude for everyone involved with the publication and sale of this book, including my editor, Nicole Frail, my agent Peter Beren, my cover designer Lilith_C, my publicist Brianna Scharfenberg, and everyone else at Skyhorse Publishing. They have done a lot of work over the last few years to make all of this happen, and my appreciation grows with each publication.

When you write a book in an autobiographical style, many readers assume you're writing about yourself. It didn't help that *An Idiot in Love* was my first book and that everything in it was apparently very believable, even for the people who knew me ("a feckless idiot who's hopeless in love? Yeah, it's probably an autobiography"). The truth is that nothing in that book was taken from my own experiences. But there was one story in *An Idiot in Marriage* that was—as bizarre as it might seem.

So, to Mickey the Duck, who came into my life by way of my backyard, ate all of my partner's bread, cost me a fortune in organic seeds, and then flew away never to be seen again, thank you. I hope you and your feathered friend are very happy together.

Staying on the animal theme, I owe a mention to PARRT, an animal charity that does incredible work in my local area. They help countless cats find homes and gave us two adorable kittens—that have now grown into even more adorable cats—named Sheldon and Hugo. Every time I write, I do so with at least one cat on my knee and at least one tail in my face. But no matter how many cat hairs I inadvertently consume, and no matter how many times I wake up to a cat pawing my face, it's all worth it.

I should also thank my family. I can't imagine they'd be too happy that I'm putting pet cats and stray ducks ahead of them, but I'm sure they'd understand. I'd also like to thank Andrew Farrell, for teaching me to play the guitar and giving me the only non-writing-based hobby I have; Alan Fraser, Carl Ridge, and Gary Neil, for helping me when everyone else thought I was beyond help; and Steve Rutley, whose expertise makes my life that little bit easier.

At that point, everyone turned to Matthew's ex, who gave him a pitiful look. "It really is a shame what's happened to him," she said, forcing another frustrated noise from Matthew. "But I guess it was always on the cards." She paused, drawing everyone's attention as she sucked on her cancer stick. "He's crazy," she finished in a matter-of-fact way.

The friend of the neighbor's son stepped forward and I noticed the others back away as he did so. When he edged closer I realized why: he stank. Whatever he had been soaked in, it clearly wasn't water. "It's because he's a chicken," he announced. "He knows what's waiting for him and he's scared."

I surveyed the expectant faces, including Mrs. Andreasson, who had now joined the rabble. They all looked like they wanted blood, even the police officers. Matthew had excelled.

"Matthew, I think you should come down," I said, playing the part of the negotiator.

He shook his head. "It ain't happening. You don't know the story; you don't know what they're going to do to me. All of them, including your wife now. She'll kill me."

I tried to laugh it off. "Lizzie isn't going to harm—"

"Yes I fucking am," Lizzie cut in.

I stared at her for a moment and the turned to the firefighter. "Put the ladder up," I told him. "I'll have a word."

It wasn't quite how I envisaged spending my night. I wasn't particularly great with heights, but my curiosity got the better of me, and as much as I hated him at that moment, I was keen to hear Matthew out.

They all watched and waited eagerly, a few of them checked their watches, a few others looked ready to race up after me and throttle Matthew. Once I made it to the top, they took the ladder away and

I remained where I was, unwilling and unable to move as Matthew came over to me, hopping across the many bumps and turns of the roof as if it were his home and he understood every curve and every incline.

"Now, tell me," I said, feeling out of breath from the climb and the panic of being up high. "From the beginning. What happened?"

He sighed heavily and sat down next to me. "Okay." He slapped his hands heavily on his thighs and turned his attention toward the waiting faces below. "So, it began when I tried to watch a film on pay-per-view."

"We don't have pay-per—" I paused. "What kind of film?"

"It *might* have been porn."

"It might have been?"

"Okay, it *was* porn."

"You tried to watch porn with my child in the house?"

Matthew shrugged, unable to see the problem. "He was the result of two people humping, and these days he spends his days rolling around naked and sucking tits. If anything he's more suited for porn than I am."

That sort of insanity didn't deserve a response, so I moved on swiftly. "And then what?"

"When I couldn't get it, I tried phoning them up."

"Them?"

"Sky."

"You rang *my* satellite provider to ask where *your* hardcore porn was?"

"Precisely."

"And?"

"And the guy tried to tell me that there was none."

"No, *really?*" I said sarcastically.

He rolled his eyes and then continued. "I may have been a bit of a dick on the phone."

"That doesn't sound like you." I layered the sarcasm on even thicker.

"Anyway, he told me that I should have been able to access all of the adult channels, but he said that the satellite reception was down and that I probably just needed to tweak the aerial, fix the alignment, that sort of thing."

"You realize it's digital, right?"

"Yes, yes," Matthew said, swatting at me. "The guy was messing with me. I should have known, really, but he waved the promise of naked ladies in front of my face and I lost all common sense. Truth is, he just wanted revenge."

"Revenge?" I was confused at first, but then it dawned on me. This was Matthew after all. "What did you say to him?"

"I may have said he was a useless prick and that the only reason he worked the night shift in a call center was because he was too ugly to be seen in daylight hours and too incompetent to find a better job."

I nodded. "And you said this, why?"

"He made me feel like an idiot for not knowing how to work the TV."

"You were."

"Can I tell my fucking story now, please?"

"Okay, okay."

The scene below me was even more animated. Matthew's ex was talking to the police again, while the butch rugby players were thumping each other on the arms. Lizzie was the only one who hadn't moved. She was still staring up, unblinking. Even I was spooked, so I didn't dare imagine how terrified she must have made Matthew feel.

Matthew continued with his story. "So I took a ladder and climbed on the roof."

"As you do."

He nodded. "But just after I got up, the ladder slipped. By this time, I also realized that the guy on the phone had probably been fucking with me."

"It's that sort of quick wit and keen intelligence that I admire in you."

He continued, doing his best to ignore me. "I waited for a few minutes but then I began to panic. Ben was inside, alone, and short of jumping off the roof, there wasn't nothing I could do. Then I saw your neighbors, the old couple."

I looked down at Mr. and Mrs. Andreasson. She was still angry; he was now lying down in the back of the ambulance, ready to be taken away and clearly still very excited by the prospect.

"Their light was on in the bedroom and I saw them in there." The look he gave me at that point said more than words could.

"Oh God, they weren't having sex, were they?"

He nodded sheepishly. "But I didn't know that then. I tried to get their attention, jumping up and down, waving, then I figured I'd get something to throw. By the time I found a chunk of slate and tossed it at the window, the old fella had responded to the shouts and opened it."

I sucked in a breath through my teeth when the realization hit as heavily as the chunk of slate had hit poor Mr. Andreasson. I would later discover that he'd taken some Viagra in preparation for their night of passion and that the main reason his wife was so annoyed was because he had wasted a good erection, which was hard to come by.

"Next thing I know," Matthew continued, "the crazy bitch was shouting at me from the window. I saw her on the phone